HE

Please return on or before the latest date above.
You can renew online at *www.kent.gov.uk/libs*
or by telephone 08458 247 200

CUSTOMER SERVICE EXCELLENCE **Libraries & Archives**

00884\DTP\RN\07.07   LIB 7

THE LAWMAN: HELLTOWN

LYLE BRANDT

THORNDIKE
CHIVERS

This Large Print edition is published by Thorndike Press, Waterville, Maine, USA and by BBC Audiobooks Ltd, Bath, England.

Thorndike Press, a part of Gale, Cengage Learning.

The text of this Large Print edition is unabridged.

Other aspects of the book may vary from the original edition.

Set in 16 pt. Plantin.

Printed on permanent paper.

LIBRARY OF CONGRESS CATALOGING-IN-PUBLICATION DATA

Brandt, Lyle, 1951–
   The lawman : Helltown / by Lyle Brandt.
     p. cm. — (Thorndike Press large print western)
     ISBN-13: 978-1-4104-1127-3 (alk. paper)
     ISBN-10: 1-4104-1127-3 (alk. paper)
     1. Large type books. I. Title. II. Title: Helltown.
   PS3602.R364L394 2008
   813'.6—dc22   2008035382

BRITISH LIBRARY CATALOGUING-IN-PUBLICATION DATA AVAILABLE

Published in 2008 in the U.S. by arrangement with The Berkley Publishing Group, a member of Penguin Group (USA) Inc.
Published in 2009 in the U.K. by arrangement with The Berkley Publishing Group, a division of Penguin Group USA Inc.

U.K. Hardcover: 978 1 408 42171 0 (Chivers Large Print)
U.K. Softcover: 978 1 408 42172 7 (Camden Large Print)

Printed in the United States of America
1 2 3 4 5 6 7 12 11 10 09 08

THE LAWMAN: HELLTOWN

1

Jack Slade was twelve miles from Gehenna, hoping he could reach the town by nightfall, when he heard the first gunshot. A rifle. He was on alert before the hills around him damped the sound, absorbing it.

One shot could be a hunter, he decided. Could be anything, in fact. Slade had a job to do, and chasing echoes through the Oklahoma badlands wasn't part of it.

He changed his mind when two more shots rang out, a pair of rifles, firing over one another. That could only mean a shooting contest or a killing party, and the U.S. marshal's badge he wore entitled Slade to find out which it was.

His roan responded to a light touch on the reins, diverting from its north-by-northwest course to southward, where the source of gunfire lay concealed by gentle peaks and valleys in an undulating landscape, as if God — perhaps frustrated with his work — had wadded up the land in one great fist and never took the time to smooth it out again. If Slade were ant-sized, he supposed, it would've been like traveling across a rumpled sheet.

A shooting contest or a killing party?

When a shotgun joined the chorus, Slade decided it was murder in the making, with a chance that he was already too late. He didn't know the territory, had to navigate by ear and instinct, homing on the source of gunfire that continued and grew louder by the moment.

In his mind, Slade hastily reviewed the possibilities. He hadn't seen a farmhouse in the past two days, but there could be some in the neighborhood, now that Gehenna was within his reach.

A stage route? He was traveling along the main road from his destination to Enid and points east, had camped beside it for the last two nights, and there'd been no coach yet to make him taste its dust.

Could be a weekly, he decided. *Maybe every second week.* Erratic schedules were the norm out here, where life was hard on good days, and the bad could make a strong man old before his time.

Some kind of raid or ambush, Slade decided. Never mind the target. Big-time shooters liked an audience, in his experience. Their game was all about building a reputation, getting new jobs when the smoke cleared. None of them worth anything would stage a fight in godforsaken country where the only witnesses were rattlesnakes and prairie dogs.

Slade urged his roan to greater speed, trusting the animal to watch its own step on the grassy turf. The hills weren't tall or steep enough to be a challenge, though Slade guessed that jogging over five or six of them would leave him winded. Lucky for the pair of them this day, the roan had better stamina and it was only three hills, not the full half dozen.

At the crest of number three, Slade reined his gelding to a halt beside a solitary oak that shaded them and made them inconspicuous. Or so Slade hoped, at any rate.

Below him, in the swale, Slade saw a small farmhouse and somewhat larger barn. The place had a corral, two horses in it, while another five or six stood clustered on the far side of the barn, barely restrained by a short man who held their reins.

The other riders, now dismounted, had besieged the farmhouse. Puffs of gunsmoke from their weapons helped Slade spot them from a distance, counting heads.

Yes, it was six.

Someone inside the house was fighting back. Slade read it as a bid to keep the enemy outside and at a distance from the house, with no great emphasis on injuring or killing anyone. As for the shooters in the yard, they obviously had no care for anyone on the receiving end of their gunfire.

Two possibilities, thought Slade. Either the shooters were a posse, bent on rooting out a fugitive, or they were bad men targeting a homesteader. Slade couldn't think of any third alternative, and either of the two scenarios required attention from a lawman who was dropped into the middle of the mix.

Helltown would have to wait.

"How many of them are there, Melody?"

"I can't tell. Five or six at least," she answered.

"If we knew for sure —"

"Hush up and let me aim!"

"Sorry." The small voice at her elbow sounded penitent and frightened, which was only natural.

Another bullet struck the window frame above her, to her left. It made her flinch, but Melody still saw the shooter's gunsmoke. He was crouched at the west end of the corral, face shaded by the fence posts and the rolled brim of his hat.

Not that she would have recognized him, necessarily. These men weren't neighbors. They were hired to do a job, and she was it. When she was dead, they would collect their pay and go find someone else to terrorize.

Not this one, she decided, as she braced herself. The Henry rifle was unwieldy for her size, but she could handle it. She still remembered Mickey teaching her to hold it steady with the stock against her shoulder, leaning into it with muscles rigid. Take a deep breath, then release half of it. Hold the rest. Squeeze gently on the trigger, trying for the space between heartbeats.

The rifle bucked against her shoulder, smoke obscuring her vision for an instant. When the firing slit was clear, she saw her target scrambling backward, seeking better cover.

"Damn it all to hell!"

"Sister!"

"Don't *sister* me!" she snapped. "Just get the shotgun ready."

"Here. It's loaded."

Melody exchanged the Henry for a double-barreled Greener. It was lighter, with the shorter barrels and only two shots in its side-by-side chambers. It didn't have the rifle's range, but neither did it call for expert marksmanship. If one of the attackers moved in close enough, buckshot would kill as surely as a rifle slug.

They hadn't shot the horses yet and seemed in no great rush to charge the house. She didn't know how long they were prepared to wait, whether or not starvation was their game, but she supposed they would prefer to make it quick, if not entirely clean.

There was no question in her mind as to the series of events that would transpire if the attackers forced their way inside the house. With any luck, she and her sister would be killed outright. If not . . .

"Switch back," she said, when no clear target showed itself. They traded guns again, no question on her choice.

She'd want the Greener's firepower if anyone broke through the door. Two blasts could take down three or four men if she handled it correctly, and the survivors would be furious. They'd come in shooting, give no thought to anything beyond the kill.

Nothing would matter after that.

Bullets were peppering the house again, but it was sturdy, built of square-cut logs and mortar. Now and then, a slug punched through the door or shutters on the windows, but their enemies outside were firing blind. Bullets that found their way inside immediately spent their force against the inner walls, with no ricochets to keep them ducking.

Just like Mickey planned it.

He'd been more concerned with Indians, of course, but every stranger in the world was a potential enemy. The badlands hadn't earned their name because the soil was poor, the weather any worse than usual.

She wished Mickey were there to help her deal with this scum, but the wishing was a waste of time. And Melody might not have much time left.

Better to use it punishing her enemies than pining over what could never be.

She glimpsed another shooter — or the same one? — at the other end of the corral. Angling to frame him in her rifle's sights, she worked the lever action, fired, then ducked below the window as the raiders answered with their guns.

How long before they thought to set the house on fire?

It could be worse, she thought. *We go out shooting, it's the same as if they broke down the door. No prisoners.*

Above all else, she would not fall into their hands alive.

"You've got them hopping mad," said Harmony.

"I hope so," Melody replied, surprised to feel the tight smile on her face. "I surely do."

"You reckon we'll get out of this?"

"Sister, if you know any prayers, I'd say them now."

Slade circled around to approach from the west, unseen by the men who'd surrounded the farmhouse. He tied his roan in a small copse of trees, a hundred yards or so behind the barn, and took his Winchester repeater with him as he closed the gap on foot.

Shooting was out, until he had at least some general idea of what was happening. For all Slade knew, the outside shooters could be members of a duly constituted posse, trying to flush bandits from the house. Granted, it didn't *feel* that way, but he could not afford any fatal mistakes.

Edging around the southwest corner of the barn, he used the six horses for cover while stalking their minder. The man was distracted, watching the house from his safe vantage point, no idea in the world that he might be approached from another direction.

Stupid.

Slade stepped around the horses, coming up beside the man who held their reins. When he was close enough to tap the cowboy on his shoulder, Slade leaned in and asked him, "What's the deal, here?"

With a gasp, the watcher spun and dropped the reins he had been holding, gaped at Slade while reaching for his holstered pistol.

No badge on his shirt, no question on his lips.

Slade lashed out with the Winchester, driving its stock into the mouth that should've asked him who in hell he was, what he was doing on the scene of an arrest in progress. Teeth crunched with the sound of gravel underfoot, and then his man was down, shivering out of consciousness.

Slade took the six-gun from the sleepy shooter's holster, tucked it underneath his belt, and waved the restless horses into flight beyond the barn. Whatever happened next, his adversaries would be scrambling to escape on foot.

Unless they killed him first.

Slade didn't check the fallen gunman's pulse, saw he was blowing crimson bubbles through a pair of swelling lips when he exhaled. Still breathing, but no longer an immediate and pressing threat.

Which still left five, and none of them within his reach.

There were two ways to handle it. He could identify himself and call for the shooters to surrender, in which case he stood an eighty-twenty chance of having all five blaze away in his direction. Slade went for the second option, lining up a target at the nearer end of the corral.

He waited for a brief lull in the firing, whistled shrilly through his teeth, and saw a couple of the gunmen turn in his direction. One of them was squarely framed in his Winchester's sights.

Again, no badge.

He stroked the rifle's trigger, watched his target tumble over backward in a boneless sprawl. Before the others could respond, he called out to them, loud and clear, "Deputy U.S. marshal! Drop your guns and let me see those hands!"

A trifle late, perhaps, but still . . .

Four guns answered in unison, their bullets rattling the barn's east wall and raising spurts of dust around Slade's feet. He caught his second target scrambling for cover near the privy, fired, and knew a graze would be the best that he could hope for as the man dropped out of sight.

So much for playing by the rules.

At least, he had removed whatever tiny doubt remained about the shooters being lawmen. Not that being right would help him, if one of them scored a lucky shot and put him down.

What luck?

At four to one, Slade knew, the odds were on their side. They could encircle him, set up a cross fire, drive him from the meager cover that he had, and drop him on the run.

Unless he beat them to it.

Slade retreated, circling west and north around the barn, reversing the direction that his enemies would follow if they tried to jump him from behind. It was an obvious maneuver, but he had them rattled at the moment, had already cut their numbers by one-third, and maybe they would overlook the obvious.

Maybe.

It was a gamble, but he had no choice. Slade was already in the game, and he could only raise the bet.

He churned around the northwest corner of the barn and saw the shooter coming for him, guard down just enough to make the crucial difference. The man thought he was clever, didn't reckon Slade would figure out his plan — or not in time, at least — and that was his mistake.

17

His *last* mistake.

They fired almost together, Slade the precious fraction of a second earlier that made the difference. His slug drilled through the stranger's chest and dropped him, sent the shooter's wasted bullet toward the sky.

Three down, and three to go.

The odds were getting better, but Slade wished he knew who he was fighting for.

"Goddamn! Who *is* that?" Rory Duncan muttered to himself. Nobody answered, naturally, since he was huddled in the shadow of the privy, all alone.

The bullet graze across his left biceps burned like the devil, but it wasn't deep enough to slow him down or cost Rory the use of his arm. He was right-handed, anyway, but used both hands to fire his Winchester.

If he could find a target.

Zeke and Tommy were already down. He'd seen them drop and tried to nail the shooter who had come from nowhere, busting up their party just when things were coming to a head. Rory assumed his shot had missed, because the stranger fired right back at *him*. And would've had him, too, except for Rory's desperate headlong dive behind the crapper.

Almost had you, even so, the pain in his left arm reminded him.

It was supposed to be an easy job, no major fuss about it. In and out, the boss had said, all of them laughing when they thought about the women waiting for them. In and out, with no proof for the law — such as it was — to say that any certain people did the deed.

"Easy," he whispered to himself, clutching the Winchester so tightly that his knuckles blanched. "Like hell."

First thing the boss had told them was there'd be no man on the O'Hara spread when they came calling. Easy pickings. They could do whatever might come natural, as long as no one was around to testify about it later on. They all knew what that meant and didn't mind a bit. The pay was decent, with a little something extra on the side.

"Like gettin' killed," he told the dusty farmyard.

Rory didn't know where Turk and Billy were. Somewhere around behind the house, he guessed. Isaac was with the horses, and he should've seen the shooter coming, since he'd started firing from a corner of the barn.

Unless . . .

"Jesus, that's three."

Rory was well and truly worried now. He

was a hired gun, not a shootist in the sense of standing up and meeting practiced killers face-to-face. The whole walk-down-and-count-before-you-draw routine was crazy, in his estimation. Back-shooting was safer, more efficient, and it got the job done mighty fine.

His problem now was that he had no back to shoot.

He'd lost sight of the nameless, faceless enemy during his wild dash for the privy, knowing that his shot was wasted, mewling when the stranger's bullet grazed his arm. Another couple inches higher, and it would've ripped his left arm from the socket. Couple inches to the left, his lung would be as flat as a balloon after the carnival left town.

"Lucky for me," he murmured.

Sudden gunfire made him flinch and huddle lower in the privy's shadow. Somewhere around the east end of the house, he reckoned, but when Rory risked a glance, the yard was empty. Turk or Billy dying now, he guessed, unless one of them made a lucky shot and took the stranger down.

Teamwork demanded that he go to help, but Rory didn't feel like risking any more blood on this job than he'd already spilled. He felt like getting out and riding hard, until the stranger and this whole damned place were miles behind him. Then —

Riding.

Isaac was with the horses, but he hadn't joined the fight. To Rory's mind, that meant that either he was dead or he'd already run away. Which left the horses — *his* horse, damn it! — free to wander off, or spook and run with gunfire in their ears.

The thought of being stranded there, and waiting for the gunman to remember him, was more than Rory Duncan could abide. He crept back from the privy, crawling belly-down until he reached a shallow gully some yards back, then followed it in the direction of the barn.

Somebody else could finish it. Rory was getting out.

He prayed to some forgotten god that he was not too late.

Two shooters left that Slade was sure of. Maybe one behind the privy, if his shot had missed. And yet another by the barn, still breathing, who might come around if Slade's luck turned against him. Not the worst odds he had ever faced, but Slade intended to reduce them if he could.

Starting right now.

He trusted those inside the house to keep

from shooting him, since he'd identified himself. That might be fatal-foolish, but he hoped they were smart enough to recognize a friend in need.

He crouch-walked to the southeast corner of the farmhouse, waited there a moment, listening, then surged around the corner with his rifle cocked and shouldered.

Nothing.

It was like a children's game of hide-and-seek, and Slade was "it." In this game, though, the losers wound up dead.

His footsteps sounded louder to him than they should have, crunching on the soil beside the house. That was the nerves, Slade understood, but those he hunted would be equally on edge. Would it improve their hearing? Let them track him and discover where he was, before he spotted them?

Another corner coming up.

He slowed, then stopped completely. Held his breath and strained to hear the slightest sound. Was that a shuffling, or his own fevered imagination?

Christ, just do it!

On a whim, Slade took his hat off, counted down from five, then skimmed it off across the yard, beyond the corner. Two shots instantly exploded, rifles by the sound of them, and in the heartbeat gap before the shooters could prepare to fire again, Slade charged.

It was a crazy thing to do, but he was running out of options. Firing as he turned the corner, Slade saw one man take his bullet in the chest, high on the right, while his companion violently recoiled from the Winchester's muzzle flash. They pumped the lever actions of their separate rifles almost simultaneously, racing Death, and while his enemy was slightly faster, Slade got there before him with a gut shot from the hip.

His adversary staggered, crying out in pain, and triggered his round as he fell. Slade had already ducked below the line of fire, waiting to see if he had done enough, or if the shooters needed more.

The first man he had shot was dead or dying quietly. The second hadn't made his mind up yet, but he was grappling with his rifle, trying for another go. Slade didn't like to shoot him twice, but there was no alternative. He aimed to make it count and did it right.

Which still left two he had to check on, for his peace of mind. It would be nice to have a couple of the raiders breathing, maybe see if he could get them to explain their actions. Slade could always ask the homesteaders, of course, but in this portion of the territory, they might not have any clear idea of why they were attacked.

It was the badlands, after all.

Slade started back in the direction he had come from, toward the front yard and corral. He'd check the privy first, go slow, and work his way around behind it, just in case his target over there was still alive and kicking. After that —

"You bathtid!"

A dusty scarecrow figure with a crooked, blood-smeared face brandished a gun at Slade, advancing toward him with a lurching stride. Slade just had time to think — *the barn!* — before the shooter fired and something like a mallet struck his skull.

Slade fell, vaguely aware that he had dropped his rifle and was on the verge of losing consciousness. The gunman he had clubbed down moments earlier now towered over him, wearing a gap-toothed smile and drooling like an idiot who'd drunk red paint. The six-gun trembled as it moved in closer to his face. Slade saw the cylinder rotating as his would-be executioner thumbed back the pistol's hammer.

Here we go, he thought, and closed his eyes.

The blast, much louder than he had

expected, pitched Slade into darkness streaked with tiny specks of light like shooting stars.

2

Dying was damned hard work. Before they let Slade get around to it, the angels or demons — whatever they were — had some things they insisted he see and consider. Each scene in turn was slightly off, a parody of how Slade had remembered it in life. *Twisted,* he would've said, in such a way to tax his mind and make him search out what was different.

First stop, a vision of the office of Judge Isaac Dennison in Lawton, Oklahoma Territory. Slade didn't know why St. Peter's review of his life should start *there,* skipping over his childhood and all of the rest, but when he tried to ask the question, all his throat would make were little croaking sounds.

This must be hell, he thought, considering the heat and his parched throat.

Judge Dennison was pacing back and forth behind his desk, a moving silhouette against the window facing down into a courtyard where the men he had condemned were hanged on Saturdays, at noon.

"Gehenna," he was saying, through a cloud of sweet-smelling cigar smoke, "is a word traced back to ancient Greek. I don't suppose you read Greek, do you, Slade?"

Slade croaked in answer, hoped Judge Dennison could understand the *no.*

"Well, never mind. In Hebrew, *Gêhinnôm* means the Valley of Hinnom, which formed the southern border of ancient Jerusalem. We find it mentioned first in Joshua 15:8. Still with me, son?"

Slade nodded, tired of croaking.

"Good. That's good. Now, scholars tell us that the Valley of Hinnom was used as . . . well, let's not mince words: a garbage dump. The people of Jerusalem threw trash in there and burned it. Kept fires burning day and night to get rid of their trash and kill the stench. Aside from daily garbage, they would also burn the corpses of their executed criminals and any other individuals who were denied a proper burial, one reason or another. Which, my friend, is why some people use Gehenna as a synonym for Hell."

No question there. Slade didn't nod or croak.

"Now, it so happens," Dennison contin-

27

ued, "that we have a town here in the territory called Gehenna. Ever heard of it?"

Slade shook his head, heard bones and tendons creaking like old saddle leather or a rotting windblown sign.

"Well, take my word for it," said Dennison. "Gehenna *does* exist in Oklahoma Territory, and from what I've heard, it lives up to its name. A little slice of Hell on Earth, you might say. They've had murders, arson, robberies, rapes, claim-jumping, rustling. Those are just the crimes we *know* about."

Slade tried to ask a question, but he couldn't get his tongue to work.

"Good question," Dennison replied. "I think most of the trouble in Gehenna comes from two men fighting for control over the town. On one side, you've got Baron Cartwright. That's his name, they tell me, not a title. He operates out of the Rosebud Saloon. His opposition is one Buck Bjornson, at the Valhalla. Between them, they run a wide-open cesspit, vying for control. The decent people . . . well, they just hang on and pray."

Slade could've told the judge that so-called decent people have a way of picking out the leaders they deserve. Gehenna's warlords wouldn't last a day if all the men and women they had bullied got together, armed themselves, and settled old accounts. As far as gambling, whoring, and the rest of it, nothing in federal law pertained. People were free to lose their money, tip a glass, or catch diseases if they wanted to.

"You're wondering why I called you here today," said Dennison.

Another nod from Slade. God*damn* his blistered throat.

"Gehenna needs a dose of law and order, son. These bullyboys need a reminder that they're just warty little frogs in my big pond. And you're the only man available right now to do the job. Questions? Concerns?"

Hell, yes!

Slade croaked some more, then tried to beam his thoughts at Dennison by sheer willpower. Nothing. The judge looked pleased, rubbing his hands together like a man about to sit down for a feast.

"All right, then. We're all set," said Dennison. "You just go on, now, and see to it. I've got riffraff waiting for the rope."

Slade rose and turned away without a handshake, crossed the judge's office to the only door available, and opened it, stepped through —

— into a dark night, in a countryside he didn't recognize. The moon was just a thumbnail sliver, low down in the eastern sky. Slade couldn't work out if that meant it was setting or had lately risen, and he didn't care.

Where am I?

If this was Hell, apparently it wasn't all one place, and some of it was cold. Slade shivered, standing in his shirtsleeves while a night wind straight from winter ran its fingers through his hair, rumpled his clothes.

Slade looked around. He turned full circle, without any wasted movement that might draw attention to himself, keeping his right hand on his holstered Peacemaker. His eyes sought the familiar shops and offices of Lawton's long main street.

Nothing.

Somehow, he'd stepped out of the judge's chambers and a sunny afternoon into a midnight scene devoid of man-made structures. Slade smelled wildflowers and something else he couldn't place. Some kind of animal, perhaps — alive or dead, he didn't know. Above him, splayed across the sky, were stars beyond counting.

"Where am I?" he whispered, his voice better now.

Not Hell, Slade guessed, unless the nether regions made allowances for trees and grass and night birds. Something rustled in the weeds behind him, small and furtive, but he didn't bother to investigate the sound.

In front of Slade, some distance from him, was a road. Not much of one, maybe a wagon track would be a better name for it. He saw no evidence that it had been maintained, except through fairly steady use. If he stood still and strained his ears, Slade could imagine that he heard a horse approaching from his left.

Except, he realized, it wasn't his imagination. Someone *was* approaching, riding easily, with no apparent haste.

Slade stood and waited for the rider, some instinct he couldn't fathom telling him that he was hidden from the stranger's view, though standing in the open without cover. *Something* would prevent the rider seeing him, either because he simply didn't glance in Slade's direction, or because Slade had become invisible to mortal eyes.

Another moment, and he saw the rider, mounted on an Appaloosa stallion. He was tall, slumped just enough to show that he was comfortable in the saddle, but with traces of a military ramrod posture evident. The wide brim of his hat shaded the rider's face until he was directly opposite the spot where Slade stood waiting. Then, he glanced across at Slade, *through* him, and Slade gasped at the vision of a face he recognized.

Because it was his own.

The dizzy moment passed. Slade understood, somehow, that he was looking at his brother Jim. They had been twins, identical in every way that mattered, from their faces to their natural impatience with rules their elders made, enforced with straps and scoldings. They'd been separated for a decade, and the space between them now seemed greater than a continent.

Because Slade knew that Jim was dead.

He could remember *that* much, even in the dying depths of his delirium. Not only dead, but murdered by —

Four riders came from nowhere, galloping around Slade, from behind him, fanning out to block the road in front of Jim. They didn't speak, let silence carry any message they might have for him.

"I wondered when you'd get around to this," Jim said.

"Your choice," one of the riders said. "The man made you a decent offer for your land."

"And I declined it," Jim replied. "Three times."

"That's why we're here," the spokesman for the others said.

Slade knew he should do something, but

his feet were rooted to the soil. He tried to draw his pistol, but it wouldn't clear the holster, even when he strained and made the perspiration bead his forehead.

Hot again, the chilling wind forgotten. Maybe he'd been wrong, and this *was* Hell.

"You'd best get to it, then," his brother said, and just like that went for his sidearm.

Jim was quick, but his four enemies were quicker. Slade mouthed silent curses as they drew and fired in unison, their bullets lifting Jim out of his saddle, flinging him across the Appaloosa's rump.

At last, somehow, Slade broke the bonds that held him frozen in his tracks. Pistol forgotten, he ran toward his brother, arms outstretched, and —

— dropped into a chair, facing a poker table and three other players. In Slade's mind, open countryside and faint moonlight were instantly supplanted by the sounds and smells of a saloon doing a banner trade.

Slade glanced down at the pile of chips in front of him. He'd done all right so far, which might explain the dour expressions of his three companions.

Circling around the table, clockwise, he first saw a man of fifty-something, gray streaks showing in his beard and shoulder-length hair. He wore buckskins that hadn't been washed since he'd tanned them, a slouch hat pushed back from his forehead on top of a weather-tanned face.

Next, directly opposite Slade, sat a freckled redhead with fat jowls and a belly to match. He played with elbows planted on the table, the handful of chips in between them marking him as the game's big loser. A hand-rolled cigarette was tucked into one corner of his mouth, the eye above it squinting through a rising swirl of smoke.

Last on the circuit, to Slade's right, a balding man with no spare meat on his frame clutched his cards in hands gnarled by time and hard use. He didn't smoke, but kept a plug of tobacco wedged firmly into one cheek, pausing every five minutes or so to feed the spittoon that he kept on the floor by his chair.

"You gonna bet or fold?" the redhead asked, glaring at Slade.

Slade checked his hand, unable to remember whether he'd been dealt these cards or drawn them. Either way, he had a full house, aces over queens.

"Ten dollars," he announced and pitched a pair of chips into the pot.

"Too rich for my blood," said the long-haired player on his left. "I'm out."

"You mean to buy this pot," the redhead sneered, "but it ain't gonna work." One freckled hand corralled his few remaining chips and shoved them forward. "Call the ten, and raise you . . . seven."

"Seventeen to me," the balding dealer said. "No, thank you, boys. I fold."

"I'll see your seven," Slade announced, "and raise you ten."

The redhead's face flushed darker than his hair. "You know damn well that I ain't got another ten."

"You have a pocket watch," Slade said. "We'll call it even."

"That's a *twenty*-dollar watch, goddamn it!"

"Not tonight."

"Awright, then, mister." Fumbling with his watch, the redhead managed to unhook its fob and chain, then placed it gently on the central pile of chips, with something close to reverence. "I call your goddamned ten. How's that? Three queens!"

The redhead faced his cards and craned back in his chair, grinning to beat the band.

"Not good enough," Slade told him, laying out his hand. "Full house."

The redhead looked as if he would explode. His torso swelled, his face suffused with shades of purple that resembled heavy bruising. His liver-colored lips moved, whispered something.

"Speak up," Slade instructed. "I can't hear you."

"Cheat!" the redhead bellowed, kicking back his chair and lunging to his feet. "I'm callin' you a goddamned dirty cheat!"

The bald man who had dealt the hand edged backward from the table. "Now, hold on a minute, Jubal. I —"

"I'm callin' *him* a cheat, not *you,*" the redhead clarified for anyone who'd missed the point.

Dead silence in the barroom now. Slade was aware of several hundred eyes watching his face and hands.

"You need to mind your manners, friend," he told the redhead.

"I am *not* your fuckin' *friend,*" the redhead snarled. "You cheated me, and these two saw you do it!"

Graybeard cleared his throat, about to speak, but never got the chance.

"You *saw* him," Jubal snapped. "Well, *didn't* you?"

"I reckon . . . um . . ."

"And *you.*" This to the dealer. "Since you dealt an honest hand, he *musta* cheated. Am I right?"

"Best leave me outta this," the dealer said.

"You're *in* it, Roddy. Tell us what you *saw.*"

"Well, I —"

"You want to make a move," Slade interrupted, speaking to the redhead known as Jubal, "it's your play. Just you. Nobody else."

The redhead's draw was flawless, lightning fast. Slade barely reached his gun before the other's Colt was blazing at him. The bullet's impact punched him backward into —

— night. Another landscape under starlight, but the moon was nearly full this time. In this vision he stood atop a ridge or hillock, watching lines of undernourished men file in and out of mine shafts lit by torches from within. The men were all stoop-shouldered, weary from their labors. Those emerging from the mines were filthy, faces smudged, hair plastered to their scalps with sweat. Shackles combined with obvious fatigue to make their footsteps drag.

Slade watched them for a moment, then a shove between his shoulder blades propelled him toward the nearest shaft. "Get back in line," a gruff voiced snarled.

Slade didn't turn to face the man who'd shoved him. He already had a mental image of a rifle and a riding crop. Slade moved to join the line of marching men that suddenly appeared beside him, only to discover that his legs were shackled, too.

He *knew* this place. There was a resonance about it, in the grim landscape, the shuffling sound of feet in worn-out boots and shoes. Slade's fellow sufferers made room for him, letting him join the line.

Outside the adit, two more gunmen waited. One covered the new arrivals with a shotgun, while the other handed tools to each man passing by. A heap of picks and shovels lay around his feet, and he dispensed them alternately. First, a shovel to the man in front of Slade, then a pick for Slade himself.

Somebody whispered in Slade's ear, "You may not get another chance. Don't let it slip."

He didn't have to question what was meant by that. Without a second thought, Slade swung his pick and drove its rusty point into the second gunman's chest, spearing a lung and forcing him to drop his scattergun. It didn't fire on impact, and he left the skewered enemy to stagger off, squealing, while Slade dived for his weapon.

Cocking it, he turned first on the man who'd handed him the pick. Slade was in time to see his adversary draw a well-worn Colt, before a charge of buckshot sent his brains and his sombrero sailing off into the night.

Slade faced the shooter who had pushed him, and saw the man exactly as he'd been imagined. He was frozen for a moment, dropped his whip, and tried to raise his Winchester too late, before Slade shot him in the chest.

More guards were rushing at him from all sides, some of them firing now. Their bullets didn't touch him, but Slade saw and heard them ripping into others, dropping shackled miners in their tracks.

Slade hobbled to the second man he'd shot and crouched to claim his Winchester. He had no hope of winning, much less breaking free, but at the very least he'd make the bastards know that they'd been in a fight.

Slade raised the rifle, chose his targets, couldn't seem to miss them as they all came charging toward him through moon-dappled darkness. It was like a shooting gallery, except that here the targets could shoot back. They couldn't seem to *hit* him, though, and that was fine with Slade. He'd take his luck as it was dealt to him and bet the maximum.

Around his twenty-first or -second shot, Slade realized that there was something wrong. His Winchester kept firing on command, although its magazine should've been empty long ago. He paused a moment to examine it, and saw a couple of the men he'd just gunned down get up again, dust off their clothes, and keep on charging toward him.

Most of them weren't firing now, Slade realized. The ones he'd shot had dropped their guns and didn't bother to retrieve them. They came rushing at him, hands outstretched to grab and throttle him, a zombie army on the march. Meanwhile, the shackled miners who'd been shot were rising, too, turning their wrathful eyes on Slade.

Well, shit, he thought. *If that's the gratitude I get, to hell with you. As long as I've got bullets left —*

And when he squeezed the rifle's trigger, nothing happened. Instantly, before he had a chance to swing the weapon like a club, a dozen snarling dead men tackled him and bore him to the muddy ground. Their teeth and filthy fingers ripped at Slade —

— stroking his face gently, while someone with an angel voice told him, "You're safe now. Sleep."

The mines were gone. A feather bed enveloped him. He reached up for the hand that cupped his face and lightly clutched its wrist, drawing a soft gasp from its owner.

Definitely female.

Faith?

It couldn't be. And yet . . .

Faith Connover had been his brother's fiancée when James was murdered. Slade had met her for the first time when he went to settle the estate and find the men who'd killed his twin. The first time he'd laid eyes on Faith, there'd been no doubt in Slade's mind that she would have made James a good wife. Between her stunning beauty, gentle spirit, and her strength of character, Faith offered everything a man could want.

His fingers traced the arm above the angel's hand, bare skin up to the shoulder, soft and warm. His lips formed whisper-words.

"You saved me."

"*You* saved *us,*" she answered him.

Above the bare, warm shoulder he found lace and slipped his fingers under it. The angel gasped, but didn't stop him. This was not entirely new to her. They'd been together now and then, to ease the pain they shared — and for entirely different reasons.

Slade felt himself stirring, stiffening. The sharp pain in his head discouraged him, but other parts were thinking for themselves.

His hand slipped farther underneath whatever sleeping garment she had on. He couldn't make it out, dark as it was inside the bedroom, but the fabric hardly formed a barrier between them. When he found her breast, Faith gasped and almost pulled away, then stopped and arched her back instead, soft flesh filling his palm.

Slade wondered where his filthy miner's clothes had gone, but didn't miss them. Smelling them would have despoiled the moment, and he wanted no distractions from the supple body pressed against him. The chemise or nightgown shifted, gliding over Faith's skin as he moved against her.

"You should sleep," she whispered to him, breathless. "You've been injured."

"Ache for you," Slade muttered, knowing she could feel how much he needed her. She strained against him where he held her round breast captive, fingers working.

Slade remembered his first time with Faith, her hesitancy, and the way she blossomed after she'd convinced herself that nothing they could do harmed anyone on Earth. James was a memory and nothing more, while in the flesh —

Impatient, Slade pulled down the shoulder strap and ducked his aching head to find her naked breast. He suckled there and felt her squirm against him, knew that she would melt at any moment now.

His free hand traced the outline of her body, searching for the nightgown's hem. It must've ridden up when she got into bed, but Slade still couldn't find it, fingers tangling in the sheets. While searching, though, his knuckles grazed her lower belly and he felt her squirm with wanting him.

Frustrated, needing her, Slade grabbed a handful of the fabric and began to draw it upward, baring graceful legs. One corner of the garment caught beneath her hip, since Faith was lying on her left side, facing him, but Slade kept tugging on the rest until he had it bunched around her waist.

He felt her stomach flutter at his touch and heard Faith catch her breath as eager fingertips slid lower, teasing at her raven curls. Slade thrust against her, slickening her belly in that way that made her gasp sometimes, and sometimes laugh.

She was about to open for him, Slade could tell, when suddenly she pulled away, slipped through his fingers, left his lips still hungering. Slade reached for her, to draw her back, but she was quicker, rolling out of bed.

Slade woke, in time to see the woman scramble out of bed, tugging her nightgown into place. Another stood beside her, one hand wrapped around a rolling pin, a pinched expression on her face. The pain inside his head came back, full bore.

He'd never seen these women in his life.

3

"Well, Sister," said the woman with the rolling pin, "I see he's got his strength back."

Slade snatched at rumpled sheets to hide himself, already wilting under scrutiny. The second woman seemed as anxious to conceal herself, snatching a robe and struggling into it while she blushed furiously.

"Ma'am," Slade told the other, "if you plan to hit me with that rolling pin, I hope you'll make it quick. My head's already killing me."

She twitched a smile at him and said, "That's not surprising, since you nearly got it blown clean off."

The images came flooding back. Slade risked a glance in the direction of the cabin's only door and instantly regretted it. He slumped back to his pillow with a grimace, even that soft contact paining him.

"You'll mend," the woman with the rolling pin informed him. "It's a graze, is all.

You're lucky. But that doesn't mean you get to celebrate with Melody."

"Who's Melody?" asked Slade, when he could speak again.

"That's me," the blusher said, arms clasped around herself as if afraid the robe would somehow open of its own accord. "This is my sister, Harmony."

Slade rode a wave of dizziness and said, "You're musical."

"You're fading," Harmony replied and laid her rolling pin aside. "I reckon I won't have to slug you for a while."

"What happened to my clothes?" asked Slade.

Melody blushed again. It seemed to be a habit. "You've been out cold for a few hours, and you were feverish," she said. "Still are, I'd say."

"I'd say you're right," said Harmony, twitching another momentary smile that made her sister turn a brighter shade of pink.

Melody forged ahead in spite of her embarrassment. "Your clothes were dusty, and your shirt is bloodstained. We can get that out, I think. But with the fever . . . well . . . we've got no medicine, but body warmth can help with chills, sometimes. I volunteered."

"Some sacrifice," her sister murmured.

"Harmony!"

"Look at yourself. You can't stand still."

"For heaven's sake, it's cold!"

"Then put some *clothes* on, Sister. You may disappoint our savior, but he'll have to live with it."

Melody bustled off to dress, muttering underneath her breath. Harmony moved to stand in front of Slade, blocking the view from where he lay.

"We don't have much, by way of privacy," she said. "But don't allow yourself to think we're free and easy."

"No. You have my thanks, for everything."

"We're even, there," she answered. "We were in a bad way with those others, when you came along."

That jerked him upright in the feather bed and sent a wave of misery crashing between his ears. "Where are they?" Slade demanded.

"Those we didn't kill, between us, slipped away," said Harmony. "I'm sure of one, at least. By now, I reckon he's reporting to the scum that sent him out here in the first place."

"Not drifters, then," said Slade.

"It's possible, but I don't think so."

"They'll come back, then," Slade suggested.

"Not tonight, and likely not tomorrow," Harmony replied. "They lost five men. That has to give them pause."

Slade heard a rustling of fabric somewhere in the room, beyond his line of sight. "We should be ready, even so."

"We're ready now," said Harmony. "You won't be ready for a while."

"My guns —"

"Are safe and sound, in case we need them. Likewise, those the others don't have any use for, down in Hell."

"Good thinking."

"It's the way we stay alive."

Melody came back to join them, fastening the last two buttons of a high-necked homespun dress. She'd lost the blush, but got it back as Slade sat staring at her, with the sheets around his waist.

"I think your fever's broken now," she said.

"Don't be so sure," said Harmony. "I still might need my rolling pin."

Slade let that pass and asked them both together, "When you fetched the other guns, did you remember ammunition?"

"All the belts they had, and what was in their pockets," Harmony replied.

"And what about the horses?"

"Just one," said Melody. "Tied out behind the barn."

"That's mine," Slade said.

"We put it in the barn. The rest were scattered," Harmony informed him. "I suppose it's just as well."

Slade wondered if the man who got away was riding or afoot. No matter. One way or the other, he was gone.

"I hate to ask about the bodies, but —"

"We'll see to them directly," Harmony assured him.

"I can help you."

"With that head? I don't think so."

"You're wrong," he said and started to get out of bed. Remembering his nakedness, and seeing Melody begin to blush again, Slade wrapped the sheet around himself like something out of ancient Rome and rose to plant his bare feet on the floor.

The pain inside his skull was staggering. It pulled the cabin's floor from underneath his feet, as if he'd skidded on a throw rug. Slade fell backward, senses reeling. His brain felt disconnected from his body, limbs as weak as a newborn kitten's, while the agony slammed through his skull.

"You're sure it's just a graze?" he asked at last, between clenched teeth.

"I washed it clean myself," said Harmony. "There's no skull showing, much less any brains."

"I may be running short of those," Slade said.

He offered no resistance as the women wrestled him back into bed and drew the covers to his chin. Already, in his supine pose, the pain was fading.

"I suppose I'm at your mercy, then," he said.

"For now," said Harmony. "Another day or two, you should be fit enough."

Gehenna would be waiting for him, Slade supposed, unless the shooters came back for him first.

Hell always waited.

Time was on its side.

"He's brave," said Melody. "You can't deny he's brave, Sister."

"He'd have to have *some* courage," Harmony allowed, "being a U.S. marshal. Don't go dreaming he's our white knight, though."

"I didn't say that."

"But you're on the verge of *thinking* it. I know you, Sister."

"And his strength is coming back."

"You felt that, did you?"

"Harmony!"

They stood outside the cabin, nearly dark now, with coyotes baying in the distant hills. Harmony knew they'd want a meal, and she was counting on the scum who'd tried to kill her and her sister to supply it.

"We've got work to do," she said. "Forget about the marshal's *strength* and help me make up a travois."

"You're such a witch sometimes," said Melody.

"It's not my spell you're falling under, Sister."

They used spare fence rails, a pair of them, lashed to the stronger of their horses, with some spare rope for a sling. Five bodies needed moving, but she reckoned they could make it in three trips — or maybe two if they were lucky.

"Start with those two in the back," said Harmony, when they had finished the travois. "One of them's on the hefty side."

They led the horse around the west end of the cabin, to the point where Slade — they'd learned his name, at least — had dropped two gunmen in their tracks. Straining together, one on either side of the travois, they loaded up the fat one first, then wedged his lighter friend beside and half on top of him. It left them winded, but there was no time to rest.

"Come on," said Harmony, and she led the way, holding the horse's reins.

They dragged their load of death a half mile from the cabin to a deep ravine choked full of weeds. The corpses would be out of sight there, and they shouldn't smell them from the house, although coyotes would be quick enough to find them, and the buzzards after sunrise.

It was just as hard unloading the two bodies as it had been placing them on the travois. Deadweight couldn't assist in relocation, but at least it didn't grapple with them, either.

"He *is* handsome, don't you think?" asked Melody.

Considering the corpse they held between them, Harmony replied, "I doubt if he was much to look at, living. As for now . . ."

"Not *him,* you goose! The marshal. Jack."

"It's first names, is it?"

"Well, you must admit he saved our lives. And we saved his. That's worth a certain closeness, isn't it?"

"The two of you looked close, all right. If you'd been any closer —"

"Stop it!" Melody was blushing furiously. "He was fast asleep. You know it!"

"*You* weren't," Harmony reminded her.

"I stopped it, didn't I?"

"After a good long while, Sister. I must admit, you had me feeling flushed, myself."

They heaved the slim one over, neither watching as he dropped into the weeds below. The next one would be harder, with his forty extra pounds.

"It's been a long time, Harmony."

"And longer still, for me." Try *never.* "Come along and help me with this tub of lard."

"You could've married," Melody responded. "You were *asked.*"

"I didn't want to *settle,* damn it. You know that. If you don't feel it, what's the point?"

"There isn't any need to swear."

"Don't push me, Melody. We've still got three more stiffs to haul, and fat-ass isn't getting any lighter while we stand here."

In the end, they got him off of the travois by having Melody stand on his legs, while Harmony went up and led the horse away. Then, with substantial straining from the two of them, they got him into the ravine.

"We should tell him everything," said Melody.

"Tell *who?*"

"The marshal."

"We don't even know who sent them," Harmony replied. "Bjornson or Cartwright. One's as bad as the other."

"Tell him *both,* then. They'll be looking for him now."

"I'll think about it. Help me with those others now, before your precious marshal takes it in his head to try and use the privy by himself."

"Oh, Lord. What if he needs to?"

"One of us will have to help him, I suppose."

"Well, if we must."

She caught her sister smiling, with her face averted. "Melody, you little vixen."

"I'm just saying."

"Say no more, for heaven's sake. It's bad enough we're stuck with him. You can't be chasing after him like you're in heat."

"Sister!"

"I only speak the truth."

"Sometimes you say too much."

They moved back through the gray dusk toward their cabin and the bodies still awaiting transport. Harmony was not afraid of death. She'd seen her share, and more was coming.

She'd have bet on it.

"We'll tell him what we know," she said at last, "and leave it up to him what's to be done about it. Who knows what the law *can* do?"

"Protect the innocent, at least," said Melody.

"This isn't Baltimore, Sister. Remember where we are."

"If there's a marshal, then there's law. There's hope."

"We'll see," said Harmony. "Meanwhile, let's get these other bastards to their final resting place, God rot their souls."

The meal was stew of some sort, well prepared and seasoned, though Slade didn't care to ask the meat's identity. He ate it sitting up in bed, his hostesses together at a table that they'd pulled a little closer for the sake of easy conversation. Modesty was served, in Slade's case, by a clean shirt that he didn't recognize.

"It was my husband's," Melody informed him. "He was Michael, but I mostly called him Mickey. We were married two years when he died. That's why my last name is O'Hara, not Maguire like Harmony's."

"In case you missed the point," said Harmony, "I'd be the spinster."

"I'm not saying that! I've *never* said that!"

"But it's obvious."

Slade didn't want to see them fight, although the prospect of the sisters wrestling had its amusing side. "Married two years, you said," he interrupted them. "Was that out here?"

"No, no. In Baltimore," said Melody. "We came out here to get a fresh start, if you can believe it."

"Lots of people do."

"And come to this?" she asked. "I hope not, for their sakes."

"Your husband died, you said. Was he, um —"

"Murdered? No. At least, I don't *think* so. His horse came back without him on a Thursday afternoon. We found him off a ways to westward, with a broken neck. He fell, I guess. Maybe a snake or something spooked the animal. He had no other wounds, except some bruising from the fall."

"I'm sorry, ma'am. Was that before your other trouble started here?"

"Not quite. Some men came out and made an offer for the homestead, after we were here awhile, but Mickey turned them down. That made them angry, I could tell, but they were still polite. A few weeks later, more men came, speaking for someone else, but Mickey still said no. We started losing cattle after that. One shot, a couple others missing. Then . . . the accident."

"How long have you been here alone?"

asked Slade.

"She's *not* alone," said Harmony.

"He means since Mickey died, Sister. Eight months, one week, two days," said Melody.

Slade finished off his stew before he spoke again. "You said the first men who came out to buy your homestead represented someone different from the second bunch?"

"That's right."

"Did they give names?"

She bobbed her head, putting a mass of auburn curls in motion. "Yes, indeed. The first two worked for Buck Bjornson. Baron Cartwright sent the other three. They're big men in Gehenna, if you didn't know already."

"So I've heard," he answered, thinking back to what Judge Dennison had told him when he got his marching orders.

"And you know the kind of men they are," said Harmony.

"I'm learning as I go. Those men outside —"

"Not anymore," the older sister said, correcting him.

"All right. Were any of them those who came to see you earlier?"

"I didn't recognize them," Melody replied.

"No," Harmony agreed. Her hair was

longer than her sister's, straighter, darker red. It glistened in the lamplight when she shook her head.

"I don't guess any of them dropped a name before I came along?" asked Slade.

"They didn't say who sent them, no," said Harmony. "They called out now and then to one another, when the shooting started. I heard 'Rory,' 'Zeke,' and 'Tommy,' but I couldn't match the names to faces."

"Never mind," Slade said. "I hoped they might've said who sent them this time."

"Sorry, no," said Melody.

"It was a long shot, anyway," said Slade.

"We're lucky you showed up just when you did," Melody told him, smiling to reveal a set of dimples in her cheeks. "I mean, to save our lives and all."

"Of course, you *did* get shot," said Harmony.

"It happens," Slade admitted.

"From your body — from your *scars,* I mean — it seems to happen quite a lot," said Melody.

"Sorry you had to see that, ma'am."

"Oh, I think scars add character! Don't you, Sister?"

"Depends on where they are and how you get them," Harmony replied. "Some mark a person who can't take a lesson from mistakes."

"I'm learning all the time," said Slade.

"Where were you headed when we interrupted you?" asked Harmony.

"Gehenna," Slade replied. "We've had complaints of rustling and such. Judge Dennison sent me to have a look around."

"One man? He sent *one man?*" Harmony shook her head again.

"I guess I'm all he had to spare," said Slade.

"And look at you. Already shot, flat on your back."

"Not quite," he said. "I'm eating stew, and someone's lost five shooters in the bargain."

"There are plenty more where those came from," said Harmony. "Whether it's Cartwright or Bjornson, both of them have thugs to spare."

"And if it's neither of them?"

"Then I'll kiss a pig and whistle 'Yankee Doodle.' One of them's behind this and the other troubles. Likely both."

"When you say other troubles . . ."

"Other homesteaders have been run off their land," said Melody. "Their stock was stolen, houses burned. We didn't know them well, but word still gets around."

"Well, I'll be looking into all of it," Slade

said. "But first . . ."

"More stew?" asked Melody.

"No, ma'am. If I could have my boots and trousers, I'll just pay a visit to the privy."

"Oh! Well . . . yes. I mean . . . Sister?"

"You may need help," said Harmony. "The standing up and walking part of it, at least."

"I'd better try it, anyway."

"We have your clothes, of course," said Melody, all flustered as she got up from the table. "I intend to wash them for you, but I haven't had the time as yet, and —"

"Not a problem, ma'am."

She brought his dusty pants, stockings, and boots. "Those socks could use some darning," she remarked.

"I'll just get dressed, then," Slade replied.

"Of course."

The cabin had a loft, but no divided rooms. The women stood together with their backs turned while Slade dressed, fighting the headache and the trace of fading dizziness that still remained. Seeing the second bed upstairs, he wondered where they slept, and how it must have been for Harmony to lie at night and listen while her sister's husband was alive.

Standing was painful for a moment, but it helped to clear Slade's head. He tottered for a second, then regained his balance and was ready for his walk.

"My pistol, if you don't mind."

"You think someone's out there?" Melody was clearly spooked by the idea of prowlers in the darkness.

"No, ma'am. Just in case."

Harmony brought the Peacemaker without its holster. Slade checked its load and shoved it down inside the waistband of his pants.

"If I'm not back within the hour," he said, smiling, "send a search party."

"He's stronger than I thought," said Harmony, watching the marshal go.

"That's just because you didn't get your turn at warming him."

"I wasn't just referring to his *body*, Sister. I believe your Mr. Slade has strength of character."

"He *is* a good one, isn't he?" said Melody.

"Unfortunately, in Gehenna, strength of character may get him killed."

"Don't say that!"

"Do you doubt it?" Harmony inquired.

"I just don't want to think about it now."

"You always were a dreamer."

"So? What's wrong with that? Mama and Papa —"

"Spoiled you silly, Sister. Even after Michael, you still think that dreams come true."

"They *do,* Sister. Sometimes."

"Not ours."

"We're still alive and well. We're here."

"That isn't *my* dream," Harmony replied. "Sometimes I wish . . ."

"That you had stayed in Baltimore. I know. It's my fault, and I'm truly sorry."

"Nonsense! No one put me on that train or made me climb aboard the wagon with a pistol at my head. We all make choices, Sister. And we have to live with them."

"Think of the choices Jack has made. Like riding up to save our lives!"

"And now he has another scar to show for it."

"I don't think he regrets it for a second."

"No. The reckless fellows don't regret much. But their women do."

"Why mention that?"

"Because I know you, Sister."

"Poppycock! I wouldn't think of such a thing!"

"You think of it," said Harmony. And thought, *We both do.* "You came mighty close to *doing* it, this afternoon."

Melody's cheeks were flaming. "I did not! He just . . . I . . . we were . . ."

"Sharing warmth. I know." Harmony put an arm around her sister's shoulders, drew her close, and kissed her softly on the cheek. "Be careful."

"Well, of course I will!"

They saw Slade reach the privy, step inside, and close the door. It felt peculiar, watching after that, and Harmony led Melody to clear the supper things. They'd have more stew for breakfast, in the morning, then she'd have to think about their next meal and their slowly dwindling supplies.

"I won't feel easy, going into town next time," she said.

"You never do," said Melody.

"But now, especially. After they tried to kill us."

"We can always go with Jack."

"You mean, with Marshal Slade."

"Yes, Sister."

"But he has business in Gehenna, Melody. He wouldn't see us home again."

"No matter. When they meet him, things will change. They won't have time to think about us anymore."

Until they finish killing him, thought Harmony, and she bit her lip as punishment. "You may be right," she said.

"Thank you."

"I said *may be*."

"I heard you, Sister."

"He should have more help," said Harmony. "I've heard about Judge Dennison. The hanging judge. Nobody ever said he was a fool."

"Why do you say that?"

"Sending *one man* to Gehenna? Why not shoot him back in Lawton and be done with it?"

"Sister!"

"You know I'm right. That town deserves its cursed name."

"The angel found a righteous few in Sodom and Gomorrah, Sister."

"*Precious* few," said Harmony. "And Lot's wife turned to salt."

"She wasn't worthy," Melody replied. "She didn't have a badge and guns."

"You *are* a child, sometimes."

"And still, you love me anyway."

"It's true. Although I sometimes wonder why."

"My wit and charm, perhaps?"

"That must be it."

Glancing back toward the yard, Melody asked, "Do you think he's all right?"

"I don't think he needs anyone to hold it for him, Sister — though he likely wouldn't mind."

"Shameless!"

Harmony smiled. "Perhaps we are, at that."

4

Slade found both women waiting for him when he came back from the privy, watching him as if they half expected him to swoon.

"Was it . . . I mean, are you all right?" asked Melody.

"So far, so good," said Slade. "No sign of anyone outside, as far as I can tell."

"They'll lick their wounds awhile," said Harmony, "and think about how they should do it next time."

Slade wished he could promise that there wouldn't be a next time, but he didn't like to lie except in a good cause. Instead, he told the sisters, "I'll try not to let that happen."

"We appreciate it," Melody replied quickly, her eyes locked on his face.

"You're pale," said Harmony. "The head's still paining you."

"It is," he said. "But I'm convinced that

I'll be better in the morning."

"Better, I'd agree," she said. "Not fit to ride, in my opinion, but improved."

"In any case, I want to thank you. For my animal, as well."

"We owe you that much, at the very least."

"I'd like to help with any nightly chores that you may have," he said, half meaning it.

"Nonsense," said Harmony. "Go back to bed, *without* those boots, and get the rest you need."

"But if there's work —"

"We're nearly finished," she assured him, "and you'd just be in the way. We turn in early around here."

"I'm taking someone's bed."

"We'll share, up in the loft," said Harmony. "It's just another night or two. No burden to it but my sister's snoring."

"I do not! You take that back!"

"Rattles the rafters, this one," Harmony went on. "But she's asleep, of course, and doesn't hear it."

"Fibber!"

"It's the gospel truth. She'll keep you up all night, once she gets started."

"I expect I've slept through worse," Slade said.

"I *do not snore!*" insisted Melody.

"Of course not, Sister. It's the night wind in the rafters, I suppose."

"You're too much! Just too much!" So saying, Melody went off to finish with the supper dishes, leaving Harmony with Slade.

"I guess you'll want to keep those trousers handy, for emergencies," she said.

"I might as well."

"And that?" She nodded toward his Colt.

"I'll slip it underneath the pillow, if you don't mind."

"Just in case," she said.

"That's right."

"Well, if you need more in the night, for any reason, over in that corner by the fireplace is your rifle and the other guns we gathered from the dead. I saw to loading them, myself."

"That's good."

"I'd wish you pleasant dreams, if that was possible."

"The same to you."

Slade skinned his pants off while the women had their backs turned, climbed beneath the covers, and was drifting by the time they finished cleaning. There were more good-nights as they went up to share the loft bed, then a lot of fabric rustling that he didn't like to think about, in case it stirred him up again.

Slade wasn't in the middle of a dream where women took their turns at pleasing him. If anything, he'd dropped into the middle of a nightmare that had almost cost his life.

Still, there were compensations.

Almost against his will, he pictured Melody descending from the loft to join him, maybe thinking that his fever had returned. Or maybe it was Harmony, determined not to place temptation in her sister's path.

When he began to stiffen, Slade switched tracks and thought about the job that waited for him in Gehenna, made more personal by what had happened at the sisters' ranch. He'd seen how the competing big men handled business, when they thought no one could interfere.

But they were wrong, and Slade would show them.

Soon.

Breakfast was stew again. Slade didn't mind, since it was good to start with, and the flavor changed when Harmony reheated it with something extra added that he couldn't name. Cooking had never been Slade's strong point, but he knew when it was managed well.

His head felt better, aching still, but not

enough to knock him sprawling if he kept his movements simple and avoided bending over. That drove a spike between his eyes, when Slade tried putting on his boots, until he lay back on the bed and did it that way, with his feet up in the air.

Still, he was better. One more night, he reckoned, and he would be fit to face Gehenna's challenges.

They made small talk across their breakfast plates, then Slade helped clear the table. Harmony assured him that his roan had feed and water in the barn, but he could tend it in a while, when he was ready for the hike. Meanwhile, Slade felt the stubble on his face and recognized the need to shave.

Melody drew a pan of water from the pump outside and put it on the stove to heat. When it was simmering, just hot enough to sting Slade's face and fingers without scalding him, she furnished soap, a smallish mirror, and then left him to it with the razor from his saddlebags.

A rugged face stared back at Slade, the bandage tied above it making him resemble something from a battlefield, or possibly a pirate ship. He didn't take the wrapping off to see the wound himself, trusting the sisters when they told him that he wasn't leaking brains. Instead, Slade lathered up and shaved with long, slow strokes that changed his face in subtle ways. Not softening his look, but making him appear more civilized.

Slade cleaned the razor after shaving, put it back into his bag, then buckled on his pistol belt and went outside to toss the soapy water. Harmony and Melody were tending to their stock — horses in the corral and chickens that had come from somewhere overnight, unseen by Slade while he was fighting for his life the day before. He counted seven hens and one cock, which explained the crowing of a rooster that had wakened him.

Slade crossed the yard, both women watching him, and let himself into the barn. The roan was fine, as they had said, unsaddled in an open stall, with food at hand and water in a trough nearby. Checking its mane and tail, he knew they'd also brushed the animal at some point after finding it.

It gratified him that the dizziness of yesterday had not returned, and that the dull ache in his head was fading by degrees. If there had been a fracture in his skull, or any deeper injury, the pain would be increasing and he would've been unsteady on his feet. Slade knew the signs from beatings he had witnessed or administered himself, and from the knocks he'd taken in return.

Healing. And that meant he would soon be on his way.

The top men in Gehenna didn't know it yet, but they were waiting for him. When he reached Helltown, their lives were bound to change, though Slade couldn't predict the outcome of his visit. There would almost certainly be more deaths, but Slade couldn't say if he would be among the fallen when the smoke cleared.

Either way, he had a job to do.

As soon as he was fit to ride.

Harmony found Slade tending to his roan horse in the barn. He didn't seem to hear her enter, busy currying and speaking to the animal. She watched him for a moment, then stepped closer, and he turned so quickly that it took her breath away, his right hand dipping toward the pistol on his hip but stopping short of it.

Harmony gasped, surprised despite herself.

Slade smiled a bit and said, "I'm almost finished here. Be with you in a minute."

As he turned back to the roan, she said, "You don't seem like a reckless man, to me."

"This is the way I always do it," he replied, and kept on with his long, slow strokes.

"It's not your horse I was referring to."

Slade missed a stroke but didn't turn again. "What, then?" he asked.

"My sister." As she spoke, Harmony moved around to a position on his right, where she could see Slade's face. "You understand she's been a while without a husband's care. A good *long* while, in fact."

"I heard her story," he replied.

"It's only natural," she forged ahead, "that in the circumstances she might be a bit *too* grateful for a kindness from a handsome stranger. One who saved her life, especially."

"You think I'm handsome?" Slade replied and smiled at Harmony again.

She felt a pang and flutter, deep inside, but fancied that she hid it well enough. "You're easy on the eyes, all right," she answered frankly. "But I see no future in it, for my sister or myself. You're drawing danger money, Marshal, and you're only passing through."

"You're right on both counts," Slade agreed.

"And you'll be leaving us, within the next few days."

"I will."

"It would be rash, and even cruel, of you to start something with Melody that has no future to it."

73

"I hear you, ma'am. But should you maybe have this talk with her?"

"We'll have our talk, all right," said Harmony. "But I'm not sure she's in the mood for listening right now. With all that happened yesterday, before you came along and after, she'll be spinning dreams and may not realize it."

"Not much I can do about that, is there?"

"Just don't make it any worse."

"Listen, about what happened in her bed —"

"My bed," she said, correcting him. "And I was there. I know that you were half asleep and likely miles away, inside your fever dreams. I'm telling you, it doesn't matter. Women miss some things as much as men do, even if we're not supposed to talk about it. Mickey O'Hara's been a long time gone. My sister's been a long time sleeping lonely, and I'm guessing that you wouldn't need a long courtship to take advantage of her, if you had a mind to."

"Well," Slade said, "I don't."

"I'm glad to hear it, Marshal. You're a credit to your sex."

His smile came back. "I wouldn't go that far."

"And modest, too. You'll make some woman happy, I expect. If you can keep

74

from getting shot, that is."

"Always my goal," Slade said. "To keep from getting shot, I mean."

"That won't be easy in Gehenna, now that you've thumped on the hornets' nest."

"It's good to stir them up a bit," Slade told her. "Sometimes, angry hornets make mistakes."

Half turned to leave, Harmony said, "I hope you won't say anything to Melody about our talk."

"Rest easy, ma'am."

She felt another deep-down pang and spoke impulsively. "You know, I'm only two years older than my sister. Not a *ma'am* at all, really."

"You'll both be ma'am to me," Slade said, "until I can repay your hospitality."

"Saving our lives should cover that, surely."

"I haven't saved them yet," the marshal answered. "All I've done is buy some time."

Supper was beans, salt pork, potatoes, and some fresh greens on the side. The sisters had a garden patch to supplement their table, and with three meals down, Slade had to grant that they were decent cooks. He wondered if the late Michael O'Hara had appreciated what was granted to him in his life, before an accident or murder cut it short.

Slade had appreciated Harmony's frank tone when she addressed him in the barn. She'd been propelled into a mother's role where her sister was concerned, and Slade thought Melody was lucky to have someone looking out for her. The last few words that Harmony had spoken cast a different light upon her, though.

Slade understood that he was dealing with *two* vulnerable women, and without a trace of egotism he supposed he could've bedded either one, if he'd been so inclined. There was a chance he might have bedded *both,* though likely not together. Some men he had known — some men he *still* knew — would've grabbed that opportunity and run with it, but Slade wasn't inclined toward conquest for its own sake.

Certainly, the images his brain had conjured were arousing. Coupled with his first glimpse of the sisters, pressed up close to Melody with nothing much between them, those delicious images distracted and excited him.

And it was the *distracted* part that worried Slade.

He had a hard job still ahead of him, perhaps made harder by his injury and by the fact that someone in Gehenna might be able to describe him. Might've spread the word that he was on his way.

No harm in that, Slade thought, *as long as they're not certain what I've come for.* And, in truth, he wasn't sure exactly what Judge Dennison expected from a single man. Sort out the trouble, maybe. Work out who was doing what to whom. But as for cleaning up the town, Slade didn't see that happening without a troop of reinforcements.

Take it easy, then. For now.

He'd felt both women watching him throughout that day, concerned that he was overdoing it with little chores. They took turns nagging Slade to rest, and he obliged, nursing a headache that annoyed him, but that never came within a rifle shot of rivaling the pain he'd suffered one day earlier.

Slade felt no dizziness to speak of on his second day with the sisters, unless he stooped over too quickly. In that case, the sick rush of blood to his head nearly floored him, but Slade thought he'd covered it well. At least, he thought so until supper.

He had nearly cleaned his plate when Harmony remarked, "You're looking peaked, Marshal."

"Am I?"

"Too much sun and labor, I expect."

"With all respect, ma'am, you have no idea how I look or act during the best of times."

"That's true," she granted. "But I'll wager you don't stagger with your face screwed up and grimacing when you bend down to pluck a weed."

"As bad as that, am I?" Slade asked.

"Not bad exactly," she replied. "But still not fit to face what's waiting for you in Gehenna."

"Why don't you enlighten me on that?" Slade said.

"Not much to say, really. With Cartwright and Bjornson feuding, each one grabbing whatever he can, it's like a little piece of Hell on Earth."

Slade slept alone that night, no fever dreams or woman's flesh to trouble him. He woke refreshed and didn't argue after breakfast when the ladies changed the dressing on his head.

"You likely won't need bandages tomorrow," Harmony advised him. "Just be careful with the scab and don't do anything to overtax yourself."

"Like getting shot, you mean."

"I'd rank that as a bad idea, along with letting people punch you, throw you off a building, drag you through the streets behind a horse —"

"I take your meaning, ma'am," Slade interrupted her. "Hard to believe Gehenna holds such rude surprises for a stranger passing through."

"It might not," she agreed, "if you were that."

"She makes the place sound worse than what it is," said Melody. "Sister, you know we've been to town at least two dozen times and only saw one man shot in the street."

"Michael was with us more than half those times," said Harmony. "He wouldn't stand for insults of the sort we suffer now."

Melody blushed at that, and focused on her plate, leaving Slade to imagine the remarks that might be passed by hoodlums in her unescorted presence.

"Well," Slade said to break the mood, "I'm not concerned that anyone will find me winsome."

"No," said Harmony. "It will be worse in your case, Marshal. They will find you dangerous."

"Only to criminals."

"That means the men in charge, and most of those who serve them," she replied. "Your judge would have been wise to send a troop of cavalry."

"He hadn't one to spare," Slade said. "I was the last bean in the pot."

"Be careful, then," said Harmony, "that they don't eat you up alive."

"They'll find me hard to swallow," Slade assured her. "And a damn sight harder to digest."

He put more sweat into the chores that day and felt the better for it. Working with his shirt off, in the sun, Slade caught both women watching him from time to time, and took it as a compliment. He'd never thought himself God's gift to womankind, but he was lean and reasonably fit. What was it Harmony had called him?

Easy on the eyes.

Slade wore his Colt all day, hoping he wouldn't need it, and by dusk there'd been no call for him to draw it. If the sisters' enemies were planning further mischief — and Slade had no reason to believe they weren't — then it had been postponed.

How long?

Would men with guns come riding up the moment he had left the ranch? Or would they wait for dark some night, come creeping when the women were asleep to force their way inside, or torch the place and burn them up alive?

Slade had no answers to those questions,

and he kept them to himself.

Slade washed up at the pump outside and was shaking water from his hair when Harmony passed by him with a hatchet in her hand. "Chicken for supper," she informed him. "It's my specialty."

"Be looking forward to it," Slade replied.

And wondered how it felt to be the chosen bird.

The bird was tasty, none the less because Slade might've met it pecking in the yard that afternoon. He didn't get confused about his place in nature, always conscious of the fact that he who ate today might be the meal tomorrow. Anyone who thought himself invincible was in for a surprise.

They didn't talk about Gehenna over supper, and Slade waited for the coffee afterward to tell the sisters he'd be leaving in the morning.

"What, so soon?" asked Melody.

"He's fit enough," said Harmony.

"We don't know that."

"It's not our business, Sister. This man wears a badge, you understand?"

"I know, but —"

"That means he must put himself in danger's way."

"But since he helped us —"

"Not just *us,* Sister. He wasn't sent from Lawton to become our guardian."

"I didn't say that. Did I *say* that, Harmony?"

"I hope," Slade interrupted them, "that when I get to town, the men who've been disturbing you may be distracted for a time. That's not a promise, but I'll do my best to keep them occupied."

"They'll notice you, all right," said Harmony. "Cartwright and Bjornson like to have things their own way. They challenge one another, but there's been no law around Gehenna since the last elected marshal disappeared."

Slade raised an eyebrow. "When was that?" he asked.

"Nearly a year ago," said Melody. "Word has it that he up and left one night, without a by-your-leave."

Something Judge Dennison had failed to mention when he briefed Slade on the situation in Gehenna. Now, Slade had to wonder if the marshal had been frightened out of town, or if he'd been disposed of in some way designed to make his end mysterious.

In either case, he would be dealing with a pair of men, both wealthy and supported by small armies of their own, who weren't concerned about the law. They might believe themselves untouchable, beyond the reach of courts and all the rules that governed civilized society. Experience would reinforce that feeling of superiority.

In fact, Slade would be counting on it.

Men with inflated visions of themselves were prone to critical mistakes. They didn't listen when they should, and sometimes bit off more than they could chew. Big men would not believe a single marshal had the wits, the courage, or the strength to bring them down.

And maybe they were right.

But Slade wouldn't believe that until he had seen Gehenna for himself and met the men in charge. He would assess the situation then, decide if help was needed to achieve his goals.

What help?

That was the rub, of course. Whether he needed help or not, Jack Slade was on his own.

He saved his final thank-yous for the morning, after breakfast, and went out to check his horse a final time before lights-out. Standing in darkness near the barn, Slade watched and listened to the night, heard nothing but the normal sounds of birds and insects undisturbed.

Slade didn't think the raiders would be

coming back that night, but he would sleep with weapons ready just in case.

The sisters had their heads together, arguing, he thought, when Slade returned and shut the cabin's door behind him. Moments later, they were on their way upstairs, taking the lamp along and dousing it before they changed into their nightgowns.

Listening, imagining, Slade found it hard to sleep at first. He lay awake until the sound of gentle snoring reached his ears, then for a little longer, half expecting Melody to sneak downstairs and join him in his narrow bed.

It didn't happen, though, and when he drifted off to sleep at last, Slade dreamed of castles burning, wreathed in bitter smoke and somewhere far away.

5

The sisters made too many eggs for breakfast, feeding Slade as if he'd been two men instead of one. He did his best to put it all away, but had to call a halt at last.

"It's mighty good," he told them, "but I'm worried that my horse may suffer if I don't stop now."

"Nonsense!" said Melody. "You need your strength."

"I've got back all I had to start with, thanks to both of you," Slade said.

"It may not be enough," Melody told him. "If you only stayed another day or two —"

"Sister, he has a mind to go and do his job," said Harmony.

"Of course." Another blush from Melody. "Don't pay a bit of mind to me."

"That's easy said," Slade answered as he pushed back from the table. "But you're right, Miss Harmony. I've got a fair ride to Gehenna, and a day's work waiting for me when I get there."

"At the very least," said Harmony.

"You *will* be careful, won't you?" Melody demanded.

"That's a promise." *And the only one I'll make,* Slade thought.

"If you get back this way, by any chance . . ."

"I'll surely try," he said. "It's hard to say how things will go, from this point on."

"I understand."

Slade hoped that he only imagined tears welling behind Melody's eyelashes. "Meanwhile," he said, "you've got enough guns here to make an army think twice about marching through this way. My best advice would be to keep them handy. Anyone shows up you don't feel just exactly right about, use them."

"We're not afraid," said Harmony.

"It never crossed my mind," Slade said in answer to her lie.

The sisters obviously *were* afraid, and with good reason. They were under siege by enemies who'd shown a willingness to murder women. If Slade hadn't come along precisely when he did, two days ago, the job would likely be complete, one of the local robber barons moving in to claim their land. In fact, although Gehenna's warlords didn't know it yet, that very fact gave Slade the angle he required to take them on.

It was a federal crime to jump claims on a homestead granted by the U.S. government, which gave Slade jurisdiction over those who did the jumping. With sufficient evidence in hand, he could deliver them to Lawton and Judge Dennison for trial — or kill them if they offered any serious resistance.

On the other hand, his jurisdiction wouldn't matter if they killed Slade first.

Something to keep in mind, before he took another wild swing at the hornets' nest.

Both sisters trailed him to the barn, watching Slade saddle up the roan, holster his Winchester, and strap his saddlebags in place. Before he mounted, Slade thanked them again for tending him and waved off any further thanks for intervening in their time of need.

"My job," he said and felt himself begin to color as they stepped up, one behind the other, planting kisses on his cheeks.

"Take care," Melody whispered in his left ear.

"Go with God," Harmony whispered in his right.

Slade had his left foot in the stirrup when Harmony said something to her sister.

Melody immediately caught his belt and blurted, "Wait! Don't go yet!"

She turned and ran back toward the cabin, Slade and Harmony watching her go. "She made some food for you to take along," said Harmony. "It slipped my mind until just now."

Slade doubted that, his doubt confirmed as Harmony addressed him in her sister's absence. "Don't take any foolish chances in Gehenna, will you? Trust no one. There may be decent people there, but Cartwright and Bjornson have corrupted most of them. The rest . . . well, they still have to live. They go along to get along."

"I hear you."

"I hope so. You won't have any friends there. Anyone who *seems* to be your friend bears watching, more than those who scorn you. Keep your back against the wall."

"Why do you stay?" he asked on impulse.

"I'd leave in a minute," Harmony replied, "but Melody won't go. She dreamed this place with Michael — Mickey — and she can't give up the dream. Also, he's buried here. I think she feels that giving up and leaving would be spitting on his grave."

"I'll see what I can do to make it right," Slade said.

"Good luck to you, but I won't hold my

breath," said Harmony.

Melody came back moments later with a parcel wrapped in cloth. Slade thanked her for it, stowed it in his saddlebag, and stood for one more kiss before he mounted. Riding out, he paused to look back once and saw the sisters waving to him from the dooryard.

Swallowing a hard knot in his throat, Slade left them there and focused on the road ahead.

His roan was happy to be traveling again after its long hours in the barn. Slade had to rein it in, to keep the animal from trotting and wasting energy.

He had twelve miles to cover, more or less. A steady pace would put Slade in Gehenna shortly after noon, with ample time to find lodgings both for himself and his horse. After that, he'd be left to explore and discover the town on his own.

Slade knew wild towns. He'd seen his share while gambling for a living, over half a dozen states, before his brother's death had led him to his present situation. Finding out that James was murdered put him in the mood to seek revenge, but Judge Dennison had anticipated Slade's reaction, stepping in to intercept him with an offer

Slade had grudgingly accepted. He could wear a badge and make the hunt legitimate, try every means within his power to *arrest* his brother's killers short of using deadly force, or he could murder them and make his own date with the gallows.

Slade had chosen the badge and secured the arrest of the man who had ordered James killed. Some of the big man's underlings refused to take their chances with a jury, and he'd had to kill them anyway. That hadn't bothered Slade at all, and Dennison seemed satisfied that justice had been served.

That would've been the time to quit, and no one had been more surprised than Slade himself when he decided to stay on, keep riding circuit for Judge Dennison, and tracking those who broke the law. It was a far cry from his old vocation as a gambler, in some ways, but he still played for high stakes.

Each time Slade donned his U.S. marshal's badge, his life was riding on the line.

The countryside through which Slade rode was much the same as earlier, a landscape sculpted into gently rolling hills with grassy slopes, some bristling with slender trees on top. He tried to picture Melody's young husband, riding back from town and

90

suddenly encountering a rattler on the ground, horse rearing, tossing him at just the proper angle where the fall would snap his neck.

It was a possibility, of course. Slade knew a man in Lawton who'd been thrown while herding cattle and was paralyzed below the waist. That injury had been a lucky one, compared to severing the spine where it connected with his skull. Slade guessed that someday, in the distant future, doctors might find ways to keep a man alive with such an injury, maybe invent machines to breathe for him — but why?

What good was living, he thought, when a man couldn't scratch his own nose or perform other chores that a body required? Would a survivor in those circumstances count himself as lucky? Would he pray for strength enough to lift a gun and curl his finger through the trigger guard?

In any case, Mickey O'Hara didn't have a choice. He had been dead when Melody and Harmony discovered him.

"Too late to prove a murder there," Slade told the roan, "unless somebody squeals."

It was a subject he could probe, and maybe agitate the guilty parties, if there *was* a crime involved. Most criminals, in Slade's experience, were not the most intelligent of men or women. And when stupid folk got scared, they made mistakes. He only needed one loose tongue to build a case, refer it to Judge Dennison.

And failing that, maybe the killers would come after Slade himself. One of them had escaped the shoot-out at the homestead. Whoever sent them on that mission might be hungry for revenge.

That thought was foremost in Slade's mind when he first glimpsed Gehenna as a smudge on the horizon, drawing closer by the moment. He was still too far away to make out buildings, much less people moving through the streets, but now he had the place in sight.

So far, it didn't look like Hell.

Slade rode into Gehenna from the east, along a main street wide enough for two wagons to move abreast and riders free to pass on either side. Raised wooden sidewalks fronted stores and offices on both sides, busy with people passing to and fro. None of them seemed to notice Slade, and yet he had a brooding sense of being watched.

With no attempt to hide his badge, Slade rode along the main drag, following a wagon piled with hides, perhaps bound for a tannery. Scanning the signs on either side of him, Slade noted that Gehenna offered most of the amenities he found in Lawton, though they served a population less than half of Lawton's size. In fact, he quickly noted, there were *two* of many shops, competitors positioned to face one another from across the street, as if a line was drawn, demanding that the populace choose sides.

There were two dry-goods stores, for instance, and two barbershops. Two lawyers' offices, two groceries, two gunsmiths, two hotels, two liveries. The marshal's office was a solo act, and it was closed, according to a faded sign fixed to the door with rusted nails.

Most prominently, there were two saloons, both doing decent business for a weekday afternoon, in Slade's opinion. On his left, as he approached them, the Valhalla spewed piano music through its bat-wing doors. The trim was red and gold, all freshly painted from the look of it. Upstairs, three modestly attractive women dressed in little more than corsets followed traffic on the street below with dull, disinterested eyes.

Across the street — and no less musical, with a trombone for some variety — the Rosebud featured blue-and-silver trim. Slade counted four girls on its balcony, two of them smoking cigarettes, none any more excited by the prospects on display than were their sisters on the south side of the thoroughfare. One of them winked at Slade in passing, but she didn't seem to mean it. Maybe, he reflected, she had something in her eye.

Outside each saloon, Slade also counted half a dozen gunmen lounging near the doors. Some sat on stools, while others leaned against the walls or hitching rails of their respective dives. Slade knew they might be customers, but from their placement and appearance he supposed they were assigned to guard the premises and stare each other down.

Two warring camps.

That could be helpful in the long run, but for now, Slade counted all of them as likely enemies. Which ones were friends of those he'd killed on the O'Hara homestead?

At the moment, he had no idea.

Slade's choice of lodgings was split between the Bonanza Hotel, on what he already considered Buck Bjornson's side of Main Street, or the Gehenna Arms directly opposite, on Baron Cartwright's side. Because he didn't fancy sleeping in the arms of Hell, Slade veered off to the south and tied his roan to a rail outside the Bonanza.

Taking his rifle and saddlebags with him, Slade pushed through the hotel's front door.

A bell mounted above the door jangled to herald his entrance. At the registration desk, a clerk with hair slicked down and parted in the middle met Slade with a smile that stretched from ear to ear.

It faltered when the greeter saw his badge.

"Yes, sir . . . um . . . may I help you?"

"You can let me have a room," Slade said.

The clerk seemed to consider that as if it were an odd request for a hotel, more likely wishing that he had a chance to ask his boss for guidance. Still, with six of eighteen room keys dangling on their hooks behind him, there was no way that the clerk could claim a lack of vacancies.

"Yes, sir. Of course! Welcome to the Bonanza. I'm afraid the quality of service offered makes our rooms a bit expensive. That is, fifty cents per day. If that's —"

"I'll take it."

"Certainly. Would you prefer a front room, or —"

"Something where I can see the street," Slade said.

"As good as done, sir. If you have luggage —"

"You're looking at it," Slade informed him.

"And how long will you be staying, sir, if I may ask?"

"I'm not sure yet." Slade put two dollars on the counter. "Here's four days' worth, for a start."

Slade signed the register with a fountain pen made up to look like an old-fashioned quill. He listed Lawton as his home address, and Judge Dennison as his emergency contact, giving the clerk and the man behind him some food for thought.

"You'll be in number six," the clerk informed him as he slid a key across the countertop. "That's at the northeast corner of the third floor, sir. Toilets at the far end of the hall on every floor."

"Indoor?" Slade asked him.

"Nothing but the best at the Bonanza, sir!"

As Slade turned toward the stairs, he wondered how long it would take the clerk to warn Buck Bjornson of his presence — or if someone else had done the job already as Slade rode along Main Street.

After depositing his saddlebags and rifle in his small-but-tidy room, Slade washed his face and hands, then went back down to claim his horse and take it to the nearest livery. From there, he had his choice of two fair-looking restaurants, Bjornson's Longhorn versus Cartwright's Chuck Wagon.

It would be good to keep the opposition guessing, he decided, until someone made a move.

"A U.S. marshal," Eulis Baker said to no one special. He was planted on a stool outside the Rosebud, leaning back so that his shoulders pressed against the wall, his boot heels dangling.

None among the shooters who surrounded Baker answered, since he hadn't asked a question and did not appear to be inviting comments. Learning Baker's moods was a prerequisite for working on his team — or, rather, for surviving as a member of the chosen few.

"He could be passing through," Baker continued, thinking aloud, "but it's early to stop if he's bound somewhere else. I don't like it."

The others muttered to themselves, a couple of them merely grunting. It was good to go on record as agreeing with the man in charge, but offering opinions could be dangerous.

"Why would he go to the Bonanza?" Baker mused, shifting to ease the weight of two matched pistols on his hips.

That *was* a question, granted, but the others grouped around him had no answers, so they wisely kept their mouths shut. Some of them kept busy glaring at their rivals outside the Valhalla, Damon Shakespeare lounging on his own seat while the others propped up walls and hitching posts. Much of their work these days was glaring at the enemy, waiting for orders to do worse.

"Louis."

"Yessir?"

"Go in and tell the Man we've got a lawman visiting. Be sure and tell him that he's got a room at the Bonanza."

"Right."

"And don't stop for a drink first."

"Nosir."

It probably meant nothing, Baker thought, as far as choosing hotels went. The marshal came from Outside, wouldn't know the way things stood around Gehenna, where the lines were drawn.

Unless . . .

Could Bjornson have a lawman on his payroll? Not just *any* lawman, either, but a real, live U.S. marshal?

Baker doubted it, but nothing was impossible. He had known crooked constables and sheriffs all his life. Why should a federal badge be anything but more expensive?

"Joey."

"Yeah?"

"Somebody needs to go across and check the register at the Bonanza. Find out where the lawman's from and such as that. You're it."

"Go over there?"

Baker could hear the hesitancy in his flunky's voice. "Not *straight* across, for Christ's sake. Use your head, for once."

"Okay. But . . ."

Jesus wept.

"Go down our side until you hit the livery, then cut across and work your way back up to the hotel. Nobody's down there, anyway. Mix in and find out what you can from the desk clerk. Slip him a couple dollars if you have to."

"S'posin' he won't talk for money?" Joey asked.

"Persuade him," Baker answered. "Just don't be too rough about it. Nothing that needs doctoring or undertaking."

"Right. Okay."

Joey set off without enthusiasm, moving west along the sidewalk, rubbing shoulders with the good folk of Gehenna.

Good folk, Baker thought, smiling. *Now there's a laugh.*

Across the street, Shakespeare was watching him. Baker put on a mocking smile and crossed his ankles where they dangled from his stool. He knew Shakespeare had marked the lawman's passing and had sent a man through the Valhalla's swinging doors to pass the word, but did it come as a surprise?

Was Bjornson raising in the deadly game they played?

We'll see, thought Eulis Baker. *Yes, indeed. And when we know for sure, we'll make our move.*

Damon Shakespeare snarled a smile across the street toward Eulis Baker, wishing he could simply grab a Winchester and drill the smirking bastard where he sat. Things would be so much easier around Gehenna — *everywhere,* in fact — if people followed their basic instincts and did whatever they wanted to, with no fretting after the fact.

Sadly, Shakespeare was not a law unto himself. He answered to a boss who could and *would* dispose of him if he strayed too far from the beaten path of orders from above.

The order for today, like every other day: Watch out for strangers riding into town, particularly those with badges on their vests.

And now he had one, riding past the Rosebud and Valhalla without stopping, heading on to one of the hotels. Not just a lawman, either, but a U.S. marshal who could throw his weight around most anywhere inside the Oklahoma territory.

Shakespeare sent a man inside to tell the boss, same thing Baker had done across the street, then watched as the stranger stopped, tied his horse, and went inside the Bonanza Hotel.

That was a puzzler, making Shakespeare wonder if the choice was random, or if there was something happening he ought to know about, something Bjornson had neglected to mention. That thought raised the short hairs on his nape, Shakespeare reflecting that the first step toward eliminating someone from the payroll was to keep him in the dark on pivotal events.

Bullshit!

He'd served Bjornson well, with no complaints so far. There was no reason for the boss to cut him out, much less in any underhanded way. Why would Bjornson send out for a marshal, anyhow?

No reason in the world, unless the badge was *on his side.*

Shakespeare dismissed the very notion as ridiculous, but made a mental note to have a look at the Bonanza's register and find out who the lawman was, start asking questions up and down Main Street of anyone the marshal spoke to on his rounds.

If he was straight — or worse, allied somehow with Baron Cartwright — there were ways to make the lawman disappear. Doctor the hotel register, warn certain people to be smart and keep their mouths shut, and it would appear that he had never reached Gehenna. Anything could happen to a marshal in the badlands, passing through. People were dying out there every day.

And more to come, thought Shakespeare. *More to come, before the end, whatever that might be.*

One thing was certain: Shakespeare meant to back the winning side and get his just desserts for helping put Buck Bjornson on top of the heap. Any attempt to cut him out along the way would have surprising consequences for the folks involved.

Shakespeare considered sending out one of his men to trail the marshal, then dismissed it as a waste of time and energy. The lawman couldn't move along Main Street without a swarm of eyeballs tracking him, the brains behind them logging every stop he made. Shakespeare would save his spies for later, if the stranger started branching out, prowling the backstreets, maybe taking off for rides around the countryside.

"Jason."

"Yeah, Day?" one of his shooters answered.

"Who's it on the desk at the Bonanza?"

"Pinkus."

"Okay."

"Any trouble with 'im?"

"Nope."

" 'Cuz I can kick his ass, you want me to."

"No, thanks. I want to ask him something later. Just forget about it now."

Trouble was coming. Shakespeare smelled it on the arid breeze, but not from Myron Pinkus clerking down at the Bonanza. Shakespeare wanted, *needed* to be ready when it happened, but for now his first job was to strike a pose and make Cartwright's gunslingers think that everything was fine as frog's hair.

Let *them* worry. Let *them* sweat.

Shakespeare disliked the game, but he was in it now, and all that he could do was raise his bet.

6

Slade thought it best to keep the opposition guessing, so he lodged his horse at Cartwright's livery, then crossed the street again and walked back to the Longhorn Restaurant.

There was no question now about that sense of being watched. The shooters ranged outside both saloons were tracking every step Slade took, most of them frowning as they tried to take his measure from a distance.

Slade responded with an enigmatic smile, hoping the look would puzzle them, and maybe worry them as well.

The Longhorn had a decent crowd for one o'clock, when Slade supposed most townsmen would be working, with their womenfolk at home. The restaurant had fourteen tables, eight of them already occupied by diners when he entered. The largest group was three men, seated near the door, whose conversation faltered as Slade entered. Five more tables hosted two diners apiece, all male except for one young lady dining with a man who could've been her husband. Anyway, she wore a wedding ring. The solitary diners, both men, were positioned at two corners of the dining room, facing the street.

Slade took an empty table in the southeast corner, where he had a blind wall at his back and all the room in front of him.

Perfect.

The waitress wore her jet-black hair tied back into a ponytail that reached her waist. The olive cast of her complexion indicated mixing, somewhere farther back. The only violet eyes that Slade had ever seen examined him before he took a printed menu and began to read.

"Something to drink, sir, while you're making your decision? We have beer and —"

"Coffee, please."

"One coffee. Milk or sugar?"

"Black."

"I'll be right back with that."

The Longhorn's menu wasn't anything elaborate. It offered beef, pork, chicken, with a list of trimmings that included beans, potatoes, onions, and a specialty the chef called Texas toast.

Slade made his choice and sat back, waiting for the waitress to return. She joined him in a minute, give or take, and set a steaming mug of coffee on the table near his curled left hand.

"Black coffee. What else would you like, sir?"

This would be the point, Slade guessed, where some young rogues might ask if she was on the menu. Others might be sly about it, asking her about the chicken breast or thigh to see if they could make her blush. There'd been a time when Slade himself might've enjoyed that game, but he was older now and weary from the road.

He glanced up, caught the waitress looking at the graze along the left side of his head, and said, "Don't worry. Any brains I've got are staying on the inside."

"Sir, I'm sorry. Please —"

Slade interrupted her apology to say, "I'll have the steak, well done, with beans and fried potatoes on the side."

"Yes, sir." She stood with eyes downcast, hands clasped in front of her.

"Am I correct in thinking that the Texas toast is just big bread?" Slade asked.

"Cook melts a little cheese on that, sir."

"Better still. I'll have that, too."

"Yes, sir. Forgive my staring, please."

"What staring?"

"Thank you, sir!"

She swirled away, quick-stepping toward the kitchen with Slade's order. He enjoyed his coffee, one sip at a time, to keep from ruining his taste buds with its heat. While waiting for his meal, Slade scanned the other faces in the restaurant and found them carefully avoiding his. Whenever he made eye contact, the other person flinched and made a show of looking elsewhere, even if it meant turning to stare across one shoulder at the street.

Ten minutes passed, and Slade was nearly finished with his coffee when the waitress brought his meal. The steak was large enough to overflow its platter, crowding beans and cubed potatoes off to either side. Two slabs of bread with cheese toasted a golden brown on top rated a small plate of their own.

"I'll bring more coffee, if you like," the waitress said.

"Yes, please."

She brought the pot and filled Slade's mug up to the brim, making his next sip something of a challenge.

"Sir, if you need anything at all —"

"I'm fine. Rest easy."

"Thank you, sir."

Slade tucked into his meal, slicing his steak and savoring the first bite while he scanned the street outside. A moment later, as he bit into the Texas toast, a heavyset young man with two guns on his belt paused at the window, cupping hands against the glass to peer inside. He spotted Slade, then swaggered to the door and made his way into the restaurant.

Slade waited, seeming to ignore him while the visitor approached his table. Only when the young man stood before him, shadow falling over Slade's plate, did he formally acknowledge the newcomer.

"You want something?" Slade inquired.

Gene Cordry wasn't sure why he'd been picked for this chore, but he hadn't felt like arguing with Eulis Baker, much less with the Man himself.

Now he was standing in the Longhorn, staring at the marshal looking back at him, and felt a tight knot twisting in his stomach.

"You want something?" asked the marshal.

Cordry started to reply, but then the Longhorn's half-breed waitress interrupted him. "Will you be dining with us, sir?" she asked.

"No, ma'am, he won't," the lawman told her, without letting Cordry answer for himself.

Stubborn, he answered anyway. "We're goin' in a minute," Cordry said.

The waitress looked confused, glanced at the lawman's plate still heaped with food, then turned and left them to it.

"You said 'we.' " The lawman spoke around a bite of well-done beef. "I don't suppose you've got a chipmunk in your pocket?"

"Huh?" Cordry suspected that the marshal was insulting him, but couldn't get a handle on it yet.

"Forget it, son. What makes you think *we're* going anywhere?"

On safer ground, Cordry replied. "I come from Mr. Baron Cartwright. He sent me to fetch you over to the Rosebud."

"Fetch me, eh? You get a bone for that?"

"A bone? I don't —"

"This Mr. Cartwright," said the lawman, interrupting. "Does he always get his way?"

"Mostly."

"Mostly's not *always*," said the marshal. "He's experienced some disappointment, then, along the way."

"I don't know anything about that," Cordry said, confused again.

"There's always time to learn, son. You go back and tell your Mr. Cartwright that I'll be along to see him when it suits me."

"I can't —"

"What I *won't* do is get up and leave this meal I've paid for, and run off to see him like some pup he's whistled for, my belly growling from the trail."

"Listen, mister —"

"Marshal." Reaching up, the lawman tapped his tin star with the fork in his left hand. It made a tiny ringing sound.

Cordry felt angry color rising in his face. Blunt fingers twitching near the curved grips of his pistols, he replied, "I don't care who you are. When Mr. Cartwright says come see 'im, you come see 'im."

"Just drop everything and trot down to the Rosebud."

"It's be a good idea," Cordry replied.

The lawman laid his knife down, and his right hand disappeared beneath the table. "So, what happens if I don't? Suppose I just sit here and finish up my meal. What happens then?"

Gene Cordry felt a headache starting up behind his eyes, the way it did sometimes when he spent too much effort thinking.

"I was told to bring you," he replied.

"I see. You'd best get to it, then, before my food gets cold."

It took a second for the import of the

marshal's words to settle in his brain, but Cordry got it. He would either have to *take* the lawman, or go back to Baron Cartwright empty-handed. Worse, go back with an insulting message from a stranger that would put his own neck on the line.

"I'm waiting, boy."

The marshal didn't blink or move a muscle as he sat there, staring up at Cordry. In his mind, Cordry could almost see the lawman's weapon — would it be a pistol? possibly a sawed-off shotgun? — pointing at him underneath the table. He was dead before he made a move, but pride demanded *something* of him.

Straining to recall the Man's precise words, Cordry told the marshal, "Mr. Cartwright told me to *invite* you. That was it."

"Invite me."

"Yessir."

"That's a good deal different, don't you think?"

"I reckon so."

"All right, then. You go back and tell him that I'll be along to see him when I'm finished here. Maybe an hour. I might have some apple pie."

"I'll tell him," Cordry said, and back-stepped from the table, keeping both eyes on the lawman as his right hand surfaced, reaching for the steak knife.

I could take him now, Gene Cordry thought. Mr. Cartwright hadn't mentioned shooting anybody. Just a talk, he said, and Cordry knew there'd be no thanks in store for him if he shot someone who could help the Man.

Embarrassed, angry, and dejected, Cordry left the Longhorn and began his trek back to the Rosebud, temples throbbing as he tried to write a short speech in his head. Instinct dictated that a touch of eloquence might save his life.

And that was frightening, indeed.

Slade watched the hulking errand boy depart, waiting until he cleared the doorway and the sidewalk visible from where Slade sat, before he let himself relax. He'd played a risky game, baiting the shooter, but Slade's instinct told him Cartwright hadn't sent the man to kill him, and he bet the gunman would be scared of overstepping Cartwright's orders.

Less than two hours in town, and he'd already made a splash. Now Slade would let the ripples spread a bit, dawdle over his meal, before he went to hear what Baron Cartwright had to say.

But he could guess.

Three broad scenarios occurred to him. The first involved a general welcome to Gehenna, Cartwright playing host and offering to make Slade's visit comfortable, help him out with anything that needed doing while he was in town. A variation on that theme had Cartwright taking Slade into his confidence, pretending he was glad the law had noticed what was going on around Gehenna, offering to help Slade cleanse the place of evildoers. In the third scenario, Cartwright would offer bribes and favors to ensure that Slade went blind and deaf to any evidence of criminal activity on Cartwright's part.

"Is everything all right, sir?"

Slade smiled at the waitress, noting little worry lines around her striking eyes. "Couldn't be better," Slade replied, "unless I had a bit more coffee."

"Yes, sir. Right away." And yet, she hesitated. "Sir, I hope that fellow didn't trouble you."

"No, ma'am." Mindful of who she worked for, Slade explained, "He had an invitation for me, but I told him I was otherwise engaged."

"I'll get that coffee for you, sir."

"Appreciate it."

As Slade finished his meal, taking his time,

he thought about Gehenna. It was split between two wealthy, ruthless men, not only physically but also in the hearts and minds of its inhabitants. *Trust no one,* Harmony had told him, and he saw the wisdom of her words.

There might — indeed, *must* — be some decent people living in Gehenna, but Slade wouldn't place his trust in anyone until he knew the individual and had a chance to test his loyalty.

Slim chance of that, he thought. The way eyes recoiled from his badge, Slade knew he couldn't count on finding any public allies in Gehenna. Everyone depended on the goodwill of one local warlord or the other to survive. Gunmen and spies would likely watch his every move, making it hard — if not impossible — for Slade to ferret out the discontented citizens and rally them behind him.

Once again, Slade wished that he could call for help.

But there was no help to be had. Judge Dennison had made that clear enough.

This time, Slade *was* the cavalry. He'd rescued two young women — for the moment, anyway — but rescuing Gehenna from itself might prove to be impossible. Slade ranked it with the labors set for Hercules, but those were mythical.

Slade's task was real. He was a man of flesh and blood, no more, no less.

Sadly for him, it wasn't difficult to puncture flesh or spill warm blood. In fact, it happened all the time.

Slade's plate was clean before he knew it, and the waitress stood beside him yet again. "Will there be something else, sir?" she inquired.

Slade thought about it, checked his pocket watch, and smiled at her. "Do you have any apple pie?"

"The marshal turned me down?" asked Baron Cartwright, dark eyes staring holes into his nervous errand boy.

"Nuh-no, sir," Cordry answered, worrying the rolled brim of his hat with restless hands. "Said he'd be coming up directly, when he finished with his meal."

"I see." Cartwright half turned toward Eulis Baker, startling his chief enforcer with a smile. "I like it. He's got nerve. I like a man with nerve, don't you, Eulis?"

"Depends on who he works for, Mr. C.," Baker replied.

"You've got a point there. Nervy men on the wrong side are bad for business."

"Yes, sir."

Cartwright faced the messenger again. "Gene, give me your impression of the marshal."

"Sir?" Chaos behind the piggy eyes.

"What did you *think* of him?"

"Well, sir, he didn't rattle easy. Got the nerve, there, like you say. I'm purty sure he had me covered underneath the table, too."

"A careful man, as well," said Cartwright. "Nerve and caution. Those are qualities a lawman needs to stay alive, wouldn't you say?"

Head bobbing, Cordry hastened to agree. "Yessir. I mean, if *you* think so."

"I do, indeed. What else, Gene?"

"Um."

"I realize you didn't see him draw, but do you think you could've taken him?"

That brought a frown to Cordry's face. "It's hard to say, Boss. He was *calm,* you know? Not rattled, like. I couldn't say if he was fast or not."

"Of course. We'll find out in due time. Gene, go and have yourself some fun downstairs. All right?"

"Yessir! Thank you."

"We need a better class of soldier, Eulis," Cartwright said after the door had closed on Cordry's back.

"Gene may be next door to an idjit, but

he's fast enough," Baker replied. "Also, he lost his conscience when his wits went out the window. Killing doesn't faze him."

"You know best," Cartwright agreed, although his tone implied the opposite.

Baker leaned forward in his chair. "Well, now, if you want me to lose him, Boss, he's gone. I mean —"

"No, no. We have a need for oxen, Eulis. But it wouldn't hurt to have more foxes on the payroll, either."

"Yes, sir. I'll keep that in mind."

"This marshal, now."

"His name's Jack Slade, according to the register at the Bonanza."

"Bjornson's place," said Cartwright. "He's sleeping under Bjornson's roof, stables his mount with us, then goes across the street to eat Buck's beef. Is there a method to his madness, Eulis?"

"My guess," Baker said, "is that he hasn't figured out the way things are around Gehenna. The way things are divided, if you follow me."

"I'm miles ahead of you," said Cartwright. "And I can't help wondering if Marshal Slade was sent, or summoned."

"Sir?"

Despairing, Cartwright closed his eyes. When he reopened them, he found Baker perched on the edge of his seat, anxious to please at any cost.

"The difference may be crucial," he explained. "If old Judge Dennison *sent* Slade to look around Gehenna and report on what he finds, it means trouble for Bjornson *and* myself. If, on the other hand, Buck *summoned* him to help their side . . . well, then, you see the problem."

"Yes, sir. I can take the bastard out, you want me to."

"Let's not be hasty, Eulis. I've invited Marshal Slade to have a word and see what's on his mind. There is a chance that he'll deceive us, or attempt to, but I count myself a fair judge of humanity, all things considered."

"Yes, sir."

"If it appears he has designs to side with Bjornson, we'll dispose of him, but carefully. He's still a U.S. marshal, after all. We don't want more of them investigating what became of one, now, do we?"

"No, sir."

"No, indeed. That kind of scrutiny can only lead to grief, in my opinion."

"You're the boss."

"Assuredly. You'll make it clearly understood, then, that none of our idjits jump the gun and try to drop him without orders, yes?"

"Sure thing."

"And if it comes to that, perhaps we'll shift the onus back to Bjornson."

"Own us?"

"Just a fancy word for blame. Nothing to fret about."

"No, sir."

"Go on downstairs now, Eulis, and make sure to send the marshal up as soon as he arrives. No confrontations."

"None at all."

"Good man."

Alone inside his office, Baron Cartwright lit a fifty-cent cigar and settled in to wait.

Slade dawdled with the apple pie, taking his time, then washed it down with one more cup of strong black coffee. The caffeine banished whatever weariness still lingered from his morning ride. The waitress brought his bill, then took his money off somewhere and came back with his change.

Slade left a tip he thought would please her, without going overboard, and left the restaurant. His fellow diners watched him go, Slade turning on the threshold just to catch them at it, smiling as he tipped his hat to one and all.

Showboating.

And why not, he asked himself. Unless he stirred things up around Gehenna, he might not learn anything. Unless the men responsible for raiding the O'Hara homestead tried to settle their account with Slade, he might leave empty-handed, nothing but a new scar for his trouble.

More than an hour had passed since he'd dismissed the errand boy dispatched by Baron Cartwright. He imagined Cartwright fuming in an office, somewhere, and decided he could wait a little longer for their meeting.

From the Longhorn, Slade walked east along the wooden sidewalk to the swinging doors of the Valhalla, passed the gunmen clustered there, and pushed his way inside. A fog bank of tobacco smoke enveloped him, the common atmosphere of most saloons, with music from a small band in one corner forcing men to raise their voices when they spoke.

Slade worked his slow way toward the bar, past poker games in progress, shrugging off the bar girls garbed in next to nothing when they tried to intercept him. At the bar, he ordered beer and got a hard look from the barkeep as a chaser.

Slade knew saloons. He'd gambled in

them from the time that he was old enough to sit in on a poker game, and fancied there were no more mysteries in store for him behind a pair of bat-wing doors. One thing about the Valhalla surprised him, though.

It was a cage of sorts, mounted against the railing of the second-story landing, where the working girls would take their customers to bed. A gunman sat inside the cage, a pistol on each hip, a shotgun and repeating rifle leaning on the bars at his right side. Slade also saw a pull cord beside the shooter, dangling from the ceiling of the cage. It took another moment, but he worked it out, noting the flaps of steel that stood out like three sides of a dissected box, waiting to drop in place and turn the cage into an armored safe as needed.

There would be gun ports in the metal flaps, Slade guessed, so that the sniper could keep firing, even under siege.

Slade wondered whether there was any call for that kind of security at the Valhalla, then he shrugged it off and drained his beer. A short walk to the swinging doors, and he was on the street again, breathing trail dust instead of smoke.

Better.

He let Bjornson's gunmen watch him cross the street, hoarding their thoughts.

The more confused they were right now, the better Slade liked it.

More shooters flanked the entrance to the Rosebud, eyeing Slade suspiciously, but none saw fit to challenge him. He passed them, felt a tingling at his back as some kept watching him, then stepped into another smoke cloud on the far side of the swinging doors.

More poker tables, faro making money for the house, more rough types at the bar, and women dressed in filmy nothings cruising for a trip upstairs. Slade saw the shooter who'd approached him at the Longhorn angling toward him through the crowd and racket, wearing an expression of annoyance on his doughy face.

"An hour, you said," the shooter groused.

"I hate to rush that apple pie."

"The Man don't like to be kept waiting."

"Let me make a note of that."

The gunman waited, as if he expected Slade to rummage through his pockets for a pencil and a scrap of paper. When it didn't happen, his frown deepened toward a scowl.

"You ready to go up, or what?"

"No rude surprises, eh?" said Slade. "Because you'll be the first to go."

"I'm shakin' in my boots."

"I see that. Can you handle it, or should I

go along without you?"

Muttering, the chunky shooter turned and led Slade toward the stairs that served the Rosebud's second floor.

7

Slade followed the waddling gunman upstairs and along a landing with a rail on his
right side, which overlooked the teeming
barroom down below. Smoke rose to meet
him, as if he were walking on a bridge above
a pit where trash was burned. The music,
clinking glass, and bursts of manic laughter
seemed incongruous.

The big man's office sat dead center on
the second floor, flanked on either side by
smaller rooms where bar girls did their
major business. Slade heard snuffling,
grunting sounds from several of those
rooms as he passed by, adding a barnyard
touch to his impression of the man-made
Hell.

Slade's escort knocked on Cartwright's
door and waited for a booming voice to bid
them enter. The shooter went first, stepping
aside to let Slade pass, while muttering,
"The marshal's here, Boss."

"Excellent! Gene, you can leave us now."

The flunky left and closed the door behind him, while his lord and master came around a desk so large, Slade thought it must've been assembled in the office, since it clearly wouldn't fit the narrow doorway.

"Baron Cartwright, at your service," said the Rosebud's boss. He pumped Slade's hand three times, then let it go and waved Slade toward a stylish captain's chair that stood before the massive desk. "Please, won't you have a seat? Something to drink, um, Marshal . . . ?"

"Slade. Jack Slade. And nothing, thanks."

Slade gave the chair a quick look over, saw no manacles or blades concealed, no trapdoor underneath it. Likewise, there was nothing to suggest a weapon hidden in the desk and pointed at the seat of honor. Just a chair, then, he decided, and sat down.

"You're wondering why I invited you to visit me, eh, Marshal?"

"I admit it crossed my mind."

"Truth is, I like to meet all the important people passing through Gehenna. Get a feel for them and see if I can help them somehow, to our mutual advantage."

"I'm afraid you're wasting time, then," Slade replied.

"How so?" asked Cartwright, looking

puzzled.

"First, I'm not all that important. Second, I'm not passing through. And third, I have a feeling that our interests don't coincide."

"May I address your points in order, sir?"

"Your office," Slade agreed. "Your time."

"First, let me say that any man who wears a U.S. marshal's badge and carries that responsibility in Oklahoma Territory ranks as an important person in my estimation. Some may disagree, but I stand fast in my opinion."

"Suit yourself," said Slade.

"Secondly, I'm curious at what you mean, *not passing through*."

"Just what I said. Gehenna's the end of my road. I've got work here, and I'm back to Lawton when it's finished."

"Lawton and Judge Dennison, that is?"

"The very same."

"Him that they call the hanging judge."

"I've heard it said, but never to his face."

"May I inquire as to your business in Gehenna?"

"Investigation of reported crimes."

"Such as?"

"I've got a list somewhere," Slade said, while making no move to produce it. "Rustling and murder come to mind, right off the top."

"I see." The big man's smile was like a grimace etched in stone. "An honest person must admit we've had our share of troubles in Gehenna, growing almost overnight the way it has. There *have* been killings, Marshal, and I've heard some tales of livestock being taken from outlying farms. The killers, I regret to say, were either hung or else got clean away. As for the rustling . . . well, I wish you luck."

"I thank you for it," Slade replied. "Fact is, I ran into some claim-jumpers myself, when I was riding in. One of them got away, but I believe I'd know his face."

Cartwright busied his fingers lighting a cigar. "One got away, you say. How many were there, Marshal?"

"Six, as I recall."

"You brought the rest along with you, as prisoners?" asked Cartwright.

"Nope. I left them out for buzzard bait."

"You've had quite an adventure, then," said Cartwright, blowing smoke.

"It isn't over yet. Your third point?"

"Sir?"

"You were addressing my responses, point by point. We just got stuck on number two."

"Of course!" Cartwright leaned forward, elbows on his desk, and peered at Slade across the broad expanse of polished hardwood. "I'm confused over your meaning when you said our interests might not coincide."

"It's just a feeling," Slade replied.

"But based on something, surely?"

"Only what I've heard."

"You'll find Gehenna is a seething rumor mill, Marshal. Some of its people live for feuds and gossip. You've been here no more than three, four hours, yet I fancy we could walk out in the street right now and hear fantastic tales about you, spun by fools and liars."

"Gossip's not my stock in trade," Slade said.

"I'm glad to hear it."

"I was thinking more of the complaints filed with Judge Dennison, in Lawton, and some things I heard after my little dustup with your men."

"*My* men? Marshal, you must —"

"Or Buck Bjornson's. Either way, I see you've both got shooters on the payrolls."

"And why not? We're businessmen who deal in cash, livestock, and real estate. Out here, there's no law to protect us. When you leave, that is."

"You had a constable or marshal, as I understand it," Slade replied.

"That's right, we did. He left us unexpectedly."

"Too bad. I would like to have heard his story."

"I'm afraid that he was high-strung, unreliable. If you succeed in finding him, please tell him that we're holding his last paycheck. If we only had a forwarding address . . ."

"Sounds inconsiderate." Slade pushed up from his chair. "Speaking of which, I'm sure I've taken up more time than you can spare."

"Nonsense! A pleasure, Marshal. Stop back anytime."

"I might just do that," Slade replied, then paused with one hand on the doorknob. "I just have to ask: What kind of name is Baron? If your parents wanted royalty, why not go for Prince, or King?"

Cartwright's reply was icy. "It's a family name, sir, from my mother's side."

"Well, thanks for clearing that up, anyway," Slade said and closed the office door behind him as he left.

"Well, dear?" said Cartwright, making no attempt to raise his voice.

The door to an adjoining bedroom opened on his left. The woman who emerged was blond, blue-eyed, with a complexion that some admirers compared to peaches and cream. In fact, face powder had a lot to do with it, but she was pretty all the same.

"He baits you in your inner sanctum," she commiserated. "That must be embarrassing."

"The name thing?" Cartwright fanned the air as if dismissing pesky flies. "I've heard that bullshit all my life."

"And yet, it irritated you," she said, taking the seat lately vacated by the marshal. As she sat, the uplift of a corset filled the low-cut bodice of her gown with alabaster cleavage.

"He *troubles* me, Sabrina," Cartwright granted. "It's been two years since a U.S. marshal passed this way, and he was looking for a fugitive. Now, of all times, we have *this* one, telling me Judge Dennison has sent him to investigate reported crimes."

"That leaves me out, I guess." Sabrina Abbott ran the Rosebud's working girls and ordered the saloon's supplies, all legal in the territory as of now. Cartwright considered her a junior partner — one who also warmed his bed from time to time — but he did not keep her apprised of his illicit dealings on the side. As to how much she'd worked out for herself, Cartwright could never guess.

"Rest easy, then," Cartwright replied. "It's me he's after."

"Not just you," Sabrina said. "He also mentioned Buck."

"That's right. He did."

"And there's your answer," she pressed on.

"How's that?"

"It doesn't suit you, being coy."

"Sabrina . . ."

"All right, then. Why not let Buck take all the bows for villainy? God knows, he's bad enough. And with a little help from us . . . well, who's to say the marshal might not blame all of Gehenna's problems on the Swede?"

"He didn't strike me as an idjit," Cartwright said.

"He wouldn't have to be. Just practical," Sabrina said. "What wise man fights *two* armies, if he can make do with one?"

"Damn it! I should've offered him a little something, while I had him here."

"And ruin everything? For shame!"

"How so?" asked Cartwright.

"Marshal Slade didn't impress me as a grafter. He's a missionary, looking for a devil he can exorcise. Why don't you give him one?"

"Screw Buck six ways from Sunday, as it were?"

"Before he does the same to you," she said.

"By God, you're right! He's bound to offer something. It's his style."

"I hope so. If I'm right about this lawman, it will put him off and focus his suspicion where we want it."

"Square on Buck," said Cartwright.

"That's the ticket, lover."

"It defies all odds, you know."

"What's that?" she asked.

"Such beauty *and* intelligence."

"You make me blush."

"All over, would that be?" he leered.

"Maybe I'll show you, later. Meanwhile, what was that the marshal said about claim-jumpers?"

Cartwright frowned. "Some kind of trouble on the road apparently. Could be big talk, to spook me."

"Five men dead? That's hard to fake," Sabrina said.

"It must be Bjornson's people, then. I'd damn well know if five of mine were missing."

"Baker plays it straight, I guess?"

"He'd better, if he wants to play at all."

"Well, you know best."

A frown creased Cartwright's face. "You want to tell me something, angel?"

"Not a thing," she said. "He's *your* man."

"Right. That's right." *But maybe,* Cartwright thought, *it wouldn't hurt to ask some questions anyway.*

Rising to leave, Sabrina said, "I'll have my ladies keep an eye out for the marshal, just in case he feels a need for some companionship while he's in town."

"No bribes, you said. Remember?"

"Maybe just a discount, then. Or something special on the side, to sweeten him a little."

"How much sugar have you got, Sabrina?"

"I've had no complaints so far."

"Don't get your hopes up," Cartwright muttered. "I believe it's *me* he's set on screwing, not your girls."

"Or Buck," she said. "Remember what we talked about."

"I'm not forgetting anything."

"And if you have a chance to put a slant on things that helps your case, don't hesitate."

"I'm thinking," Cartwright said. "Don't hurry me."

"I wouldn't dream of it," Sabrina answered. "But you really shouldn't wait too long."

■ ■ ■ ■

The shooter known as Gene was waiting at the bottom of the stairs as Slade descended, practicing his scowl. His hands weren't on his pistols, but he kept them close enough to make Slade wonder if the big man might've buzzed a message on ahead of him.

Something like, *Kill the lawman.*

Slade was halfway down the staircase when the gunman stepped into his path. "The boss all done with you?" he asked.

"I'm done with him," Slade said. "For now."

"I've been considerin'," said Gene.

"Must keep you busy."

"I been thinkin' that you owe me an apology."

"For what?"

"Your goddamned smart-ass attitude."

The background music didn't stop, but Slade was conscious of a hush falling around them at the near end of the bar and its adjacent tables. This was entertainment, and it didn't cost a thing unless a stray shot plugged some member of the avid audience.

"You reckon I insulted you," Slade said, not making it a question.

"Damn sure did," said Gene.

"And now you want to fight."

"You're heeled. Why not?"

"Maybe you ought to ask your boss first. Find out if he'll need you, later on."

"The hell is that supposed to mean?"

"In case you're not around," Slade said.

"I ain't afraid a you."

"I see that. It's a sign of your intelligence."

"Damn right!" said Gene, a stranger to the finer points of sarcasm.

Slade had released the hammer thong on his Peacemaker when he entered the saloon. The piece was ready, anytime he chose to draw and fire.

"All right," he said. "Let's do it, then."

"Say what?"

"You heard me, Gene. You think I owe you something. Here I am. Either collect, or get the hell out of my way."

"We oughta go outside," said Gene.

"So you can have one of your buddies shoot me from the alley? I don't think so."

"There's nobody out there," Gene protested.

"This is where you braced me. Make your move, or let it go."

"Goddamn your eyes! We ain't suppose to shoot in here."

"Says who?"

"The boss. Who else?"

"I say again, you ought to have a word with him before you take the leap."

Gene squinted, tried to wrap his mind around the warning. "Are you workin' for him now, or somethin'?"

"No."

"It makes no difference, then."

"Your call," Slade said. "Your play."

"What if I lose my job?" asked Gene.

"Least of your worries," Slade replied. "That only matters if you live."

"You think I'm slow," Gene said, "because I don't talk good sometimes."

"I don't know if you're slow or fast. We'll find out in a second."

"I'm faster than you think, lawman."

Slade took a chance, descending two more steps, to put his holster on a level with Gene's face. "You talk a good fight, anyway," he said, and nodded toward the shooter's guns. "Are those for show?"

"You just insulted me again."

"Can't help it. You're a natural."

At least two dozen witnesses were watching now, although their confrontation went unnoticed by most gamblers and carousers in the spacious barroom. For the majority, gunshots would be their first and only warning of a fight in progress.

Slade's eerie calm didn't surprise him

anymore. It had, the first few times he'd toed the line with sudden death, but now it just seemed . . . natural. He waited, watched Gene's eyes and hands for any flicker that betrayed a draw.

"You got me in a corner, lawman," said the shooter, almost whispering. "I can't just let you walk away."

"Why not?" Slade asked. "You called the play, and you can call it off. Somebody asks you later, make up any reason that sounds right."

"It ain't that easy."

"Dying's easy," Slade informed him. "Living takes some work."

"Can't do it, mister."

"Then go on and make your move."

The shooter hunched his shoulders, bracing for it. He was no more than a dozen feet from Slade, too close to miss unless Slade's first round put him down and kept him there. A head shot was the only guarantee, but also the easiest to miss.

"All right, goddamn you! I —"

"Gene Cordry!" Cartwright's voice lashed out from somewhere overhead. "What in pluperfect hell has gotten into you? Will you explain that to me?"

Cordry slowly turned to face his lord and master. "Mr. Cartwright —"

"Shut the hell up, and get out of the marshal's way. You hear me, boy?"

"Yessir."

He shuffled to the side and slumped against the banister. Slade's shoulder brushed the shooter's as he passed, then he was navigating through the maze of poker tables, feeling eyes upon him from all sides.

"Sorry about that, Marshal," Cartwright hollered from his balcony. "Come back real soon. We're all friends, here!"

"Not all of us," Slade muttered to himself as he pushed through the Rosebud's batwing doors into the night.

"You need to put a leash on Cordry, damn it!" Cartwright seethed. "He came *this close* to spoiling everything, just when I've got our plan in place."

Standing beside the captain's chair in Cartwright's office, Eulis Baker asked, "What plan would that be, sir?"

"I had a chin-wag with the marshal, as you know. Turns out Judge Dennison sent him to have a look around our little town. *Investigate reported crimes,* he says. Supposed to have a list, I understand."

"You saw it?" Baker asked.

"Hell, no. He could be bluffing. Either way, my plan should cover it."

"And that would be . . . ?"

"We're dumping everything on Bjornson, Eulis. Is that perfect? I'm inclined to think so."

"Well . . ."

"You see a problem?"

"Bjornson isn't one to just sit still and take it, is he? Suppose the lawman talks to him, and Bjornson tries to throw it back on you?"

"Throw *what?*"

"Whatever. If you're gonna frame him, you need evidence and witnesses. Judge Dennison's nobody's fool."

"I'll handle it," said Cartwright. "Leave all the thinking up to me, son."

Baker bit his tongue and nodded mute agreement, wondering how tricky it would be for him to slip out of Gehenna and get lost for good, someplace where Cartwright and the lawman couldn't find him.

"I've got something in mind to hang on Buck," Cartwright continued, "but I need to ask you something first."

"What's that, sir?"

"Slade — the marshal — told me that he had a run-in with some claim-jumpers along his way to town. I'm not sure when or where it was. Could be he's lying, but I didn't get that sense."

"Claim-jumpers." Baker's mind was racing.

"Meaning, I suppose, one of the homesteads hereabouts. My question to you is, were *you* involved?"

Not *we*. Baker fought to keep from sneering at the man who paid his salary. "We've run homesteaders off," he said. "You know that, Boss. Bjornson's done it, too."

"According to the marshal, he shot four or five of these dumb shits and left them where they fell. So, now I'm *asking* you —"

"No, sir. We've got nobody missing."

"Are you positive?"

"I'd know if four or five boys never made it home."

"No secrets, Eulis?"

"No, sir!"

"I admire initiative, you understand. But if you try and hang me out to dry on this, you'll soon be looking for another job — in Hell."

"I'd tell you, straightaway."

"So much the better, then," said Cartwright. "Take for granted they were Buck's boys. Maybe we can still find out their names, get something for the marshal that will put him on Bjornson's trail. There's nothing motivates a man like nearly being killed. He'll want the sumbitch who's behind it for the court at Lawton."

Baker saw the pristine logic of it, but he also saw the difficulty. "Mr. C., how am I gonna find these dead men if I don't know where to look?"

"I worked that out already, Eulis. Think about it! Slade was sent from where?"

"You just said Lawton."

"Right! And you confirm he rode in from the east?"

"That's right."

"Last time I checked, the shortest way between two places was a straight line, Eulis. Check the map for homesteads east of town, along the way to Lawton. Get the names and go a-calling. Be all friendly-like. Concerned. Find out who Buck's been leaning on, who's had a dustup with his shooters in the past few days."

"And when we find the homestead?"

"Find the bodies, if you can. Watch out for anything that links them back to Bjornson."

"Could be nothing," Baker said.

"Oh, there'll be *something,* Eulis. You can count on that. I guarantee it."

"Something like those business cards he likes to pass around," said Baker.

"Now you're talking. Something *just* like that."

"I'll see it done, Boss. Don't you worry."

"I have every confidence. Good hunting, Eulis. Do me proud."

Outside the office, Baker paused to think about the problem set before him. Planting Bjornson's fancy cards on corpses wouldn't be a problem, but he had to *find* the bodies first. Cartwright supposed it would be easy. Just ride out and ask the friendly farmers if they'd had a problem with claim-jumpers lately, and if any had been shot of late, where were they planted?

"Damned fool," he muttered.

Cartwright coveted the same homesteads that Bjornson lusted after, and he *knew* that Baker's men had squeezed the farmers just as hard as Bjornson's raiders ever did. Dumb luck was all that let him answer honestly when Cartwright asked if any of their men were missing at the moment.

The farmers Cartwright and Bjornson hadn't driven off were mortal enemies of both. Baker had never shown his face to them — he wasn't stupid, after all — but none of them would welcome strangers asking questions about murder and the like.

Unless . . .

A sudden inspiration gripped him, making Eulis Baker smile. He knew exactly how to lull the stupid sodbusters and make them help him. All he needed was the proper costume for himself and those he picked to join him. Just a little something from the office of Gehenna's former constable.

He'd have to force the back door's lock, of course, but that was easy. Once inside, he'd find exactly what he needed and be out again before the neighbors knew it. Not that anyone on Cartwright's side of Main Street had the nerve to try and stop him.

No. They wouldn't be that stupid, even with the law in town.

8

It was dark on Main Street as Slade left the Rosebud. He sidestepped from the saloon's lighted windows, declining to present himself in silhouette for any marksmen lurking in the shadows, and stood watching the town for a while.

He marked a change in the pedestrians on Main Street, from the crowd he'd seen that afternoon. No women were in evidence, now that the sun had dropped from sight, and the men who passed him on the sidewalk seemed to represent a rougher crowd than daylight's shoppers.

It was much the same in any frontier town, Slade knew from long experience, and even Lawton had its raucous nightlife under Judge Dennison's very nose. Gehenna, so far, didn't seem much different from the other towns where Slade had tried his luck at poker, prior to putting on a badge, but there was something in the air — more a *sensation,* or the scent of danger — that had put his nerves on edge.

"Imagination," Slade half whispered to himself, his voice drowned out by three drunks tottering across the street from the Valhalla to the Rosebud. Cartwright and Bjornson plainly shared their customers, milking the suckers for their last dime if they could.

Like gamblers, barkeeps, and whoremasters everywhere.

What made Gehenna different, then?

Perhaps it was *two* bosses vying for control, though Slade had seen the same thing played out in a dozen other towns. Most often, the contenders found some way to live and let live, but it wasn't guaranteed by any means. Luke Short had learned that fact the hard way, down in Texas, and the Earp brothers in Tombstone, Arizona.

You could forget about the Golden Rule, where money was concerned. There was another standard in that case: The fellow with the gold could make the rules, at least until some bigger, tougher hombre knocked him off his pedestal and took his place.

Slade didn't know if Cartwright and Bjornson were well matched, or if one held the winning hand at present, but he planned to make himself acquainted with those facts as soon as possible.

First, though, he had a mild headache demanding his attention, and the only thing that Slade could think to do for it was sleep it off. He planned a final look in at the livery, to satisfy himself that there had been no trouble with his roan, and then he'd make the short walk back to the Bonanza, where his bed awaited him.

Too bad Faith wasn't there to share it, or a pair of sisters bent on banishing his fever dreams. The thought of either one failed to relax him, but Slade hoped at least they'd make for some diverting dreams.

The livery was never closed, a service to its customers who might need transportation at odd hours of the day or night. The hostler had a small room near the broad front doors, where he was bound to hear them rumbling open after nightfall and could greet a paying customer — or a potential thief — without delay. Slade let himself into the stable, then stood waiting while the night man grumbled out to greet him by lamplight.

"Just checking on my horse," Slade told him. "You can go on back to sleep."

"No problem, sir," the aging fellow said, retreating even as he spoke. Based on his size, he could've been a jockey in his prime,

146

but that was far behind him, leaving a love of horses and a lack of any other useful skills as ties that bound him to the livery trade.

Slade's horse seemed fine, well fed and watered, groomed again before the hostler traipsed off to his lonely cot. Slade whispered to it for a while and got a whinny in return, then left the stable by its back door to confuse whoever might be watching him out front.

Maybe no one, he thought, but couldn't swallow it.

While Main Street had been dark enough away from the saloons, the strip behind the livery and other north-side shops was black as pitch, with only distant freckled starlight for illumination. Slade considered turning back, then loosened his Peacemaker in its holster and proceeded on his way.

After a long block, when he reached a narrow alleyway between two stores, Slade turned and walked back to Main Street. He lingered in the shadows there, waiting and watching for a sign of anything amiss, and peered back toward the livery to check for any lookouts on the street, down there.

Nothing.

When he was satisfied, Slade stepped onto the elevated sidewalk and resumed the journey back to his hotel.

He almost made it.

Half a dozen strides from the Bonanza's recessed doorway, Slade saw movement there and gripped his Colt as two men came into the open. One was slightly taller than the other, and he did the talking for them both.

"Good evening, Marshal. My name's Damon Shakespeare. This here's Ernie Gantt."

"Looking for me, are you?" Slade asked.

"In truth, we are. Our boss — that's Mr. Bjornson — would appreciate a word with you at the Valhalla, if you've got the time."

"And if I don't?"

"I was requested to inform you that it's urgent."

"As in now or never?"

" 'Urgent' was all he said," Shakespeare replied.

Despite Slade's weariness, it wasn't late. "Let's get it over with," he said.

"You know the way, I take it?"

"Hard to miss," said Slade. "But you can take the lead."

"My pleasure," Shakespeare said and started back along the sidewalk, headed west.

The constable's office smelled musty inside. It made Eulis Baker's nose twitch, standing there in the darkness and breathing dead air. A scuttling noise in the far corner made him pivot toward the sound, hand gliding toward his gun, before he figured out it must've been a mouse and let himself relax.

Not *too* much, though.

He didn't know if it was burglary or not, to force his way inside a long-abandoned place and steal things from a man who wasn't coming back. Some might describe it as a salvage operation, but the fine points of debate were lost on Baker. He had plans and needed certain things to make them work. Beyond that, he was conscious of the fact that he was stealing, and he didn't want someone to catch him in the act, despite the fact that there was no law in Gehenna.

Well, no *local* law.

He didn't think a U.S. marshal cared about a little common burglary, but why take chances? Baker didn't strike a light as he moved through the dark cave of an office, edging slowly, carefully in the direction of the former lawman's desk.

The office wasn't large — one room in front, one in back — but it would probably have rented to some merchant if it wasn't for the back-room cells. Removing metal bars and doors would be a costly proposition, and the one man who'd considered it

— old Moses Guttenberg, who ran Bjornson's dry-goods store, had claimed he saw a ghost hanging around the place. From that point on, the office had been pretty much taboo.

No ghosts tonight, thought Baker, as he reached the desk. Nothing on top of it except a stub of pencil and a piece of paper — blank. Behind the desk, a corkboard had old WANTED posters tacked upon it, curling now from age and fluctuations in humidity. Baker would need a light to read about the bad men profiled on those flyers, and the truth was that he didn't give a damn about them. Most were dead by now, he reasoned, or had gotten clean away.

More power to them, in that case.

He tried the desk drawers, one by one, and found all of them locked. Sighing, he eased into the missing lawman's chair, remembering to dust it off before he sat. As Baker drew his knife from its belt sheath, he thought about the absent constable and what might've befallen him.

If anyone had polled the folks in town, opinion would've split around the sixty-forty mark, between those thinking that the constable was dead and those who claimed he'd simply run away. Baker was in the dark, himself, and could only say that *he* had no hand in the lawman's disappearance, nor had any of the shooters under his direct command. There had been incidents, of course, provoked by Cartwright's men, and more from Bjornson's side, but Baker had been honestly surprised to wake one April morning and discover that the lawman wasn't with them anymore.

If he'd been forced to wager, Baker would've bet that Shakespeare's crew had killed the constable — maybe by accident, on one of their adventures in the night — and planted him somewhere to keep the people guessing. That idea did not disturb him, any more than stepping on a scorpion. It simply would've pleased him to be certain of the truth.

He cracked the old desk's middle drawer and found what he was seeking right away. Loose badges, half a dozen of them, slithered on unfinished wood as Baker pulled the drawer open with more force than the job required. He pocketed all six, then thought he might as well go on and search the other drawers while he was at it, just to satisfy his curiosity.

The top drawer on his left contained another pencil and a notepad with approximately half its sheets of paper missing. Lower left, a deeper drawer held nothing but more dust. The upper right revealed some empty envelopes, an inkwell long gone dry, and its companion fountain pen. Beneath the envelopes, one hand of a brass-knuckles set lay hidden. Baker smiled and claimed it for his own.

The last drawer, bottom left, concealed a hidden treasure. There, Baker discovered two shot glasses and a bourbon bottle, still half full. He brought the glasses out and frowned at them, wondering who had been the lawman's secret boozing friend while he was ostracized by damn near everyone in town.

A secret friend, unknown to either of the warring sides that crushed the constable between them in their struggle for control? Was he — or she — still in Gehenna, maybe waiting for revenge to be served as a cold dish, sweet and fine?

Someone had reached out to Judge Dennison in Lawton, prompting him to send his marshal for a look around. Someone, perhaps, who hated and despised both factions equally?

That was a mystery to ponder, but the night was slipping through his fingers, and there was a wench back at the Rosebud who had promised Baker something extra for his trouble if he joined her in her crib upstairs.

He liked the French approach to things and didn't want to miss it on account of sitting in the dark, woolgathering.

He took the bourbon bottle with him, rose, and left the two shot glasses on the desktop, drawers still hanging open on both sides. Next time someone broke in, they'd have another little mystery to solve.

Impulsively, he twisted off the bottle's cap, sniffed it to verify the contents, and threw back a gulp of liquor that brought water to his eyes. Good stuff, not watered like most of the rotgut at the Rosebud and, across the street, at the Valhalla. Rivals they might be, but Cartwright and Bjornson were soul brothers when it came to operating on the cheap and screwing customers six ways from Sunday.

Pausing at the office's front window, well back from the glass and hidden from the street by shadow, Baker saw three men passing along the sidewalk opposite. He picked out Damon Shakespeare in the lead, one of his shooters keeping pace — and then the U.S. marshal following a step behind them, easy-like.

None of the three had pistols drawn. It didn't look like kidnapping. That only left a social call, and they were heading down to the Valhalla, sure as anything.

Baker forgot about the bottle in his fist and made for the back door. The Frenchy girl would have to wait a little longer, until he had a moment with the Man and broke what damn near had to be bad news.

Sabrina Abbott liked to watch Main Street's nocturnal traffic from the Rosebud's second-story balcony. Her room, next door to Baron Cartwright's office, had a six-foot window that swung open like a door and granted access to the balcony.

Sometimes she felt like God up there, if only God had been a woman, looking down on all the puny mortals from above.

Most times, she just felt like a whore.

She'd graduated from the two-bit cribs when Cartwright took her on, made her the madam of his stable, but the work Sabrina did was whoring, just the same. Her price was triple or quadruple what the other girls could charge, depending on the service rendered, but she still had regulars who asked for her specifically and wouldn't go upstairs with anybody else.

At one point in their curious relationship, she'd hoped that it would bother Cartwright, seeing — well, say *hearing* — her with other men, but that had worn off in a while. Despite their little interludes, for which he never paid, she'd come to understand that Cartwright was unique among the countless men she'd known. He didn't form attachments of the personal variety, felt nothing in his heart for anyone, except contempt for suckers and abiding hatred for his mortal enemies. He had no friends, per se, only the people who agreed for reasons of their own to help him on his journey toward control of everything within his reach.

Sabrina guessed that Buck Bjornson was the same way, more or less. She'd never met him personally, but town gossip told her that he had no wife or steady lover, no relations he acknowledged, no trusted advisers when it came to business dealings. One tale claimed that Bjornson had apprenticed under old Al Swearengen, in Deadwood, back before the town got civilized. Sabrina didn't know or care if that was true. She recognized Bjornson as her master's enemy and worked to undercut him any way she could.

Spying was what Sabrina Abbott did the best — no, make that second best — and she was practicing her craft that evening when Damon Shakespeare came into her line of sight. Beside him, one of Bjornson's other gunmen, Ernie something, tried to keep pace with his boss. The third man in their little triangle was Marshal Slade, who'd left the Rosebud barely half an hour earlier after his little talk with Cartwright.

What the hell?

She watched them disappear through the Valhalla's swinging doors, then hurried back inside her crib and went directly to the door connecting her bedroom to Cartwright's office. Knocking was the last thing on her mind as she barged in, to find one of her girls — redheaded Annie Lassiter — kneeling between the Man's splayed legs, head bobbing like a derrick in an oilfield.

"Christ, Sabrina! Privacy!"

"No time for that," she answered sternly. "Day Shakespeare just sashayed your U.S. marshal into Bjornson's place."

"The hell you say!" Instead of rising or allowing Annie to escape, Cartwright splayed fingers in her hair and kept her at it. "Were they prodding him along?"

Sabrina shook her head. "He *followed* them, all friendly-like."

"Goddamn it! Do you think he's going over, then?"

"I don't read minds or lips," she said and shot a glance at Annie with the last bit. *Talk about your fiddling while Rome burns,* Sabrina thought, but wisely kept it to herself.

"All right," said Cartwright, leaning back with eyes closed, speaking through clenched teeth. "We've got our man inside, across the street. He'll find out what they . . . what they . . . Yes! *Yes!! Yes!!!* . . . and let us know, first thing." His eyes opened again. "I'll see to it, Sabrina. Don't you fret."

"No skin off me," she said and softly closed the door.

Slade didn't trust his escorts, but he reckoned having them precede him was the best that he could do under the circumstances. Any ambush waiting for him on the street should claim them first, while Slade had time to dive for cover in the dark.

And he was looking forward to his meeting with Gehenna's other boss man. Why deny it? Baron Cartwright hadn't managed to surprise him, and he doubted Buck Bjornson would, but that was for the best. By all accounts, they had a rough game going in Gehenna, each man vying for control. Slade was the new man at the table, sitting in without an invitation from the others.

And he might turn out to be the wild card, after all.

Slade's two watchdogs made no unwelcome moves during their hike to the Valhalla. Shakespeare glanced back but once, to see if Slade was still behind him, then seemed perfectly at ease. Slade likely could've let himself relax, but he kept his right hand on the handle of his Colt, regardless, stubbornly refusing to be lulled.

If Gantt or Shakespeare thought his badge would stop him shooting either of them in the back, should they be ambushed, they were fatally mistaken. But it didn't come to that, and moments later Slade was standing at the threshold of Bjornson's pleasure palace, battered once again by the discordant music from inside.

He paused and glanced across the street, to find a woman watching from the Rosebud's balcony. She wasn't one of those who'd lined the rail on his first pass that afternoon. The night obscured her age, but Slade thought that she had an almost stately quality about her, as if in defiance of the odds she found a certain dignity in whoring.

She was watching Slade and his companions from her aerie, there could be no doubt of that. Slade almost tipped his hat to her, then reconsidered it and let the moment pass. She might report his movements back to Cartwright, which would help to stir the pot, but any feint toward friendship on his part in front of Bjornson's men, at least right now, could prove to be a critical mistake.

Keep everybody guessing, while you can.

Upstairs, the watcher stood with elbows planted on the railing, leaning slightly forward, so that midnight shadows gathered in her cleavage. Slade imagined he could hear her garments rustle when she moved, but that could only be illusion. Maybe wishful thinking.

Never mind.

"You coming, Marshal?" Shakespeare asked him, standing with the bat-wing doors propped open by his body.

"Right behind you," Slade agreed and crossed the threshold of Valhalla for the second time that evening.

No one appeared to notice him this time, a benefit of strolling in with two of Bjornson's men, he guessed. The ragtag corner band kept playing, never missed a beat, and most of those not busy playing cards were focused on four dancing girls, high-kicking on a little stage beside the slumped musicians. Slade imagined it was meant to be a variation on the cancan, spiced up by the fact that all four dancers had forgotten to wear any underclothes.

"You like that, Marshal?" Ernie Gantt inquired.

"I've seen worse," Slade allowed.

"I bet you have." The gunman sniggered, grimy fingers swabbing moisture from a corner of his mouth.

"Remind me, Ernie. Which one is your sister?"

Gantt stopped dead, turned purple from the collar up, and would've rushed Slade then if Shakespeare hadn't gripped Gantt's arm and whispered something deadly cold into his crumpled ear. It sobered Gantt enough to let him stand without restraint, but hatred flickered in his little rodent eyes.

"I guess you be a joker, lawman," he replied at last.

"Go have a beer," Shakespeare instructed Ernie. "Cool off for a bit. Remember who you're working for."

"I ain't forgettin' nothin'," Ernie told them both, then turned and stalked off toward the crowded bar.

"You shouldn't bait a wildcat, Marshal," Shakespeare offered.

"How about a skunk?"

"They'll bite you when you least expect it, I imagine."

On stage, the dancing girls had turned their backs to the hooting audience and hoisted their skirts to reveal pallid cheeks. A wiggle here and there brought down the house.

"Mr. Bjornson's waiting, Marshal, if you've seen enough."

"That ought to hold me for a while," Slade said.

"Of course, the girls do private dances, too, sometimes."

"Do tell."

"It's mostly up to Mr. Bjornson. Nothing's too good for his friends."

"Right generous, I take it."

"To his friends," Shakespeare repeated. "Now, his enemies . . . that's something else."

They'd reached the stairs at one end of the bar and started climbing toward the second floor. Slade had a sense of reliving his visit to the Rosebud.

"Enemies are something I relate to," Slade told Shakespeare. "Does he have a lot of them in town?"

"Fewer and fewer all the time," Shakespeare replied. "They seem to have bad luck."

"Do tell."

"No doubt about it, Marshal. You can take that to the bank."

9

Bjornson's office was another second-story job, but that was where the resemblance to Cartwright's layout ended. Instead of looking down upon his operation from the middle of the second floor, Bjornson had claimed a large room at the southeast corner. He was farthest from the inner stairs, that way, but Slade already knew from checking the Valhalla's grand exterior that other stairs led from an alleyway on the saloon's east flank up to the second floor.

Bjornson had himself a private access route — a getaway contingency if things got too rough for his liking in the place he'd built and named for Viking heaven.

Shakespeare led Slade to the office door and rapped his knuckles on the polished panel, just below a brass plate reading PRIVATE. There was no discernible trace of Scandinavia in the voice that replied with a hearty "Come in!"

Shakespeare preceded him and made the introductions, while Buck Bjornson stood behind a desk that rivaled Cartwright's, planted at an angle in the northeast corner of his office. Close at hand, no more than three strides distant from his high-backed rolling chair, Slade saw the exit that would put Bjornson on the outer stairs.

Something to file away for future reference.

"Boss, this is Marshal Slade," Shakespeare announced.

Slade hadn't dropped his name in conversation with the shooter, meaning that the Cartwright team must have a leak, or else someone had checked his hotel registry.

"Go on and have a drink, now, Day," Bjornson said, moving around his desk on stout, strong legs. As Shakespeare closed the door behind him, Bjornson's massive paw enveloped Slade's right hand and pumped it twice, then let it go.

"Buck Bjornson," he announced. "As if you didn't know. Whiskey? Cigar?"

"No, thanks."

"Well, have a seat, at least."

The chair planted in front of Bjornson's desk turned out to be a rocker, of all things. Its seat was nearly wide enough for two slim people, sitting side by side. Slade scooted to his left, leaving his pistol and his right hand free.

If Baron Cartwright was a wolf, Slade thought, then Bjornson had to be a bear. His size and movements were exaggerated, hinting at a hearty friendship in the offing, but Slade took for granted that his mood could turn with lightning speed from fellowship to rage. Slade made a mental note to stay out of Bjornson's reach if he was ever in a killing mood.

"How are you liking our fair city, Marshal?"

"It seems friendly, on the face of it," Slade said.

"Gehenna *is* a friendly town," Bjornson granted. "We've got something here for everyone, I fancy. But they don't all get the same greetings as *you.*"

Slade raised an eyebrow, questioning, but otherwise his face was deadpan. He said nothing.

"Come, now, Marshal!" Bjornson urged him. "Surely you're aware of getting special treatment? You've already been across the street to see my old friend Baron Cartwright, and I've asked you here, myself. You can believe most paying customers don't get a private audience, much less a pair of them."

"I'm flattered," Slade replied.

Bjornson laughed and said, "I doubt that very much. Fools fall for flattery, and I don't take you for a fool, Marshal. You *do* know why you're here with me, right now."

"You want to see the wild card," Slade suggested.

"Marvelous! Exactly right! We've had a static game here in Gehenna, no great wins or losses tallied up for either side. Life gets a little . . . dull. Wild cards spice up the game, sometimes. Of course, like Cartwright, I prefer to have them in *my* hand."

"This wild card's on the table," Slade informed his host. "It could go either way."

"A challenge. Excellent! May I assume, then, that my competition didn't ante up sufficiently?"

"I'm sure I don't know what you mean," said Slade.

"No, no! Of course not! I'm just saying that a winning bet, to sweep the table, should be damned impressive to the . . . er . . . wild card."

"There was some talk of cash," Slade mused. "And women."

"Basic staples," Bjornson said, waving his hands with a dismissive air. "The man . . . er, *wild card* . . . who could help me win this game, once and for all, would find me *very* grateful. Money? Not a problem. Shall we take five thousand dollars as the starting point of our negotiations?"

"Well . . ."

"Women? You'll find that the Valhalla's ladies rival and surpass whatever's offered at the Rosebud. Now, I don't refer to Baron's private stock, of course, but I can promise that you'll never get a taste of *that one* in your lifetime. Otherwise, I've got redheads, brunettes, Chinese, something for every taste."

"It sounds inviting," Slade allowed.

"But for the clincher, I propose a guaranteed position on my staff. Damon's a good boy, follows orders to a T, but when it comes to raw initiative . . . well, let's just say I should've won this game six months ago. Maybe a year. Sometimes I think he actually holds me back."

"You're tired of that," Slade said.

"Indeed I am! The man who wins this for me will have Damon's spot — with a substantial raise, of course."

"It's tempting," Slade admitted, "but the thing is —"

"Yes?"

"I've got a job already. I was sent here by Judge Dennison to get a feel for what's been happening, crime-wise, and round up anyone I catch breaking the law."

"That's a tall order, Marshal." Bjornson slumped back in his rolling throne. "Some hereabouts might reckon it's impossible."

"I won't know till I try."

"And what would happen if I buzzed Damon back here to deal with you, right now?" asked Bjornson.

"Buzz away, fat man. You'll be in Hell before he's in the office."

"I begin to fear we'll never be the best of friends, Marshal."

"Don't let it pain you," Slade replied, rising. "My guess would be we've both got friends enough, for now."

"Sadly for you, Marshal, my friends are *here*."

"All of them?" Slade inquired, while drifting toward the door. "None missing, lately?"

Bjornson frowned. "I'm sure I don't know what you mean."

Slade shrugged. "It's likely my mistake. I thought maybe the five claim-jumpers that I killed, a day's ride out from town, might be the kind of trash you take for friends."

"Our business is concluded, Marshal. You can find your own way out?"

Slade smiled and said, "I wouldn't be surprised."

"You're quakin'," Shakespeare said, eyeing his slim companion. "What the hell is wrong with you?"

"Nothin'," Rory Duncan answered, reaching out to down his second shot of whiskey in as many minutes. "Nothin', Boss."

"Nobody's askin' you to *fight* the marshal," Shakespeare chided. "I just want to know if it's the same man who dropped Isaac and the rest but let you get away."

The last remark made Duncan tremble all the more. "I told ya how that happened, Day. There wasn't nothin' I could do to stop 'im. All the other boys was dead. *Somebody* had to come back here and tell you what went wrong."

"And I appreciate it, Rory. But your job's not done until you tell me whether *this* lawman's the same hombre who butted in and killed five of our friends."

"Okay," Duncan replied. "I'm here, ain't I?"

"Just keep an eye peeled," Shakespeare ordered. "Either way it goes with Buck, it won't take long."

"I'm watchin'," Duncan told him. "I just need another shot to —"

"No! You're cut off till you do this for me, understand?"

"Aw, Jesus, Day."

"Don't *Jesus* me," Shakespeare mocked him. "I never knew a worser heathen in my life."

"I been to church," groused Duncan.

"Sure. The day your folks got married, you were in your mama's belly."

"Now, you wait a —"

"There he is!" Shakespeare clutched Duncan's arm with painful urgency. With grim reluctance, Duncan raised his head and peered from underneath his hat brim at the balcony above the bar. He saw a pair of boots passing, and raised his chin farther until the full man was in view.

"Well?" Shakespeare challenged. "Is it him, or not?"

"I only see his back, Day."

"Shit! Keep watchin' then, when he comes down the stairs."

So Duncan watched, reliving panic from the shoot-out in the farmyard, picturing a man who ran hunched over, dodging bullets, rapid-firing with a Winchester repeater.

"Is it *him,* goddamn it?"

"I don't know," Duncan admitted as the lawman made his way downstairs. "He's 'bout the same size as the man I saw, but *he* was runnin' all around and shootin'. I believe the shirt is different."

"People *change* their shirts, for Christ's sake! You should try it, sometime!"

"Day, I'll lie and swear it's him, if that'll please you. But the only thing I'm *positive* about is that I need another drink."

"Drink and be damned, you useless wretch," Shakespeare replied. "And when you've had one more, get on that fleabag you've been riding. Get the hell out of Gehenna, Rory, do you hear me? If I see your worthless ass tomorrow, you're a dead man."

Shakespeare didn't wait for a response, just turned and stalked away into the crowd.

Damn right, I'll go, thought Rory Duncan. *Get out while the getting's good.*

And to the bartender he said, "One more. Make it a double, wouldja, please?"

"Here's how we do it," Eulis Baker told his five assembled men. Five pairs of eyes glittered with lantern light, fixed on his face. "All nice and legal-like."

"Ain't there a U.S marshal here in town, right now?" one of them asked.

"That's right," Baker replied. "And that's exactly why we have to watch our step."

Lifting a hand, he let the badges tumble

from his fingers, one by one, onto the tabletop. The first one rattled with a lonely sound, while those that followed clinked and clanked together like metallic poker chips.

"What's that?" one shooter asked.

"What does it look like?" said another. "Badges."

"*Badges!* We don't need no stinkin' —"

"Yes, we do," said Baker, interrupting the complaint. "For *this* job, with the law in town, we need this very thing."

"Awright, you say so," the complainer granted, slouching back into his chair.

They occupied a back room at the Rosebud, commonly reserved for high-stakes private games. Tonight, there were no cards involved, but Baker knew the stakes might well be life or death.

"Now, here's the thing," he told them. "Slade, this law dog, told the Man he had some kind of dustup with a pack of shooters on his way to town, out east there, somewhere, on the way from Lawton. Claims he *killed* five of them and just left 'em there."

"Man must be purty fast," one said.

"Bullshit, I says," another offered.

"*Any*way," said Baker, "whether he dropped five or only one, they weren't *our* boys. We need to find out whose they *were*."

"Who else, but Bjornson's?" asked a grizzled hand whose left eyebrow was interrupted by a zigzag scar.

"It isn't good enough for us to know that," Baker answered. "We need some *proof,* get it? Something the courts call *evidence,* that we can feed the marshal and Judge Dennison, so they'll go after Buck and leave the Man alone."

At mention of the hanging judge, the scarfaced gunman ran a grimy fingertip around his collar, as if he could feel the chafing of a noose. The others shifted nervously, exchanging furtive glances.

"Still," a balding shooter said, "I don't see why we need no badges."

Baker kept his temper with an effort. "It's like playacting," he said. "Just think about it. If we go around the homesteads as we are, them sodbusters will either put us off with lies or hunker down to fight. They see a lawful *posse* ridin' through, why, they'll just naturally cooperate."

"Says who?" one of them muttered.

"Says the Man," Baker snapped in reply. "You wanna go upstairs and argue with him?"

"Naw. I reckon not."

"Good choice. Now, let me finish, will you? What we're gonna do is wear this tin and ride a circuit of the farms out where I told you. Shouldn't be more than a dozen, maybe less. We ask 'em *nice* and get their confidence. Somebody has to know what happened. They can either point us to the stiffs or maybe give us something else that's useful. When we've got it, then I give it to the Man, and he hands it to Slade."

"One helpful citizen," a freckled gunman said, grinning with half a dozen teeth.

"That's it exactly. Now, if everybody's clear . . . ? All right, then. Have a few drinks if you want to, but I don't want any god-damned hangovers tomorrow. Understand me? Any man can't ride directly after breakfast, I will beat until he can't walk, neither."

Grumbling, they rose and left him, each man picking up a badge before he traipsed back to the bar. Alone, Baker examined the remaining star and wondered whether it would bring him luck — or if, by tempting Fate, he'd bring disaster down upon himself.

"Fate, hell," he sneered, at last. "Who needs it?"

Buck Bjornson roamed his office like an animal confined against its will. He gnawed on a cigar, clutching big hands behind his back and leaning forward slightly, as a man will do when slogging up a steep or muddy hill. Off in a corner, Damon Shakespeare tried to keep out of his way.

"I don't like this at all," Bjornson said, and then repeated it for emphasis. "I *don't* like *this* at *all*."

"No, sir."

"It's one thing if the lawman doesn't want to help us, right? I've known that kind before. Dead honest, some of them, and they're the quickest ones to wind up dead. But is he *really* all that clean, or is he helping *someone else?*"

"You mean Cartwright?"

"Could be. Why not? They met before I had you bring the marshal over here. What did they talk about, I'd like to know?"

"Maybe the same thing you did, Boss. I know that Baker sent one of his boys to the Bonanza for 'im, and the law dog come down to the Rosebud after."

"Fine. But was he *fetching* Slade, or just confirming an appointment? Do you see my point?"

"Well . . ."

"Damn it, Day, we need to get a handle on this thing. Get out in front of it before it runs us over."

"Yes, sir."

"If the law weighs in on Cartwright's side, we're finished in Gehenna. One way or another, they can hang or lock up anybody they've a mind to. That is *not* the way I plan to end my days."

"Um, Boss . . . if you don't mind my saying so, maybe you've gone a mite *too far* in front of this. It sounds to me like you're already giving up."

"Hell, no!" Bjornson snapped. "Not even close. But if the law's against us, now, we have to be prepared. We can't put all our eggs together in one bucket."

Shakespeare frowned and tried to work out what was wrong with Bjornson's turn of phrase, then let it go and simply said, "No, sir."

"We'll fight for what we have. Hell, yes! But if we reach a point where anyone can see that we don't have a hope of winning, then we need *another* plan. You see?"

"For getting out, you mean."

"For getting out *alive,*" Bjornson said, "with all that we can carry."

"Yes, sir."

"I know you don't like this defeatist talk, Day. Christ, I hate it more than you do. But we need to think ahead of Cartwright and his shooters. Think ahead of Slade and old Judge Dennison, as well."

"Boss, I can't swear to it, but ever'thing I've heard about the hangin' judge claims that he's arrow-straight and won't take any kind of favors. That could be a crock of shit, but I know men — well, *one* — who tried to buy him off and didn't fare well."

"Maybe just a rotten marshal, then?" Bjornson smiled at that, grasping a slender reed. "That's better, anyway. If Dennison's so straight, he'll be the first to scorn a crooked deputy. Should something happen to our Mr. Slade, and there be evidence that he was taking Cartwright's side against the law, it just might do us proud."

"Kill him, you mean, and put some money in his pocket?"

"I'd prefer a bit more subtlety," Bjornson said. "Besides, we don't know how much cash he carries ordinarily."

"Oh, right."

"We need something *embarrassing.* First thing you do, get someone watching Slade around the clock, but *careful,* so he doesn't even smell them. Understand?"

"That's easy, Boss."

"And when he makes a slip, you let me know."

"Suppose he don't?"

"We all slip, Day. It's human nature. Hell, boy, it's what keeps us all in business."

■ ■ ■ ■

Slade felt weary, walking back to his hotel from the Valhalla. He had played Bjornson fairly well, baiting the big man just enough to agitate him, maybe to provoke a critical mistake. He didn't need a shooting war between Gehenna's major rivals, but an increase in dissension might make Slade's job easier.

It might keep him alive.

One thing Slade *didn't* want was Cartwright and Bjornson meeting privately, comparing notes about their conversations with the new lawman in town. If they conquered suspicion of each other, even for the short run, then Slade's life span in Gehenna might be short, indeed.

The good news was, Slade didn't see that happening. From all appearances, Gehenna had two would-be rulers, each intent on owning everything the town and its environs had to offer. Slade didn't foresee that either one of them would yield or slink away until the issue was decided in dramatic style, winner take all.

But it was his job to ensure that both men lost.

That was a tall order, and Slade couldn't

achieve his goal that night. He'd start fresh in the morning, build upon the groundwork he'd already laid, and maybe see what happened when the town's two bosses squared off for the main event.

Slade would prevent bloodletting if he could, but dealing with a lawless breed, that wasn't always feasible. In which case, Slade's job was to make sure that the right folks did the bleeding, while the innocent — or nearly so — were safe outside the line of fire.

But first, he needed sleep.

No one was waiting for him this time as Slade entered the Bonanza. When the bell jangled behind him, a young clerk he hadn't seen before popped up behind the registration desk, spotted his badge, and said, "Good evening, Marshal Slade."

"So far," Slade said and passed on toward the stairs, feeling the stranger track him all the way.

Two flights was nothing, but Slade felt it in his legs before he reached the second floor. His headache had receded to a bit of soreness centered on the healing wound itself, mostly forgotten unless Slade's hat shifted to the left and made direct contact. He'd have to sleep on his right side again, but that was fine. It kept his right hand near the Peacemaker beneath his pillow.

Nearing his corner room, Slade took it slow and easy, staying near the wall, where floorboards naturally had less give and creak to them. He held his key in one hand, pistol in the other, as he stood to one side of the door and turned the lock. With luck, if there were gunmen hiding in his room, their first shots through the door might miss.

But no one fired. The empty room was perfectly indifferent to Slade's return.

He put the Peacemaker away and lit a lamp, took off his hat, and locked the door behind him when he went to use the indoor privy. Staying on the safe side, Slade left that door open, sacrificing modesty to keep a sharp eye on his room. No one surprised him, and ten minutes saw him back inside his rented bedroom, locked in for the night.

What had he learned so far? That Cartwright and Bjornson were two ruthless men, at odds with one another in a contest that would ultimately leave one wealthy and the other broken, if he lived. It was the kind of game Slade understood, though as a gambler he had never played for so much cash and property.

He had, however, gambled with his life. *That* was a game that Slade knew very well, and on the last deal he had always drawn a winning hand.

So far.

It would be reckless to assume that he was wiser than his new opponents. Cartwright and Bjornson hadn't reached their present states by acting foolishly. Greed did strange things to men, however, all the more when it was aggravated by emotions such as anger, fear, uncertainty, and lust.

Slade's clear advantage was that he had no designs upon Gehenna, planned to take no profit from it for himself. In theory, he'd been sent from Lawton to protect the town, but in reality, Gehenna's *people* were his first concern.

The law-abiding ones, at least.

Sometimes — *most* times — the cleansing of a place involved damage and loss. The guilty would be injured, certainly. Perhaps some of the righteous, few as they might be, would also suffer. Such was life. So had it always been.

Slade started to undress for bed, determined to put Cartwright and Bjornson out of mind for now. He had his shirt off and was starting on his belt buckle when he heard someone rapping softly on his door.

10

The woman on Slade's doorstep was a looker. Blond hair framed a heart-shaped face with blue eyes and a button nose above pink bee-stung lips. Slade saw those eyes flick toward the six-gun in his hand. All smoky-voiced, she said, "I hope you don't intend to shoot me, Marshal."

Slade stepped out to check the corridor, found that she was alone, and let himself relax a little. "Not just yet," he said.

"I'm glad to hear it. May I step inside?"

"Who are you?" Slade inquired.

"Sabrina Abbott," she replied. "We haven't met."

Still barring access to his room, Slade said, "No, I'd remember that, ma'am. What's your business?"

"Since we're being blunt, it's best discussed in privacy."

Slade thought about refusing her, then stepped aside. At the same moment, he remembered he was shirtless, with his belt unbuckled and his trousers sagging slightly on his hips. After he'd shut and locked the door against intruders, Slade holstered his Colt and picked his shirt up from the bed.

"Oh, please, don't dress on my account," Sabrina said.

He slipped the shirt on, leaving it unbuttoned. "We were getting to your business, ma'am."

"Call me Sabrina, please. *Ma'am* makes me feel a hundred years old, if you want to know the truth. I'll call you Jack, if that's all right."

She knew his name and plainly lived in town. The tailored and expensive dress she wore told Slade that she was almost certainly employed by either Cartwright or Bjornson.

"I was just going to bed, Sabrina."

"That's a trifle sudden, Jack. We ought to talk a little first. May I sit?"

Slade felt heat in his cheeks, and hoped it didn't show. He waved Sabrina toward the only chair and sat down on the bed, six feet away from her. A silence fell between them, strained and brittle.

Finally, she said, "I'll start, shall I? I missed you at the Rosebud earlier, when you stopped by to visit Mr. Cartwright."

There it was. "Were we supposed to meet?" asked Slade.

"No, not *supposed* to, Jack. I try to keep abreast of business that affects me, though. It's only wise, don't you agree?"

"I might, if I had any business with your Mr. Cartwright."

"Don't you?" She put on a knowing smile.

"None that will turn a profit for the house," Slade said.

"I hope that you don't mean him any harm."

Slade marked that she said *him,* not *us.* Was there a difference?

"I don't mean harm to anyone," he answered diplomatically. "I have a job to do here, on the law's behalf. No one who's playing straight has anything to fear from me."

"Define 'straight,' Jack."

"You must've talked to Cartwright."

Nodding, she replied, "Of course. He said something about claim-jumpers. It was all confusing, I admit. Such things are . . . well . . . *beyond* me."

"But not entirely foreign."

"Oh, I've heard about them. From customers, perhaps. I'm in the entertainment business, Jack."

"With Cartwright."

"For the moment. Circumstances change, of course."

"Meaning?"

"I'm an *employee,* Jack. A manager of sorts. I'm neither slave nor master of the operation. Are we clear on that?"

"You work for Cartwright, not the other way around."

She nodded, smiling. "When I give advice, sometimes, it's limited to business at the Rosebud. If, perchance, Baron has gone astray in other fields, I can't be held responsible."

"I see."

"That's not to say I think he *has* done anything malicious. Please be clear on that, Jack. Baron has been good to me. I have no reason to believe that he's been wicked in a vicious way."

"All right."

"You don't believe me, Jack?"

Slade shrugged. "You're saying what you *feel,* not what you *know.* I can't take that to court, for good or ill."

"You have a court case, then?"

"Not yet. I'm working on it."

"May I ask what it's about?"

Why not? Slade thought. "Claim-jumping, as you said. Rustling. Harassment, maybe murder, of homesteaders on the land around Gehenna."

"Bloody business, then."

"I'd say."

"Nothing about the conduct of saloons or their accessories?"

"Offhand, that doesn't sound like federal business," Slade replied.

"Well, then, our interests don't conflict," she said.

"Not even if your boss goes down?"

"Oh, bosses come and go, Jack. They're like lightning rods. I don't wish Baron ill, you understand, but he can always be replaced."

"You have another candidate in mind?" asked Slade.

Her smile was positively sinful. "Now, that's something we can talk about."

"Well, I'll be damned and go to hell," said Ardis Flack.

I wouldn't be surprised, thought Rory Duncan.

What he *said* was, "What's the matter?"

"Don't go blind on me. You *saw* her, right?"

"The lady? Yeah."

"Lady, my ass! You don't know who that *is?*"

They were staked out across the street

from the Bonanza, watching out for Marshal Slade in case he wandered out of the hotel for any reason. Flack and Duncan would be stuck there until dawn, most likely, unless Shakespeare took it in his head to send early relief. Duncan despised the task, hated the dull pain in his lower back. He wanted whiskey and a warm bed, but his hopes of getting either were minute.

"Guess not," he answered Flack. "Why should I?"

"Thought maybe you'd been saving up your pennies for a go at her," Flack told him, snickering.

"She's on the game?" asked Duncan, with a bit more interest now.

"Old son, she *is* the game, if you go sniffing after poon around the Rosebud. That's Sabrina Abbott. She's in charge of Cartwright's whores. Does turns herself, from what I understand, if anybody can afford her."

"All right, then. We saw a whore. So what?"

"You ain't real swift, I take it. Why's she goin' into the Bonanza, do you reckon?"

Duncan made a sour face. "To get some sleep. We oughta try it."

"Not so fast," said Flack. "She makes her nest down at the Rosebud, next to Cartwright."

"So, she's visiting," said Duncan.

"Right! But *who?*"

"Now, how in hell would I —" Duncan was thrilled by sudden understanding, and a bit embarrassed it had taken him so long. "The marshal?"

"Give the idjit a cigar!"

"You go to hell, Ardis!"

"I been there. Didn't care much for the scenery." He paused. "Why do you s'pose she's visitin' the law dog?"

"*If* she is, it could be any reason."

"Wrong, old son. It's either business or it's pleasure. Maybe some of each."

"You're jealous now," said Duncan. "Picturin' the two of them."

"That may be true, but I ain't thinkin' with my pecker now. You know what Damon told us."

"We're supposed to catch the marshal doin' somethin' that he ain't supposed to."

"That's the ticket. And I'd say we've got him now."

"Bedding a whore? What's wrong with that?" asked Duncan. "There's no law against it."

"But Sabrina Abbott ain't just *any* whore. I told you that. She's Cartwright's *special* poon. Her bein' with the marshal has me thinkin' he's in bed with Cartwright, don't you see? I reckon anyone would say the same — even the hangin' judge."

"I see it, now."

"Hail, Mary! Better late than never."

"So, what now?" asked Duncan.

"Now, I do what Damon *said* to do and tell him what we got here."

"He's most likely sleepin'," Duncan said.

"I don't care *what* he's doin. 'Any time of day or night' is what he told us, right?"

"I guess."

"All right, then. I'll skedaddle back and help him rouse the others. You stay here and keep your eyes peeled, just in case."

"In case of *what?*"

"I don't *know* what. Maybe they'll take a midnight stroll around the town. Just watch, and follow Slade if he goes out."

"You won't know where to find me, then."

"That's my lookout," Flack said. "Just do exac'ly like I said."

With that, Flack darted from the alleyway and scuttled back toward the Valhalla. Duncan watched him flitting between clumps of shadow, then turned his full attention back to the Bonanza.

They had marked Slade's corner room, light showing through the curtains even now. Whatever Slade was doing with the whore, they hadn't bothered turning down the lamps.

Duncan, who'd only done it in the dark — and mostly with his eyes closed — found that thought arousing, in a scary kind of way. It heightened his alertness as he stood and stared at the hotel, mind churning with the fear that Slade *would* leave and wander off while Flack was gone.

"Stay put," he whispered to the man who couldn't hear him. "Just stay put and have your fun. It's almost over, now."

"I'm listening," Slade told Sabrina Abbott. And he was, though not with any thought to joining in her plans, whatever they might be.

"It just occurred to me," she said, "that should unfortunate events befall poor Baron *and* Buck Bjornson, then Gehenna would be . . . how should I phrase this?"

"Ripe for the picking?" Slade suggested.

"In a word."

"Sounds like the same problem you have right now," he said.

"Except, without the competition," she replied. "Assuming someone moved in quickly to control the situation."

"Someone like yourself?"

"My heavens, no!" Her shock seemed

189

nearly genuine. "I've told you, Jack, I'm not a master. And I have no aspirations to become one. To control a town like this, one needs a certain strength and ruthlessness. One needs a set of balls."

"Did you have one in mind?"

"I might," she told him, rising from her chair and settling beside him on the mattress. "It occurs to me that any man with strength enough to topple Buck *and* Baron should be able to consolidate their holdings. Naturally, if he wasn't too familiar with the business, he might need some counsel."

"Which you'd happily provide," Slade ventured.

"I might be persuaded." As she spoke, Sabrina's left hand lightly slipped inside Slade's open shirt, her fingertips tracing the muscles of his stomach.

His reaction was involuntary and immediate.

"If asked," she said, "I'd make myself available to render any service possible, of course. At any hour of the day or night. If I was wanted."

"I can see where some might find that guidance useful," Slade replied, around the hard lump in his throat.

"Useful," she said. "And maybe not unpleasant."

"No," he said. "*Unpleasant* didn't come to mind, right off."

"I have all sorts of skills," she said, hand dipping lower still. "Until you've seen me work, you really can't imagine."

"Then again, maybe I can."

Her fingers found him, teasing through the fabric of his pants. Slade wore his sternest poker face, but couldn't stop the rest of him from answering the primal call. When she stopped stroking and attacked the buttons on his fly, Slade caught her wrist and slowly but decisively removed her questing hand.

"Forgive me, ma'am, but I just can't help thinking that your heart's not in it."

"Jack, it's not my heart you're thinking of right now."

"That's true enough," he granted. "But I'd like to think you'll know I'm in the room."

"Then prove it to me."

"Not tonight."

She struck a pouting attitude. "Is that your final answer, Jack?"

"It is."

"I see. It pains a girl to ask, but do you find my other proposition any more appealing than my humble self?"

"First off, you may be many things, but

humble isn't one of them. As for the business offer, I can't see myself as anybody's pimp."

"Too bad." She rose and said, "You don't know what you're missing."

Guiding her in the direction of the door, Slade said, "I have a pretty fair idea."

"Another time, perhaps?" Sabrina asked.

"Depends, now, on what you're referring to."

"I must confess, I'm thinking strictly of myself. Rejections are . . . unusual. You shake my confidence."

"No need for that. Most other circumstances, I'd be happy to oblige."

"Well, then, I'll hope for different circumstances," said Sabrina. "You can make this up to me."

"Maybe I'll see you when the dust settles," Slade answered, not believing it.

She clutched Slade's hand as he was reaching for the doorknob. "Jack, you *will* be careful, won't you? There are people in Gehenna who would kill you for the fun of it. With money in the pot, and plenty of it, you won't find a single person on your side."

"Not even you, Sabrina? What a disappointment."

"Now you're mocking me," she said.

"Just holding up a mirror. If you don't

like what you see, maybe it's time to change."

"Easy for you to say." She stepped into the corridor. "If I were you, I'd sleep with one eye open, Jack."

"I always do," he said and closed the door.

"She's comin' out!" hissed Rory Duncan.

"What the hell? He couldn'a done it that fast," Ardis Flack replied.

Duncan began to ask, *Why not?* but caught himself in time. Humiliation lay in that direction, so he said, "Maybe he didn't want her."

"Jesus, are you blind *and* stupid?" Flack demanded. "Lookit 'er, for God's sake."

"Awright, but she's leavin' anyway."

Duncan had seen her through the hotel's lobby windows, and now Sabrina Abbott stepped onto the sidewalk, gently closed the door behind her, and turned back toward the Rosebud. It was on the far side of the street, meaning she'd have to get her shoes dusty, but when and where she'd cross was anybody's guess.

"You think they's ready?" Duncan asked.

"Let's wait and see," Flack answered.

Duncan wasn't sure what to expect. He knew that Flack had gone for help, and that their reinforcements should be on the scene by now, but he'd seen none of them and didn't know how many Shakespeare might've sent — or where they were, for that matter.

They were supposed to wait until the lights winked out in Slade's hotel room, meaning that he'd settled in with Cartwright's whore to pass the night. When that happened, the lot of them were meant to slip inside, do whatever was necessary with the clerk, and make their way upstairs all quiet-like. The final rush would take them through Slade's door and have them firing all together at the bed where Slade was bundled with his little friend.

As Duncan understood the plan, it was supposed to kill Slade *and* embarrass him — or, more correctly, shame Judge Dennison in Lawton that his marshal was caught dallying with Cartwright's hooker. Duncan wasn't clear on how that would excuse the bunch of them for shooting Slade, but Bjornson and Shakespeare came up with the scheme, so he reckoned there must be an answer.

If not, he could always slip out of Gehenna and make his way westward.

The plan was starting to unravel now. Who would've guessed that Slade would send Sabrina Abbott packing without poking her a time or two, just for the fun of it? Duncan had gotten to the point of thinking she was just a messenger, but that did him no good. Whichever way he sliced it, she was *leaving,* and —

Across the street, a crouching figure lunged out of a pitch-black alleyway just as the Abbott woman passed its mouth. A hand smothered her scream, and she was yanked back out of sight, into the shadows.

"Got her!" Flack exulted. "Come on, Rory. Let's get over there."

They ran across Main Street, Duncan whipping his head from side to side in search of witnesses. He spotted none, but knew a hundred people might be watching from the blank windows on either side, upstairs and down. For all he knew, their little drama would be playing out in front of half the town.

So what?

Gehenna's sheep were powerless to intervene, so cowed and beaten down that Duncan knew they wouldn't even dare to try. Between Cartwright and Bjornson, they had bought or bullied everyone in town, until the whole damn population were the next best things to slaves.

Except for Marshal Slade. And soon —

Duncan was panting when he reached the

alley, almost stumbling into Flack. Four other boys were waiting for them in the dark, their faces hidden, but he recognized their voices and their smells. Shakespeare had sent his best, but hadn't come to join the fun himself.

Why not?

Duncan remembered from his short, unhappy army days — before they slapped him in the brig, then drummed him out — that most high-ranking officers remained behind the lines when there were battles to be fought. They made the plans, pored over maps at headquarters, and left it for their underlings to lead the charge against massed bayonets and cannon.

Just one man, he told himself. *It's just one man!*

"Hard to believe the law dog didn't want you," said one of her captors.

"Hell, *I* want her," said another.

"We should have a little fun, before we take her up," a third suggested.

"No, goddamn it!" snapped the fourth. "We got a job to do, and pokin' whores for sport's no part of it."

The woman gasped in sudden pain, a heartbeat later, and the fourth man said, "You're gonna take us to the marshal's room and get us past the door. Agreed?"

She hesitated, then produced another squeal.

"I said, *agreed?*"

"Yes! Yes! Please, don't —"

"Shut up and lead the way."

Uneasy with the change of plans, Duncan fell in behind the rest and trailed them into the hotel.

Slade wasted no time getting into bed after Sabrina Abbott had left his room. His long, strange day was winding down at last, and he'd begun to get a feel for how things happened in Gehenna, but he still had nothing for Judge Dennison.

Not yet. But he was getting closer.

Slade could feel it in his gut and in his bones.

Cartwright and Bjornson had both tried to bribe him, but he had no proof that would support that relatively minor charge. He'd spoken to Gehenna's dueling masters privately, no witnesses, and Slade didn't believe Sabrina Abbott would consent to testify.

But if she did, what of it?

So, a pimp had offered Slade a whore — without attaching any strings to the transaction or requesting payment — in a town where hooking was permitted. That proved nothing, and Sabrina might contend that it was all her own idea.

That thought intrigued Slade, but it didn't lead him anywhere. He didn't buy Sabrina thinking that he could or would step into Cartwright's shoes, after eliminating both her boss and Buck Bjornson from the scene. In other circumstances, if he didn't wear the badge, Slade granted that the proposition might be tempting. But the truth was that she'd never have approached him in the first place if he weren't a lawman. The whole thing was a tease — but to what end?

Slade stripped down to his underwear and washed his face again, using the smaller of his two white towels to pat it dry. The mirror set above his basin framed a tanned, trail-weary face, with hair spiked up in places that embarrassed him, thinking about Sabrina Abbott sitting with him on the bed.

"Surprised she didn't laugh out loud," Slade told his image in the glass. *Or run straight back to Cartwright and complain about the lousy job he'd given her.*

Unless it was, in fact, her own idea.

Slade frowned, searched his reflected eyes for some hint of belief, but couldn't find it.

"Go to sleep," he told the mirror man. "Start fresh tomorrow."

Right.

But he'd have trouble dozing off, Slade realized. Sabrina Abbott's touch had stoked a fire inside him, following his brush with Melody O'Hara's heat that hadn't truly faded yet. Slade closed his eyes, thinking of Faith, of Melody, of Cartwright's store-bought woman, and he couldn't quench the need by willpower alone.

"Tough guy," he said and smiled back at himself.

At least the women still saw something in him that appealed to them, although the more Slade thought about it, he began to wonder whether it was *him,* or circumstance.

He'd met Faith after James, his twin, was murdered. She was vulnerable, and it hadn't hurt Slade's case that he resembled James exactly, to the smallest detail. Melody, another not-so-merry widow, had felt the need to nurse Slade mingle with her gratitude.

Sabrina, now . . . well, she was something else. Slade had no doubt that she could teach him things, but he imagined that the price tag on those lessons would be more than he was able — or prepared — to pay.

Slade hung his gunbelt on the bedpost near his head and placed his Winchester repeater on the floor beside him, within easy reach of his right hand. Thus armed and ready to defend himself against nightmares, he doused the bedside lamp and closed his eyes.

11

The clerk was easy. Ardis pistol-whipped him to the floor, then gave him one to grow on, making sure he wouldn't stir and cause a fuss while they were on their way upstairs. It seemed a trifle harsh to Rory Duncan, but he'd seen worse in his time — done worse himself, in fact — and griping would've done no good at all.

The place was quiet once they finished with the clerk. Duncan supposed that the Bonanza's guests were either fast asleep or still out on the town. He didn't know or care which, simply hoping no one stumbled into it while they were dealing with the lawman.

Brett Cooper led them up the stairs, clutching Sabrina Abbott's arm in his left hand, holding a six-gun in his right. Behind him, Charlie Eastman and Ben Kelly both had scatterguns, with pistols in reserve. Clem Borden paired with Ardis Flack, their handguns drawn, while Duncan was the lone man at the rear, just halfway up the stairs when Cooper and the woman reached the second floor.

He could've turned around and left then, likely without being noticed. No one else appeared to care much whether Duncan tagged along or not, but it would soon get back to Day Shakespeare and Mr. Bjornson if he tried to weasel out of finishing his job. Shakespeare was looking at him funny, as it was, since Duncan had survived his first skirmish with Slade unscathed.

Wearing a coward's label was the quickest way to get out, or worse. Duncan was bound to see this killing through and do his part, regardless of the fact that he had horned toads scuttling around inside his stomach at the very thought of it.

When all of them were huddled on the landing for the second floor, Cooper let Eastman hold the woman for a minute, while he went to check the privy. Duncan hadn't used an indoor toilet yet, himself, and only had a vague idea of how they worked. He moved around to watch as Cooper tried the door, found it unlocked, and wrenched it open quick-like, crouching with his pistol pointed at an empty seat.

In other circumstances, Duncan might've

laughed at that, but Cooper got his sense of humor from a rattlesnake, and in their present situation he was almost guaranteed to lash out violently toward anyone unwise enough to laugh at him. So Duncan bit his cheek to keep from snorting, then stepped back and followed as the little group moved down the corridor toward Slade's room, on the end facing the street.

When they got there, the shooters formed a semicircle around Cooper and Sabrina Abbott, all their weapons leveled at the door. Duncan was on the left-hand side of the formation, nearest to the stairs if they were routed, but he steeled himself to face whatever happened next. He thumbed his Smith & Wesson's hammer back, clutching the gun so tightly that he feared its walnut grips might crack.

Cooper prodded the woman, and she rapped lightly upon Slade's door. "Marshal?" she almost whispered to him.

"Louder, damn it!" Cooper hissed.

She knocked again, with more authority, and raised her voice. "Marshal? Hello?"

No answer came back to Sabrina from the silent room. She tried again, rapping more urgently, as the gunman beside her jabbed the muzzle of his six-shooter into her ribs.

Sabrina tried to make her voice seductive, something she could do almost unconsciously when panic hadn't gripped her throat.

"Jack, wake up now! We need to have another word before I go."

Nothing.

Damn it! Where was the man?

"What's goin' on here?" asked the leader of her captors, pressing harder with his gun against her rib cage.

"How should *I* know? He was in there when I left!"

The leader spun toward someone on her left. "Duncan?"

She saw a little rat-faced gunman shrug. "He didn't come out through the front while I was watchin'."

"What about the *back?*"

The rat eyes narrowed, glinting. "How'n hell am I supposed to watch *both* sides, when Ardis up'n left me on my own to fetch you all?"

"I wasn't gone that long," another said, presumably the awkward Ardis.

"Jesus Christ, you clumsy bastards!" fumed the gunman at her side. Fuming, he clutched Sabrina's arm and shook her. "Where'd he go!"

"I wasn't *with* him! Are you stupid?"

The snarling gunman shoved his pistol underneath her chin. "I'm smart enough to blow your head off, bitch! We mean to kill someone tonight, and if your boyfriend ain't at home, you're it. Now, try again!"

"All *right!*"

She fairly hammered on Slade's door this time. "Jack, darling, will you *please* get up and let me in? You're starting to embarrass me."

Silence.

Sabrina's shoulders slumped, despite the gun wedged underneath her jaw. Mind racing, she imagined all the places where Slade might've gone, if he had dressed and slipped out through the hotel's back door, while she went out through the front.

There was the Rosebud, the Valhalla, and . . . exactly nowhere else. None of the other shops were open at that hour of the night. Unless he simply felt an urge to roam the streets, there were no other options.

"I don't believe this shit," her escort muttered through clenched teeth.

"What are we waitin' for?" another member of the party asked.

"You're right. Screw this!"

The gunman shoved Sabrina to her left, making her stumble, nearly falling to her knees before the one called Duncan caught her arm and saved her from a tumble. When their eyes met, he seemed troubled, verging on apologetic, but he did not speak.

They turned together, saw the leader of the pack rear back, raise his right foot, and slam his heel into the door beside its knob. The first kick rattled Slade's door in its frame, drawing more curses from the kicker, then he tried again and got it right the second time. The door crashed inward, pieces flying from its shattered latch and rattling across the floor, as shooters rushed into the darkened room.

Slade shot the first man through the doorway with his Winchester, letting the lamplight from the outer hallway frame his target as a silhouette. He didn't try a fancy shot, just aimed directly for the center of the lead man's chest and put him down, then rolled away before the rest could draw down on his muzzle flash.

He'd heard them coming down the corridor, guessed there wouldn't be that many neighbors in the room next door to his, and rose to meet the new arrivals well before they reached his room. He'd buckled on his gunbelt, slipped into his boots, and found a place against the wall to watch and wait, as far off from his bed as he could get without cutting a new door for himself.

The knock hadn't surprised him, but Sabrina's voice had drawn Slade's mouth into a scowl. Thinking she'd set him up for killing made Slade's trigger finger itch, but he'd resisted that first impulse to fire blindly through the door. Straining his ears, he'd picked up on the sound of angry voices arguing and then framed another possibility — that someone might've grabbed Sabrina on her way back to the Rosebud, forcing her to front for them on Slade's doorstep.

Perhaps.

He'd boiled it down to fifty-fifty when the door caved in, and gunmen spilled into the room. After his first shot and the shoulder roll, Slade crouched beside the chest of drawers and chose another target in the light spill from the doorway.

Slade could see three shooters on their feet and figured there were likely two or three more waiting in the corridor outside. He couldn't spot Sabrina and decided that he wouldn't gun her down unless she faced him with a weapon in her hand.

As for the rest . . .

Slade shot the second gunman high and somewhere right of center, just a trifle jerky on the trigger in his haste. The bullet's impact spun his target back and to Slade's left, jostling the man behind him hard enough to spoil the startled shooter's aim.

The second wounded man was falling, crying out in pain and triggering another shot that might've grazed his lurching, dodging sidekick. Slade pumped the Winchester's lever action, rolled again to dodge incoming fire, and fetched up hard against the foot of his abandoned bed. Bracing his rifle on a corner of the mattress, he was ready for a third shot as his final target turned and fled.

He nearly missed the third man, ducking as the runner was, but Slade saw blood spurt from the shooter's left sleeve as he spun and dropped out of view. Two hulking bodies filled the doorway then, both firing double-barreled shotguns without taking time to aim.

They nearly bagged Slade, even so, but he was wriggling underneath the bed by then, and frightened shooters have a tendency to point their weapons high, a trait exaggerated by the recoil from their shotguns. Slade fired twice from underneath the bed, missed once, and heard one of his adversaries bleat a curse as lead ripped through his shin.

Outside, a jabber told him the survivors were reloading and regrouping, working up their nerve to try again. Slade cast around the bedroom for a weapon that could save him — and he found it, just in time.

It took unprecedented strength, in Rory Duncan's case, to keep himself from running like a frightened rabbit from the hotel corridor, downstairs, and out into the street. His jaw ached from the way he ground his teeth together, and it felt as if his bowels had turned to water, but he stayed.

He stayed and *fought.*

Granted, his random shots into the lawman's room accomplished nothing, but at least no one could say he'd hung back on the wall and watched the others carry all the burden. He was doing what he could to help, and by God, none of them were doing any better.

Brett Cooper was dead, he reckoned. First man through the door and first to fall, with Clem Borden behind him. Borden hadn't come out of the bedroom, either, and the marshal's third shot had winged Ardis on the run. Charlie and Ben — shortened from *Ebenezer,* Duncan understood — had sprayed the room with buckshot, and the lawman *still* kept firing, plugging Eastman through one leg.

It was a bloody mess, and now they all were huddled in the hallway — four of them, at least, together with the woman — trying to decide on their next move. Duncan was damned if he would be the next man through that doorway, and he didn't care *who* ordered him to make the move. Cooper had been in charge, and now the lead was up for grabs, as far as Rory Duncan was concerned.

Why not command the team, himself?

That startling thought was echoing in Duncan's mind when a sudden light flared in the darkened bedroom, a kerosene lamp flew tumbling through the open doorway, bouncing off the wall directly opposite and then smashing on the floor. Its fuel splattered, caught fire, and rapidly began to spread.

It wasn't just the floor on fire, either. Some of the kerosene had splashed on Ardis Flack and Charlie Eastman, catching in their clothes and causing them to dance erratically around the hallway, yelping curses as they spun and slapped the biting flames. Duncan recoiled from contact with the human torches, standing ready with his pistol just in case the clever lawman made a break for it in the confusion.

Which, of course, he did — but not before he triggered two more rifle shots from the recesses of his rented room. One slug drilled

Ardis through the head and put him down immediately, like a puppet with its strings slashed. Eastman took the second hit while he was lurching past the doorway, but it struck him somewhere in the hip or lower back, cutting his legs from under him while leaving him alive and thrashing on the floor.

And *then* the marshal came for them, a wraith of vengeance who broke Duncan's will, despite his firm resolve to stand and fight. Cursing himself as seven kinds of coward, Rory Duncan fired two hasty shots, and then he ran.

The lantern was his only surefire way to get out of the room. Slade's hands were trembling as he struck a lucifer to light it, almost certain that his enemies would choose that moment for another rush and catch him with his guns down, helpless.

But they didn't, and his pitch was perfect, spraying fire across the hallway when the lamp shattered on impact. Slade was hoping for confusion and a smoke screen that would cover him, but he got more, setting fire to a pair of his would-be killers and watching them struggle to beat out the flames.

He shot them both, of course, not caring that their backs were turned, nor wasting time on any other frontier niceties, which he'd observed were honored more in the omission than in practice. One — the same man Slade had winged a moment earlier — was dead before he hit the floor. The other benefited from a hasty shot and lived, but lost the full use of his legs.

There'd never be a better time to rush them, and Slade knew it. Moving in a crouch, letting his rifle take the lead, he scuttled to the door and through it, leaping wide across a pool of liquid fire that was devouring the rug and wooden floor beneath it.

Sound the fire alarm, before the whole place goes, he thought. And then, *To hell with it.*

Slade saw two shooters on their feet, a third rolling around the floor in blood and burning kerosene, together with Sabrina Abbott huddled off to one side by herself. Slade glimpsed a portion of her skirt smoldering and pointed to it, calling to her, "Watch yourself!" before he spun to face his enemies.

One of them triggered two wild shots, then turned and ran, quitting the fight before he really got a piece of it. Slade focused on the one still standing and the deadly sawed-off shotgun in his hands. At that range, aiming was a luxury with such a weapon. All the shooter had to was point —

And fire.

Slade dropped as if he'd stepped into a snare and it had yanked his feet away. The double buckshot swarm passed over him and pocked the nearby wall. Before he could reload, Slade shot him in the gut, and then once more, under the chin, as he was falling over backward.

That left two — one fleeing, and the other just now struggling to his hands and knees, smoke rising from his clothes and from his greasy hair. Shaky he might be, but the toasted gunman had a pistol in his hand, and it was aimed rock steady at Slade's face.

Slade flinched at the gunshot, then realized it wasn't loud enough to be a Colt. A hole appeared above his enemy's left eye. The astonished shooter stared past Slade, then crumpled to the floor as if his bones had turned to dust.

Slade turned to find Sabrina Abbott standing with a derringer still smoking in her hand. Instead of waiting for his thanks, she said, "You missed one, Jack. He's on his way downstairs."

Rory Duncan reached the hotel lobby, ran halfway across it, toward the exit and Main Street, then stopped dead in his tracks. He could escape — but then, what?

Shakespeare already suspected him of cowardice, and Duncan running out once more would cinch the deal. He couldn't show his face at the Valhalla, then, or anywhere around Gehenna.

And beyond that, who or what would spook him next?

He *had* to stand and fight, not for Bjornson or Shakespeare, but for himself. Having decided that, however, Duncan quickly realized that waiting for his target in the middle of the open lobby would be tantamount to suicide.

More shots rang out upstairs. Duncan approached the registration desk, peered over it, then ran around behind it. The unconscious clerk still lay where he had fallen, snuffling through a flattened nose. Duncan reached down to grasp his belt, dragged him a few feet farther back, then crouched behind the counter with his six-gun drawn and cocked.

He waited, sweating out the deathwatch, wondering if Ben or someone else had gotten lucky with the marshal and disposed of him. Duncan supposed he ought to check upstairs, but staying put exactly where he was felt right.

Waiting for another chance.

He heard the floorboards creaking over-head, and smelled smoke wafting down the staircase. Duncan had a vision of the hotel all in flames, but knew he could get out before that happened. Even if the floor above him should collapse, he knew that it would start around the point where Slade had smashed the lantern, not directly over Duncan's head.

So, he had time. A little, anyway.

Outside, a cry of "Fire!" forced him to reconsider his position. Townsfolk would be rushing into the Bonanza soon, bearing buckets of water or sand to extinguish the flames. Duncan could only hope to deal with Slade quickly, before the others who came ruined everything.

The clerk stirred restlessly behind him, moaning. Was he coming back around to call for help? Duncan leaned over him, saw eyelids flickering, and whipped his pistol down across the bloodied skull. A tremor rippled through the clerk's body, then he lay still once more.

"And *stay* there," Duncan muttered to him, turning back to face the stairs.

More voices from the street, but then he heard a clamor on the stairs, boot heels galumphing down in the direction of the lobby. Duncan told himself he must be careful not to fire before he saw the target's face, in case it was Kelly or Eastman, victorious.

Ready . . .

He leaped erect, bleating a war cry, as his six-gun found its mark.

Slade hit the hotel lobby running, half expecting that his adversary would be out and gone before he got there, vanished in the night. At first glance, he supposed he was correct, then noise and movement on his left brought him around to face a shooter rising from behind the registration desk, howling like some demented animal and sighting down the barrel of a Smith & Wesson .44.

They fired together, Slade's round whispering within a half inch of the shooter's ear, the Smith & Wesson's bullet rattling past a foot or more from Slade. The pistolero made a little sobbing sound, began to cock his piece again, but Slade was faster with the lever-action rifle, and he got there first.

The Winchester recoiled against his shoulder, and he had the target in his sights this time. The kill shot wasn't perfect, but it slammed into the gunman's chest, tore through one of his lungs, and pitched him back into the bank of cubbyholes where messages were stashed for different rooms, above their dangling keys.

Slade heard the shooter's pistol clatter to the floor, and rushed around the desk to cover him, toeing the fallen pistol out of reach. The dying man coughed blood and stared at Slade with rheumy eyes.

Slade crouched beside him, mindful that his enemy might have a belly gun, but all the fight had left him with the flow of precious blood. Slade leaned in close enough to make sure he was heard.

"Who sent you here?" he asked.

The shooter's lips were moving, leaking crimson at the corners, but Slade couldn't make out any words among the little whisper sounds that issued forth. Whatever Slade's opponent meant to say was lost in one last gusher as he slithered over sideways to the floor.

Slade checked the clerk, made sure that he was breathing, then stood up in time to see the point men of Gehenna's fire brigade arrive.

"Where is it?" one of them demanded, water sloshing from his bucket.

"Second floor," Slade said. "You can't miss it."

They clambered up the stairs, nearly colliding with Sabrina Abbott on her way down to the lobby. Slade surveyed her, noting that her hair was mussed, one shoulder of her gown was ripped, a portion of its hem scorched brown.

"Not Cartwright's men, I take it?" he inquired.

"I don't know any of their names," she answered. "Two or three I've seen outside of the Valhalla."

"For a minute there, I thought you were with them," Slade said.

"I was, but not the way you mean. They grabbed me on the street."

"You're all right, now?"

"They weren't so tough. Am I under arrest?"

"For what?"

"Shooting that tub of guts upstairs."

"I try not to arrest people who save my life."

"I'll just be going, then."

"Be careful," Slade advised.

"Of what? They have no further use for me."

"I'd just feel better if you watched your step."

"Okay." She hesitated on the threshold, turning back. "What's next for you? Taking your pelts to Buck?"

Slade shook his head. "He wants them, he

can fetch them from the undertaker. I have other business, mobilizing the community."

"Sounds serious," she said, risking a smile.

"You never know," Slade said. "It just might be."

12

"I still don't feel right," Melody O'Hara said, "leaving the animals and property this way. Suppose someone —"

"They *won't,* Sister. Have faith."

"I think I've lost mine," Melody replied.

Harmony held the buckboard's reins, sharing the driver's seat with Melody. Beneath them, covered with a knitted blanket in the wagon's foot well, lay two rifles and a pair of pistols captured from the men who'd tried to kill them four days earlier.

"You mustn't say that," Harmony rebuked her sister. "God is always listening and watching."

"Is he?" There was a cutting edge to Melody's reply. "Where was he, then, when Mickey fell? Where was he when those bastards came to burn us out?"

"You know the answer, Sister. Bad things happen. We have trials. And on the second matter, you'll recall that he sent Marshal Slade."

"Oh, rubbish! He was riding to Gehenna and he heard the shooting. What does the Almighty have to do with it?"

"His hand is everywhere," said Harmony.

"It needs to fall on those who torment us. When *that* happens, maybe I'll find my way back to believing."

Harmony knew that her sister wouldn't bend on that subject, but she had done her bit to witness for the Lord. If she pursued a stronger argument, against all of the evidence, she would feel foolish.

"Anyway," she said at last, "we have a lovely day for traveling."

And it was true. A cloudless sky beamed sunshine down upon them as they followed the suggestion of a road between their homestead and Gehenna. Since they were alone and dreaded contact with the men in town, the sisters minimized their shopping expeditions, but it had been nearly three months since their last visit, and they were running desperately short on various supplies.

"You have the shopping list?" Harmony asked her sister.

"*Yes,* for the *fourth* time! Will you stop asking me?"

"I'm sorry."

"No, I am. I've turned into a shrew."

"You've had more than your share of burdens, Sister."

"This is one of them. It sets my very teeth on edge."

"I know."

"Passing along that street, knowing some of the men we see can't wait to run us off our land . . . or worse."

"Don't think about it, now."

"How can I not?"

"There's Marshal Slade," said Harmony, remembering his face, the way he moved. "He's in Gehenna now. Nothing will happen to us while he's there."

"You hope. He can't be everywhere at once, you know. Suppose he's out investigating somewhere, or —"

"You worry too much, Sister. If we have to fight, we brought the tools along."

"And that's another thing! What will we do if someone steals them from the buckboard while we're shopping?"

"They won't. We'll carry them along with us," said Harmony.

"Sister!"

"Why not? You won't see many men in town without at least one gun. The merchants keep them out of sight, but they're still there."

"I swear, you'll send our reputation straight to Hell," said Melody, smiling.

"It's pretty close already, I expect," said Harmony. "We're goldarned female sod-busters with no men of our own, no young'uns, and we don't kowtow to elders of the town. I'd be surprised if they don't call us whores right now."

"Oh, do you think so?" Melody did not sound mortified.

"At least," said Harmony. "It may be worse than that."

"Worse how?"

"It may be," Harmony replied archly, "they think we're victims of the love that dare not speak its name."

Melody laughed aloud at that, a welcome sound. "You are a caution, Sister, I must say."

"Remember, when we get there," Harmony continued, "that we won't be pushed around or cheated. Right?"

"Of course not," Melody assured her. "What would people say?"

Slade tried the Longhorn's breakfast special on his first morning in Gehenna. It included two eggs, bacon, ham, a mound of fried potatoes, flapjacks drenched in syrup, and a steaming mug of coffee.

When the smiling waitress made her second visit to his table, Slade corralled her for a quick word. "I'll be looking for your local minister today," he said. "Also, whoever runs the newspaper. Can you give me their names?"

"Sure thing, Marshal," she said. "The preacher's Reverend Trowbridge. He seems nice enough, although I'm not a member of his flock. As for the paper, that's the *Beacon*. Kester Ridley runs the whole show by himself, as far as I know."

"Thanks."

"You're welcome. Can I warm that coffee up for you?"

Slade saw the sisters in their buckboard passing by the Longhorn's windows as he rose and left his money on the table. Moments later, he was on the sidewalk, crossing Main Street to the point where they had stopped outside the dry-goods store. He caught them stepping down and reaching back for something in the well beneath the driver's seat.

"Good morning, ladies."

Both of them looked startled, yanking back their hands, then smiled to see him. Melody hurried around the buckboard, stopping by her sister, on the side closer to Slade.

"Good morning, Jack!" she said.

"Marshal," her sister said with more reserve.

"How are you both?" he asked.

"We're fit enough," Melody answered. "How's your head?"

"Still on my shoulders," Slade replied, making her smile. "And is it quiet out at your place?"

"As the very grave," said Harmony. "I trust your sleep is undisturbed in town?"

A pair of carpenters passed by them, lugging paint and tools. Slade watched them enter the Bonanza, telling Harmony, "We had a little fracas at the hotel overnight. Nothing to fret about."

"And you were in the middle of it, I presume."

"They threw a party for me, but I've never been one for surprises," Slade explained.

"A rowdy lot, I take it?"

Slade shrugged. "They got carried away."

"How many does that make it now?" asked Harmony.

"How many *what?*" Melody interrupted.

"I believe we're one short of a dozen, for the week," Slade said.

"They won't forgive that, Marshal," Harmony advised him.

"I don't seek forgiveness, just compliance

with the law."

"Considering the place, you ask too much."

"Will someone kindly tell me what you're on about?" asked Melody. "Was there more shooting? Is that it?"

"We're in Gehenna, Sister. What do you expect?"

"But, Jack," said Melody. "You *are* all right? No other injuries?"

"Fit as a fiddle, ma'am. A bit concerned about you ladies being in here, at the moment, though," he said.

"We need supplies," said Harmony. "And we can take care of ourselves."

Melody glanced back at the buckboard as her sister spoke. Frowning, Slade edged between them, flicking back a corner of the blanket in the foot well to reveal a rifle's stock.

"I see you've come prepared," he said.

"Our presents from the housewarming," said Harmony, her face stern with defiance. "If somebody wants to claim them, we're prepared to give them back. One bullet at a time."

"I'd say you've caught the spirit of this place," said Slade.

"It's with reluctance that we join them in the pit, but we must all survive," said

Harmony.

"If it's a question of your safety here in town," Slade said, "I don't mind helping with your errands."

Melody seemed ready to accept, might have replied in the affirmative, if Harmony had not reached out to clutch her hand.

"We'll be all right, Marshal," the older sister said. "You must have business to conduct, yourself."

"In fact, I do," Slade told them. "I'll be looking up their minister, this morning, and the man who runs the local newspaper."

"Good luck to you," said Harmony, already turning from him.

"Yes," said Melody. "Good luck!"

"And all the best to you," said Slade. He turned away before the sisters took their weapons from the buckboard, clutched them tight, and went into the dry-goods store.

"He knows them two," said Eulis Baker, lounging on his customary seat outside the Rosebud. "Who are they?"

None of the shooters ranged around him answered for a moment, then a grizzled, scar-faced specimen off to his left said, "I b'lieve they homestead, somewhere hereabouts."

"Somewhere," Baker replied. "We need to narrow down the field."

"What for?" another of his gunmen asked.

"A question!" He pretended to be pleasantly surprised. "And who can answer that?"

Baker sat waiting for a full minute, watching as Slade and the two women finished up their conversation, then going separate ways. His eyes picked out the weapons that they pulled from hiding in their buckboard prior to entering the nearby shop.

"No one?" he said at last. "Okay. Let's not dwell on the fact that all of you are dumb as posts. Try keeping up with me."

He counted on his fingers as he ran down the apparent clues. "Slade knows them, but he's never been in town before. They homestead, somewhere close enough to come in for their shopping and go back again, let's say before nightfall. They're glad to see him, so we know he's done them a good turn. Last thing, they brought their guns to town. What does that tell you? *Any*body?"

"Well . . ." Scarface considered it, but he had spoken prematurely. Finally, he shook his head and spat into the street.

"No one? Jesus." Baker stood up to pace the sidewalk. "*Think* about it, boys! He's new in town, but helped those ladies out with something. Something *scary,* since

228

they're packing guns to town."

Another wait. Baker, disgusted, snapped at them, "Shit fire! You idjits make my ass tired. *They're* the ones he must've rescued from Bjornson's boys. Get it? Am I the only one around here with a pair of eyes that works?"

"Oh, yeah," one of them said. "I see it now."

The others nodded, making noises of agreement. No one wanted to be last in line, seeing the light.

"But now," Baker continued, "none of you know who they are or where they live. Is that about the size of it?"

Dull nods around the circle, faces heavy with embarrassment.

"All right," said Baker. "Now, what can we *do* about it?"

"Go down there an ask 'em?" Scarface said.

"Right here, on Main Street?" Baker asked. "What happens if they get upset, maybe start shooting at us?"

"Shoot 'em back, dumb bitches," said another.

"Perfect. Kill the lawman's lady friends in broad daylight, in front of witnesses."

"I got a notion," said the red-haired, freckled gunman.

"Thrill me," Baker said.

"Why don't we follow 'em back home and ask 'em there?"

"You take the prize, J.D.," said Baker. "I believe you truly do."

Turning to scan the street, Baker removed a badge from his vest pocket and began to flip it like a coin, its small points winking in the sunlight.

Damon Shakespeare lounged in shade, outside of the Valhalla, watching Marshal Slade cross over toward the other side of Main Street. It required iron will to keep his pistols holstered as the lawman ambled into range.

Iron will . . . and fear.

Mere hours earlier, Slade had eliminated six of Shakespeare's handpicked shooters, when they should've caught him rutting with Sabrina Abbott and disposed of him in nothing flat. It was a solid plan, but Slade had turned it right around on them and killed them all.

Shakespeare had gone to see their bodies at the undertaker's place. Buck Bjornson had insisted on it, cursing all the way over and back about half-assed, pissant plans drawn up by idjits. Shakespeare had no answer for the torrent of abuse. Viewing the shot-up corpses, two of them with burns on top of fatal wounds, he couldn't think of an excuse.

That made eleven men rubbed out within a week — not even that, *four days* — and all of them apparently by one man with more luck than any mother's son deserved. If Shakespeare couldn't find someone to take Slade out, and soon, he'd have to try himself.

And that was where the fear came into it.

"Those women he was talking to, who are they?" Shakespeare asked.

"Them Irish bitches," one of his assembled gunmen answered. "Live out east of town, without no man."

The women suddenly had Shakespeare's full attention. It had all begun with them, he realized, this run of luck against him that had made his recent life a misery. On Bjornson's orders, he had sent six men to run the sisters off their spread, and only one — sad little Rory Duncan — had returned, bringing his story of a U.S. marshal who rode out of nowhere, killing left and right, to save the day.

Next thing he knew, the marshal was among them, in Gehenna, talking snotty to Bjornson and the rest of them like he thought he was bulletproof, flirting with

Cartwright at the Rosebud, entertaining Cartwright's whore at his hotel.

Shakespeare had given Rory Duncan one last chance to prove he had a backbone, sent five men along to prop him up, and now all six of *them* were dead, stacked up in rough pine boxes at the undertaker's shop.

Slade and the sisters had it in for Shakespeare. That was obvious. He tried to earn a decent living for himself, and they conspired against him, throwing roadblocks in his way like they were too damned good to share the world with common trash.

Well, he could teach them something yet. The lawman wasn't born who could embarrass Damon Shakespeare twice and live to gloat about it. As for *women,* someone must've put the crazy notion in their heads that they could deal with men as equals, but he'd change their minds on that score pretty soon.

"Billy," he snapped.

"Yeah, Boss?"

"Get four, five men together. Ride out to the sisters' place and hide up somewhere. When they come home, take good care of 'em. And bring me somethin' for the marshal. Somethin' for him to remember 'em by."

The one called Billy chuckled. "It'll be a

pleasure, Boss."

"I bet it will," said Shakespeare with a smile.

Slade was halfway to Gehenna's church, First Baptist, when a woman's voice behind him said, "I see you like them country. Maybe two at once?"

Sabrina Abbott showed no ill effects from last night's ordeal. Any bruises she'd sustained were covered with cosmetics, and her dress was new — at least, to Slade. It hugged her body like a second skin above the waist, and flounced in ruffles from her hips down to her feet.

"You're all recovered? Back at work?" Slade asked.

"It takes more than a shoot-out and a fire to get me down," she said.

"You've seen worse, I suppose?"

"We both have, Jack."

He let that pass and said, "How did your boss take it?"

"Which part? Where you rejected me, or where you almost got me killed?"

"Whichever."

"He was disappointed by the first, but then the other cheered him up a bit. Whenever Bjornson's men go down, it makes him happy."

"Glad to help." Slade tipped his hat and said, "Good morning to you, ma'am."

"Hold up! You haven't thanked me yet for saving you."

"How do I know it wasn't just revenge?" asked Slade.

"What difference does it make? That shooter would've plugged you, either way."

"You're right," he said. "Thank you."

"You're welcome . . . anytime."

"We've been all over that, if you recall," he said.

"No, Jack. If you had been all over *this,* you'd never manage to forget it."

"I suspect that's true, but I'm a busy man."

"Busy with what, if I may ask?"

Slade weighed the risks of telling her — of telling Baron Cartwright, in effect — and thought it might not hurt to show a couple of his cards this far into the game.

"First thing, I thought I'd go to church," Slade said. "And then, I plan to stop in at the newspaper."

"An interview?" Sabrina smiled. "With six dead, Ridley must be licking his chops."

"Serving the public's what it's all about," said Slade.

"Uh-huh." She raised one dainty foot and wiggled it. "Now pull the other one. Don't leave me walking with a limp."

"You question my integrity?" he teased.

"After last night? Not me. But I'd bet money that there's something going on inside that head of yours."

"I hope so."

"I won't like it, will I?"

"That depends," he said, "on how attached you are to Cartwright and Gehenna."

"What, you aim to run us out of town?"

"My plans aren't that advanced yet," Slade replied. "I'm supposed to stop the claim-jumping, the rustling, everything that goes along with it."

"The sporting, too?" she pressed.

"It's not against the law."

"So far, that is."

"You want something to worry about," Slade said, "think about who you work for."

"I've known him forever, it seems like. He isn't so bad."

"He kills people, or orders them killed."

"So do you," she replied. "Does the badge make a difference?"

"The *why* makes a difference," Slade said. "I've never shot a man to get his land or money, never out of spite."

"I guess that makes you pure of heart."

Slade held her eyes with his. "I don't

concern myself with what's inside a person's heart," he said. "Just whether they obey the law."

"Toeing a hard line makes you vulnerable, Jack."

"I'll take that chance."

"I hope you don't regret it."

With a shrug, he said, "Regrets are part of life."

"Some more than others, I suppose."

"But you don't have to carry them forever," Slade replied.

"You find someplace to leave them, let me know, will you?"

With that, she turned away and hurried toward the Rosebud, leaving Slade alone to find Gehenna's church.

It wasn't hard. He'd seen it, riding in, a white spire set against the blue sky like a finger aimed at God. Whether it was supposed to point the way or aim an accusation at the heavens, Slade could not have said.

Either by accident or by design, the church was situated at Gehenna's western boundary, so that its worshippers — if there were any to be found — had to traverse Main Street's full length to reach their sanctuary. Slade enjoyed the walk this morning, feeling eyes upon him, knowing that a few of those who watched were shaken by the sight of him alive and well.

It troubled Slade that those same eyes would have beheld him with the sisters, Harmony and Melody, but there was nothing he could do about it now. He couldn't promise that no one would move against them, and the sisters knew that. They remained, against all odds, to work the land that Cartwright and Bjornson coveted, because surrender was unthinkable. Slade understood that stubbornness and hoped it would not bring them to a sorry end.

En route to meet Gehenna's pastor, Slade stopped off to see his horse. The hostler greeted him as always, with a quick bob of the head. Slade had already paid him for the week and owed no more. He spent time with the roan, promised a run that afternoon if it was feasible, and then took solace from the fact that he could never disappoint an animal that didn't understand a word he said.

"You had some trouble last night, what I hear," the hostler said as Slade was leaving.

"Some. Who told you?"

"I don't rightly recollect, sir."

"Ah."

"Just wanted you to know, nobody messes

with the horses here. I don't allow it. Anybody tries it, either side, I blow his goddamn head off. Horses ain't to blame for nothin' that goes on 'round this place."

"I appreciate it," Slade replied.

"It's for the beasts, not you nor anybody else."

"I get it."

Slade preferred the smell of animals, of fresh hay and manure, to what awaited him outside, but he could only stall for so long. When he left the livery, First Baptist stood across the street from him, at a diagonal. Slade saw the large cross mounted on its wall, above the double doors in front, but there was no figure of Jesus visible.

Slade wondered whether it was too much for the Son of God to hang on Main Street in Gehenna, watching sinners come and go around him, plotting crimes they hoped would make them wealthy and above the law. What would the Savior think of *him,* who almost never turned the other cheek to enemies and broke most of the Ten Commandments without thinking twice.

Not stealing, though, he thought. When he'd been younger, living on the road without a skill or trade in those days, Slade had stolen to survive, but that was long behind him. He had never asked forgiveness, reckoning that it was no one else's business, and he felt no urge to grovel now.

As for the rest — swearing, breaking the Sabbath, fornication, lying, coveting, killing — he'd done it all. The killings were in self-defense, or in defense of others, and on balance, Slade spent little time worrying about his soul.

But that could always change.

Not likely, Slade decided, as he crossed the street, but anything was possible.

13

The church was cool and dark inside, after the glare of Main Street. It was lit primarily with half a dozen lamps, three on a side, suspended from hooks on the walls. The only window in the sanctuary was a stained-glass piece behind the pulpit, showing baby Jesus in his mother's arms, with golden rays from heaven falling on his upturned face.

A tall, thin man, dressed all in black except for his shirt collar, stood behind the pulpit as Slade entered. After Slade had closed the door, the parson — who else could he be? — stepped down and moved along the central aisle between the pews.

"Good morning, Marshal . . . Slade, is it?"

"They told you right," Slade said, shaking the preacher's outstretched hand.

"I'm Quentin Trowbridge, pastor of Gehenna's flock, such as it is."

"You don't get many, of a Sunday?"

"I can't complain on that account," the

minister replied. "We're nearly full, most times."

"You're getting out the message, then."

"I do that, sir . . . for all the good it does."

"I'm guessing some backslide, between the sermons," Slade remarked.

"Backsliding, I can deal with," Trowbridge answered. "I can pray for the repentant sinners, Marshal. It's the *others* who confound me."

"Others?"

"Those who dress up on a Sunday morning and present themselves to him," said Trowbridge, with a nod back toward the stained-glass window, "then go on about their business and forget him through the week."

"You have some insincere parishioners, I take it."

"I am beset by hypocrites, in fact. Not all of them, you understand. Including some who set the tone for the community at large."

"Big money," Slade suggested, glancing none too subtly at the stained-glass window.

"It's a daily struggle, I admit, sir. And sometimes, I fear I may be losing."

"You get folk from the saloons?"

"I get the ones that matter, and a few you wouldn't naturally expect," Trowbridge replied. "Don't get me wrong, please. Christ himself loved harlots — in the purest sense, you understand, not carnally. But to be saved, a sinner has to *change*, or at the very least, *desire* to change. It takes commitment on our part, as well as his."

"You get lip service," Slade interpreted.

"If that. Sometimes, I think First Baptist is a cruel charade. A social outing for some folk to flaunt their finery, before they strip it off again and wallow in the muck."

"Sounds serious."

"What could be more so, than the fate of man's immortal soul? I ask you that, sir!"

"Souls aren't really my department, Pastor. I'm concerned more with the worldly side of things."

"Of course. I understand, Marshal. What brings you here, in fact?"

"In my experience," Slade said, "parsons have influence in their communities. People look up to them, and ask them for advice."

"That's true in my experience, as well. But in Gehenna, sir, you've found a special case where few, if any, normal rules apply."

"That bad?"

"May I speak frankly, Marshal?"

"Please."

"I'm window dressing, sir. For most of those who stop here on a Sunday morning,

I have no more impact than a fly buzzing around their ears. I hope — I *pray* — to reach the younger ones, but then, I only see them once a week, while they absorb the lessons of their parents and acquaintances around the clock each day."

"Why do you stay, if it's a trial for you?" Slade asked.

"Because it *is* a trial," Trowbridge replied. "If I touch one soul here, it may be worth a thousand in a town where piety's the norm. Remember Sodom and Gomorrah, Marshal. 'If you find one righteous man . . .' "

"Suppose the fire is coming, and you haven't found him yet?"

"I live in hope."

"Seems like a lonely road," Slade said.

"It can be. But the good fight has its own rewards."

Glancing around First Baptist, at stained glass, fresh paint, and varnished pews, Slade wondered if the fight was really all that hard and lonely, or if Trowbridge simply knew which side his bread was buttered on.

"You do all right," Slade said, "for window dressing."

"Guilty consciences are often generous, Marshal. Sadly, it doesn't often indicate a will to be redeemed."

"I guess you heard about the ruckus down

at the Bonanza overnight?"

"I did."

"Will you be saying words for them?" Slade asked.

"I knew *of* the departed, but they didn't come to church. I'm sure that's no surprise. However, if I'm asked to speak for them, however undeserving they might be, it falls within my duties."

"Who might do the asking?"

"Their employer, I suppose," said Trow-bridge cautiously.

"And that would be . . . ?"

"Well, now . . ."

"I only ask," Slade said, "because he sent them down to kill me, and a lady. I've a mind to settle that, before I leave Gehenna, and I wouldn't want to be mistaken in regard to whom I owe a visit."

Trowbridge cleared his throat and said at last, "I understand they were Bjornson's men."

"That was my understanding, too." Turning to leave, Slade said, "I wish you luck, Parson. If you decide to give the slackers hell, some Sunday, I'd be pleased to come and hear you talk."

"It's possible," Trowbridge replied. "With God, all things are possible."

■ ■ ■ ■

"Come on, goddamn it!" Billy Bauer snapped. "We need to get a move on, 'fore them *ladies* start for home."

"How come we don't just wait along the way and dry-gulch 'em?" Hank Murphy asked.

"Because Day *said* so, and he's talkin' for Bjornson. Any other questions?"

"Naw. I reckon not."

"We get to have some fun with 'em?" asked Jared Cole. His brother, Jubal, snickered from the horse beside him.

"No one told me any differ'nt," Bauer said. "Main thing is to be shut of 'em, once and for all."

"They's scrappers, though," said Early Somers as he settled on his piebald mare. " 'Member what happened to the last boys went out there."

"That was the law dog," Bauer said. "He'll be tied up in town."

"You *hope* it was the law dog," Somers muttered.

"What was that?"

"Nothin'."

"Awright, then. Shut your yaps and ride!"

Bauer led by example, spurring his stallion eastward. They rode behind the Main Street buildings, keeping out of sight of those who shopped and dawdled past the stores. Someone might see them, once they cleared the town limits, but who would know exactly who they were, or where they might be going?

Bauer couldn't speak for the rest of them, but he welcomed a chance to hit back, after all the hard knocks that his friends had suffered lately. Maybe *friends* wasn't the best word for them, since he didn't really give two hoots in hell for most of them and wouldn't miss them greatly, now that they were dead. But it was still a point of honor, wasn't it, to stand up for the team and fight when it was threatened?

Right.

Plus, they were getting paid a little something extra for this job — and they could poke the women, too.

Why not?

Bjornson wanted them removed, and that meant dead. He wouldn't care what happened to them first, and might even appreciate the extra touches, after all the grief they'd caused him. Anyway, there'd be no questions as to how the women died, or if they suffered.

Dead was dead. Amen.

Bauer hoped there would be something worth stealing when they got to the homestead. Most sodbusters didn't have a pot to piss in, literally, but a few of them had family heirlooms stashed around, or so he'd heard it said. Gold would be nice, or cash, but anything that he could sell in town, after the dust settled, would suit him fine.

Old Mama Bauer hadn't raised a numbskull, never mind what certain people said behind his back.

And truth be told, he was glad to be getting away from Gehenna just now. It spooked him some, the way the new law dog had dropped six men, slick as you please. A back-shooter by nature, Billy Bauer didn't want to face Jack Slade if he could help it — most particularly if the odds were even. Give him some kind of an edge and he might try it, but the way things stood . . .

Better the sisters, he decided, than a man who'd proved that he could kill and kill again without batting an eye.

The *Beacon*'s office stood between a dress shop and a barber shop that also offered baths. Slade walked in off the street and found a whirlwind of activity produced by one man who appeared to handle everything himself — typesetting, scribbling notes, minding the press in back.

A bell chimed over Slade's head as he entered, and the frantic man called out, "Be with you in a minute! Just let me —"

He glanced at Slade and froze, his sudden stillness striking in comparison to all the hectic motion of a moment earlier.

"You must be Marshal Slade! The very man I want to see!" he said, trotting around the counter, offering his hand.

Slade cocked his head, examining the ink-stained fingers, and replied, "Maybe another time."

"Of course! Forgive me. I am Kester Ridley, editor and publisher of the Gehenna *Beacon*."

"Thought you might be."

"And *you*, I might say, are the man of the hour. Blood and thunder! Rough justice! Come, sit, and tell me all about it, Marshal. As it happens, I'm just putting out a special edition."

"On the shooting?"

"And its repercussions for the town," Ridley explained. "It isn't often that we lose six men, that way. Your first-person account would be —"

"Eleven," Slade said, interrupting him.

"Excuse me? I'm not sure I understand."

"You've lost *eleven* men," Slade said. "Or

248

maybe I already missed your coverage on the first five?"

"Um . . . No, sir. I am embarrassed to admit that I don't have the first idea of what in hell you're saying."

"So, you're not aware that six men from Gehenna tried to run a pair of sisters off their homestead, east of town, four days ago? Five of them got their due, but one slipped off. I wouldn't be surprised if he came back to town."

"Sisters, you say." Ridley screwed up his features, maybe as an aid to thought, then said, "The only homestead sisters I'm aware of are Miss Harmony Maguire and Mrs. Melody O'Hara."

Slade replied, "The very same."

"And *when* was this, again?" Ridley produced a notebook and a pencil from the pockets of his printer's apron, hands a blur as he began to write in shorthand.

"Four days back, counting today," Slade said.

"You were a witness to this happening?"

"And a participant."

"So, you . . . that is to say . . . the men last night were not the first you've had occasion to dispatch while visiting Gehenna?"

"No," Slade said. "And I suspect they're not the last who'll try their luck."

"Can you suggest some reason why these gunfighters might want you dead, Marshal?"

"Judge Dennison sent me to have a look around Gehenna and identify the men behind some recent crimes."

"Such as?"

"So far, I've documented rustling and terrorizing homesteaders. Before I'm done, I wouldn't be surprised to see some murders on the list."

"Do you have any suspects, other than the men already dead?"

"They're small-fry," Slade replied. "The men I *really* want are those who pay the freight and pull the strings."

"Can you identify them for my readers, Marshal?"

"Not just yet, but they know who they are. We've spoken, and they understand my interest in their activities."

"Sir, this is fascinating. But without the names . . ."

"You'll have them soon enough," Slade said. "As soon as they make their next stupid move."

"You don't have much respect for these opponents, I surmise?"

Slade smiled and plunged ahead. "Let's say they're not the brightest candles in the chandelier. Granted, they've managed to accumulate some wealth and local influence, they got rid of a constable some time ago, but they're big fish stuck in a tiny pond. Their shooters are a bunch of idiots. At this rate, they'll be out of guns by Saturday or Sunday, and they have to make a choice."

"Which is . . . ?"

"Either step up and do the dirty work themselves, or slink away like yellow curs. I'm betting neither one of them will stick around."

"But if they leave, won't that defeat the ends of justice, Marshal?"

"They can run, but they can't hide," Slade answered. "Cleaning up Gehenna is my first job. If the trash gets scattered, I can always track it down."

"Strong words, sir. Let us hope you don't regret them."

"I expect there'll be enough regret to go around," Slade said, "among the so-called decent folk who let things get this bad. I don't regret jailing a criminal, or shooting a mad dog."

"Terrific!" Ridley beamed. "I wish we had more time, sir, but my press awaits." He paused, arching his eyebrows, and pressed on. "Have you considered a *book,* Marshal Slade? An autobiography, perhaps?"

"Can't say I have. But if I *do,* you'll hear

from me."

Beaming, the newsman pumped Slade's hand and walked him to the door. Before Slade cleared the sidewalk, Ridley had returned to work, his agile fingers flying over rows of type.

"I don't know how men manage this," said Melody O'Hara. She was grappling with three parcels from the dry-goods store, while holding a repeating rifle pressed against her ribs, beneath one arm.

"Most of them just wear gunbelts, Sister," Harmony replied.

"We should've done that. After all, we have enough of them at home now."

"None of them would fit us, I'm afraid."

"We can punch new holes in the leather," Melody said.

"And it would be unseemly," Harmony persisted.

"As opposed to lugging rifles up and down the street?"

"Sometimes you vex me, Melody!"

Melody placed her packages in the buckboard, then turned back to face her sister. "Harmony, I *always* seem to vex you. Can you tell me, honestly, why you've remained so long since Mickey died?"

"Why have I . . . ? Why, there's much work

to be done."

"I know that, and appreciate your help, but I could manage it alone or hire a hand to work around the place."

"What would the others say to that?" asked Harmony, a stern expression on her face.

"The same things that they say about the two of us, I reckon. And you wouldn't have to hear it, anyway. You wouldn't *be* here."

"You're my sister, Mel—"

"That's right. Your *sister,* not your *child.* I shouldn't be your *burden,* either."

"I honestly don't think of you that way. It pains me that you've misconstrued my feelings all this time."

"How could I, when I don't know what they are?" asked Melody.

"You silly goose. I *love* you."

"But you're not *responsible* for me."

"Is there a difference?"

"There should be."

"I'll try to remember that . . . unless you're sending me away?"

"Not yet."

"Oh, good. I'd miss you, Sister."

"And I, you."

They climbed aboard the carriage. Harmony picked up the reins, then offered them to Melody. "Your turn," she said.

"You know I hate to drive."

"Relax, then. We'll be home in no time."

"Or the usual four hours."

When they'd cleared Gehenna's limits, Harmony said, "Sister, I apologize for lying to you."

"Lying? When?"

"Just now, and ever since your husband passed, God rest his soul."

"Lying in what sense, Harmony?"

"I haven't *only* stayed with you because you need me — though you *do.* I've also stayed because I have nowhere to go if I leave here."

"Why not go back to Baltimore?" asked Melody.

"For what? A spinster's job, teaching rich brats to read and write? It isn't worth the journey, Sister."

"If it's a man you want . . . I mean, how will you *ever* find one, where we live?"

"The pickings in Gehenna aren't too promising, I grant you." Harmony was smiling now. "And Melody, the truth is, I don't care."

"But wouldn't you prefer —"

"To be in your place? No."

"It's better to have loved and lost," said Melody.

"I know the poem, Sister. And I've seen

the way you've suffered through your loss. No, thank you."

"You're just being silly, now. Who says your man would up and die?"

"The specimens I've seen around Gehenna, I'd be lucky if he died *before* I met him."

Melody could only laugh at that. When she was able to control her breathing once again, she said, "Oh, Sister, you're a caution. But I *do* love you and need you. Every day."

"And that's when you shall have me, even when your stubborn moods say otherwise."

"We make an odd pair, don't we, Sister?"

"That we do," said Harmony. "And God help any man who tries to make us change."

Slade hoped that he had planted seeds enough to raise some hell around Gehenna in the hours ahead. In each case, he believed that he had done his best with the available materials.

Sabrina Abbott might be sharing thoughts with Baron Cartwright — or, perhaps, considering her place within a world where he did not exist. She had the wits to help him topple Cartwright, if she found the nerve, but that was something Slade could not supply.

The preacher might not have the grit to challenge wealthy sponsors from the pulpit, but at least his conscience had been pricked enough to sting him — and he might surprise the town, at that, if he displayed the courage of his own conviction.

Kester Ridley was a more straightforward case. It seemed he would print anything to sell more copies of the *Beacon.* If he included Slade's insulting comments, they might spur Cartwright or Bjornson to some further reckless action.

Angry enemies were careless enemies.

The best kind possible.

Of course, with all the men and guns at their disposal, there was still a chance that Slade could lose his gamble — and his life. He had depleted Bjornson's forces, but the robber baron still had other men on tap, while Cartwright's private army was unscathed.

Slade wished that he could set the two of them against each other with a vengeance, let them fight it out, and then mop up the stragglers. Sadly, he had not as yet devised a strategy that would fulfill that goal, and he was worried that a full-scale war might claim more innocent bystanders than combatants.

But *were* they truly innocent?

He'd touched on that theme with the newsman, with his slam at "so-called decent folk" who gave the rogues among them license to grow fat and happy by inflicting misery on others. If that stung some consciences among Gehenna's upper crust, so much the better.

Slade was not a Puritan. He had no quarrel per se with liquor, gambling, or easy women — even though the atmosphere created by saloons and cathouses inevitably spawned a rash of crimes, ranging from petty theft and battery to rape and murder. If he'd had the power to ban all vice with one snap of his fingers, Slade would not have used it.

He was only human, after all.

But some humans, like Cartwright and Bjornson, were not satisfied with simply sitting back and raking in the cash they earned from satisfying carnal appetites. They always wanted *more,* and they'd do anything to get it. Whether it was land, livestock, a lode of precious ore, crude oil — the list went on and on, but at the root lay *power.*

Slade drew a modest salary for performing a relatively simple job: He stood between the greediest, most violent of men and their intended victims, stopping human predators from acting out their base desires or bringing them to book for wrongs already done. It was a job he'd never have considered, if his brother hadn't fallen prey to such a man, but now Slade found it suited him.

He shied away from thanks and would've laughed at anyone who called his work heroic, but the fact remained that he performed a service most men were incapable of doing, or else disinclined to try. That made him stand out in the Oklahoma Territory — and within Gehenna all the more.

All right, he thought. *I've poked the hornet's nest. Now what?*

Maybe a round or two of cards to pass the time, before his adversaries made another move?

Why not?

Slade was a gambler where it counted, in his soul. He loved the risk and finding ways to turn it on his competition when he could. Winning was sweet, but he enjoyed the game for its own sake.

Gehenna offered two saloons where he could likely find a poker game — at least, for now. Bjornson's crowd at the Valhalla might be steaming, after last night's bungled effort to assassinate him. But when Ridley's *Beacon* hit the street, Slade guessed that he would have few friends in either camp.

On balance, he decided that the Rosebud would be best, for now, and turned in that direction, yearning for the feel of pasteboard in his hands, the clink of chips, the rhythm of the game.

14

Reverend Quentin Trowbridge knelt behind the pulpit in his church, eyes fastened on the stained-glass image of his infant Lord and Savior. It was there, bathed in the hues of Christ, that he felt closest to his God.

And *close* was what he needed at the moment.

Help was what he needed, but he heard no answers from on high.

Trowbridge had spent the past two hours dwelling on his conversation with the lawman. Even as they spoke, he felt the marshal's thinly veiled contempt for any man of God who welcomed criminals into His house and failed to call them on their grievous sins.

No matter.

Anything the marshal felt, Trowbridge had felt it first, about himself. He was a failure in his mission, wracked with guilt inside, although he showed an ever-smiling face to the community.

Community?

Say, rather, that Gehenna merged two hostile camps, with hapless bystanders caught in between, compelled either to choose a side and pay tribute or else fall prey to both at once. There was no safe and saintly middle ground.

Trowbridge was praying for his soul and for the town that he had failed. A true evangelist would have attacked the problem rather than accommodating it. Trowbridge had viewed Gehenna as a challenge in his early months at First Baptist, before he realized it was a quagmire on Hell's threshold, snaring men of goodwill, sucking them into its depths.

The marshal, Slade, had so far managed to resist — had even slain some of the minor demons who assailed him. Whether he could stand against the town's true rulers was a problematic question Trowbridge couldn't answer.

So, he sought advice from God and got — nothing.

Trowbridge was not surprised by the Almighty's silence. They had scarcely been on speaking terms, the Lord and he, since Trowbridge in Gehenna first began to look the other way, ignoring things that should've roused his anger and produced the kind of sermons that could fire men's blood.

In short, he sold himself.

And whether there was any coming back from that, he couldn't say with certainty.

Trowbridge was muttering his fifth round of the Lord's Prayer when he heard the left door to the sanctuary open, followed seconds later by the right. The hinges on the left door needed oiling, and they gave out a distinctive squeal. Boot heels clomped over floorboards, and he heard a muttering of voices, though he couldn't understand the words.

When Trowbridge rose behind the pulpit, his three visitors looked startled. "Where in hell did you come from?" the tallest of them asked.

"May I remind you," Trowbridge said, with all the dignity remaining to him, "that you're standing in God's house?"

"It looks like Baron Cartwright's house," the scruffy spokesman for the trio said while his companions grinned. "He staked you to it, mostly, ain't that right?"

"It's true that Mr. Cartwright is a generous parishioner. And, may I add, not one to suffer blasphemy in such a place as this."

"Thing is," the unkempt gunman said, "he sent us here."

"Indeed?" Trowbridge felt lead weights settle in his stomach. "For what purpose, may I ask?"

"You may. We're s'pose to find out what you and the law dog talked about this mornin'."

"Marshal Slade was here, I grant you. As to what we spoke of, that is confidential."

"What's that mean?" the gunman on the left inquired.

"Means preacher, here, don't wanna tell us nothin'," said their leader.

"Gentlemen . . ."

They swarmed him then, two breaking to the right, the third one circling to his left, eliminating any venue of retreat. The leader of the trio swung at Trowbridge first, driving a fist into his face with stunning force. The minister absorbed a rain of blows as he collapsed beside his pulpit.

"Feel like talkin' now?" one of the gunmen asked.

"Father, forgive them, for —"

The sharp toe of a boot took Trowbridge in the ribs and hammered the breath from his lungs. Trowbridge writhed on the floor as all three began kicking him, putting their weight and pure malice behind it.

It seemed to last forever. Finally, from a great distance, Trowbridge heard one of his tormentors call out, "Find me a rope."

Eternity swept past on waves of pain before another voice replied, "Found one!"

"Le's get him up, then," said the first voice.

Strong hands clutched at Trowbridge, dragged him upright as if he weighed nothing. They were heedless of his pain, hauling him slumped and barely conscious over floorboards where his toes made raspy scraping sounds.

Slade's fifth card slid across the table, coming to rest with its mates in the space between his hands. He scooped all five together, scanned them briefly, then arranged them in his hand. He held a pair of treys, a pair of sevens, and the ace of hearts.

He'd lost the first two hands, getting to know the other players at the table. Seated opposite, the dealer was a fat man with sandy hair and graying muttonchop sideburns. His straining vest was fashioned from a Confederate flag.

On Slade's right, the first man to bet on this hand was a beanpole who'd outgrown his black hair, pointed skull poking through with a bald spot on top like a friar's shaved scalp. He compensated with a handlebar mustache that drooped around his mouth, unwaxed.

"Two dollars," said the beanpole, reaching out to drop his chips.

"I'll see the two," Slade said and paid his dues.

The player to his left was heavyset, but lacked the dealer's corpulence. He wore a patch over his left eye and habitually held his cards close to his face, as if the one eye he had left was weak. His drab clothes could've been a parson's or an undertaker's but for the soup-stained cravat of lavender that covered half his bulging Adam's apple.

"Stay for two," he said, the Adam's apple bobbing.

The rebel dealer stayed and asked the others, "Cards?"

One went to Slade's right, where he guessed the tall man hoped to fill a straight. On viewing it, the player seemed to grimace, but it could've been a nervous tic.

"One card for me," Slade said.

It slithered toward him and he palmed it, kept his face deadpan as he revealed the seven of clubs.

Full house.

The pseudo-preacher drew two cards and swallowed hard on seeing them. It was a giveaway, but Slade still had to figure out if he was seeing disappointment or elation.

"Dealer takes one," the hefty rebel said. "Bet to my left."

"I check," the handlebar mustache replied.

"Three dollars," Slade announced, and dropped his chips into the pot.

"Too rich for me," the player on his left decreed, folding his hand.

"I'll see the three, and raise you five," the dealer said.

"I'm out," the word came from Slade's right.

"I call," Slade said and matched the dealer's bet. "Let's see them."

"Two pair," said the dealer, fanning out his cards. "Kings and jacks."

"Full house," Slade answered and displayed his hand. "Looks like my luck's begun to change."

Slade raked in the chips, leaving one dollar out as his ante. The dealer eyed him for a moment, then matched him and passed off the deck to his left. The others anted up, then waited while the handlebar mustache announced, "Same game, again."

He shuffled awkwardly three times, then passed the deck for Slade to cut. That done, the deal began, another round of five-card draw.

Slade's first three cards were clubs: a deuce, a nine, a queen. The fourth, a nine of diamonds, gave him his first pair but blew the flush. The fifth, a trey of hearts, shot everything to hell.

He was about to check when suddenly a heavy bonging sound eclipsed the Rosebud's background noise. Slade thought at first of some alarm, then someone at the bar, behind him, said, "How come the church bell's ringing?"

"Check," Slade said, raising his voice to make it heard above the tolling of the bell.

"Same here," the player to his left declared.

"I'll bet a dollar," said the rebel vest.

Before the dealer could respond, a man of middle age burst through the Rosebud's bat-wing doors and shouted, "Fire! The church is burning!"

"Jesus, what a dump," Hank Murphy said.

From where he sat, atop a low ridge overlooking the O'Hara homestead, Billy Bauer couldn't argue. Then again, *all* farms were drab and dreary places in his eyes. Farming meant work from dawn to dusk and slim reward for any of it. He'd escaped that life when he was twelve years old and never once regretted fleeing home.

"To hell with what it looks like," he told Murphy. "We ain't movin' in, just waitin'

267

for the sisters."

"No one else supposed to be here?" Early Somers asked.

"They live alone," Bauer replied. "No menfolk."

"That's what Shakespeare told the other bunch," said Jubal Cole.

"Well, now, we *know* the marshal's back in town," said Bauer. "You expectin' someone else?"

"No, Billy. I just meant —"

"Screw what you *meant*. Let's get down there and have a look around, before the fun starts."

They descended in a skirmish line, five men abreast. Despite his personal assurance, Bauer kept a close eye on the farmhouse windows, flicking anxious glances toward the barn and privy as they closed the gap. If anyone *was* home, he guessed the shooting wouldn't start until they moved in close enough for animals or faces to be recognized. Say fifty yards or so.

When they had reached that deadline without drawing fire, he started giving orders. "Jared, you and Jubal check the barn. Early, you got the crapper."

"Shit!"

"Exactly. Me and Hank'll do the house. Rest of you join us, when you've had a decent look-see."

They galloped in, hands on their six-guns without drawing them. The Cole brothers were first to reach their destination, since the barn was closest of the targets to be scrutinized. Somers dismounted at the privy's rear and walked his horse around to face its slightly crooked door.

Bauer and Murphy rode directly to the house, dismounted in the shadow of its porch, and tied their horses to the nearest upright posts. Both drew their pistols as they stepped onto the shaded porch.

The front door was secured with a padlock, confirming Bauer's sense that there was no one in the house. He first considered blasting the lock with his pistol, then drew his knife instead and dug around the screws securing the brass hasp to the door. When they were loose enough, he gave the door two heavy kicks that wrenched the hasp free of its moorings, and then pushed his way inside.

There was a smell of cooking in the house, most likely bacon, but with something else that made Bauer uncertain of his guess. The plates and pans were clean, no clues there to guide him. Murphy brushed past him, climbed a ladder to the loft, and called down, "There's another bed up here."

"What else?" asked Bauer.

"Nothin' much. Some clothes on hooks. A little chest of drawers."

"Go through it. Tell me what you find," Bauer instructed.

While the search went on upstairs, he covered the ground floor. The sisters had a double bed down there, a kitchen stove, table and chairs, and a dresser, which he guessed was larger than the one above. Bauer pulled out each drawer in turn, pawed through their things, smelling the laundry soap on some and just pure woman on the rest.

You won't need none of this, when you get home, he thought and smiled.

"Just shit up here," said Murphy as he moved back toward the ladder. "An old Bible, hairbrush, woman things."

"No money, anything like that?"

"I looked under the mattress," Murphy said, descending. "They got nothin'."

But they're in town, shopping, Bauer thought. He guessed they must've carried any money they possessed into Gehenna with them, likewise wearing any jewelry they owned. It wouldn't come to much, from what he saw around him.

Too bad.

But they could make his ride worthwhile

in other ways.

Somers arrived, still scowling from his look inside the privy. "Big surprise," he said. "They piss and all, like ever'body else."

"No gold mine underneath the crapper?" Murphy kidded him.

"Go on and sink a shaft, you feel like it," Somers replied.

"Go fetch the brothers," Bauer said, to no one in particular. "They're likely flipping coins to see who pokes the sow."

Both of his men laughed dutifully at that, then Somers left, striding in the direction of the barn.

"What now?" asked Murphy.

"Now," Bauer replied, "we sit and wait."

The belfry of First Baptist had become a smokestack by the time Slade reached it. There were no flames visible from the outside, but smoky tendrils reached out from the open doors, tainting the air he breathed.

For the second time in twelve hours, Gehenna's menfolk had formed a bucket brigade, dashing from the nearest horse troughs to the church and back, darting inside to splash the fire Slade couldn't see, all of them coughing as they came back into daylight.

Slade collared the next man through the door and asked, "Where's Reverend Trowbridge?"

"Back in there, Marshal," the merchant gasped. "He's hanging from the bell rope, dead as Sunday dinner."

Cursing, Slade rushed toward the church and through its open double doors, into a scene from Hell. The lamps that he remembered hanging on wall hooks to either side were smashed, their spilled fuel combined with paint and sun-dried wood to feed an inferno. Smoke churned along the ceiling, so reminding Slade of storm clouds that he half expected rain to douse the fire.

The center aisle was clear, though, and he had no trouble spotting Trowbridge at the far end of the chapel. Rather, Slade could see the preacher's feet and lower legs dangling. The rest of him was hidden from where Slade stood, up inside the belfry proper.

Slade ran up the aisle to stand beneath the hanging body. One glance, even through the rising smoke, told him that Trowbridge would not be resuscitated. In addition to the thick rope tied around his neck, the preacher had been beaten bloody, maybe stomped, until the blood soaked through his shirt beneath the black frock coat.

Slade thought of calling someone from the bucket line to help him, but no urgency remained for Trowbridge, and it wouldn't matter if he had another man to break his fall. Slade ducked to fill his lungs with cleaner air, held it, and scrambled up the ladder that protruded from the belfry's wall. When he was level with the preacher, he unsheathed his knife and started sawing at the bell rope.

It took longer than anticipated, but he got it, watched the body drop into a boneless sprawl below, then climbed back down to join it. Two men stood with empty buckets, gawking at the preacher's corpse, until Slade shouted through their daze and set them back to work.

Another struggle followed, as Slade wrestled Trowbridge over his left shoulder, straightened up to bear the load, then carried his deadweight out of the church. Bystanders rushed to take the burden from him, once he'd cleared the smoke screen pouring through First Baptist's open doors.

It looked as if the fire was winning, and Slade knew it when the bucket men stopped running back to fetch more water. "Troughs are empty!" one of them cried out, and dashed his wooden bucket to the ground.

The undertaker seemed to come from

nowhere, kneeling over Trowbridge, probing at the rope around his neck with long, thin fingers.

"Hanged?" he asked Slade, after rising back to his full height.

"After a beating," Slade replied. "I couldn't say if he was dead before they strung him up."

"Who's *they?*" asked Kester Ridley, suddenly beside them with a pad and pencil in his hands.

"I couldn't tell you," Slade replied. "Must have been two, at least, to hoist him up inside the belfry."

"A conspiracy?"

"Whenever two or more join forces to commit a crime, that's what you've got," said Slade.

"But who would want the preacher dead?" asked Ridley.

"Is it fair to speculate on that?" another voice demanded.

Slade turned toward the speaker, finding Baron Cartwright flanked by gunmen on his left. Sabrina Abbott had not joined them.

"Fair?" Slade countered. "I'd say it was mandatory."

"But without some evidence, your guesswork won't mean anything."

"Looks like the murderers took care of

that," said Slade. "A lucky break for their employer, I suppose."

"What's *that* supposed to mean?" asked Cartwright.

"Hellfire!" said Buck Bjornson, shoving through the ring of onlookers. "We all know what it means. We've got no crazy preacher killers in Gehenna. Someone had to be sent *special* for the job."

"Be careful where you point your dirty fingers, Buck," warned Cartwright.

"I'm a careful man by nature, Cartwright, as you have reason to know."

"Careful enough, mayhap, to put the blame on someone else for what you've done, yourself."

"You smart son of a bitch, I'll —"

"That's enough," Slade stepped between them, right hand on his Colt. "There's nothing to be done here, and I want you all to go about your business. *Now.*"

Gehenna's warlords glared at one another for a moment longer, then turned back toward their respective enterprises. Each man spared a parting glance for Slade, and neither of them had a friendly cast about him.

"May I get the dear departed off the street, Marshal?" the undertaker asked.

"I'd take it as a favor," Slade replied.

And thought, *You'd better get some extra boxes ready, while you're at it.*

"Just a few more questions, Marshal," Kester Ridley said. "If you don't mind, that is?"

"Ask what you need to, Mr. Ridley," Slade replied.

"Same question as before, then. Have you any thoughts on who might want the Reverend Trowbridge dead, his church destroyed?"

"I'd guess the fire was incidental, covering their tracks. That is, unless the killers were a bunch of lunatics, like Cartwright said."

"But you don't think so?"

"No, I don't."

"There was some *purpose* to the murder, then. What might it be? A robbery?"

"From what I saw this morning, talking to him in the chapel, Trowbridge didn't strike me as a man with much to steal."

"You spoke with him?" Ridley stood with his pencil poised, unmoving for the moment.

"Right before I dropped in at your office," Slade confirmed.

"Um . . . then, do you suspect your visit may have motivated someone in Gehenna to . . . er, shall we say, *dispose* of Reverend

Trowbridge?"

That question had been nagging Slade since he laid down his poker hand and answered the alarm. "All I can tell your readers, in respect to that, is that their minister said nothing I could use in court, for any purpose whatsoever."

"May I ask what you discussed with him?"

"The value of repentance and forgiveness."

"So, it was a *spiritual* consultation?" Ridley did a poor job of concealing his apparent skepticism.

"Not on my part," Slade replied.

"Then, I'm afraid you've lost me, Marshal."

"I asked him about his flock, how he could preach the gospel in a town founded on gamblers' money. Maybe worse."

"And were *names* mentioned?"

"Not by me."

"By Reverend Trowbridge?"

"He expressed ambivalence about his role here in Gehenna. He referred to hypocrites, big money, harlots giving lip service to God and using it as cover for their sins."

"I see." The shorthand scribbling started up again. "What else?"

"Nothing specific, but I left here with a

feeling that there might be changes in the wind."

"Such as . . . ?"

"You would've had to ask the preacher that," Slade said.

"And now, sadly, I've lost the chance."

"So, maybe you could ask yourself."

"Excuse me?"

"Think about it. I spoke with two men this morning. Now, one of them's dead. And the other is . . ."

"Me! Jesus!"

"I expected longer hair," Slade said. "Maybe a beard."

Ridley ignored the joke. He seemed unsteady on his feet. The shorthand pad and pencil trembled in his hands. He glanced swiftly to left and right, as if expecting shooters to appear and gun him down.

"You think I'm *next?*" he whispered, leaning in toward Slade.

Slade shrugged. "It may be that they started out just asking Trowbridge questions, and he put them off. Maybe they worked him over, still got nothing from him, and decided he could serve as an example."

"But he didn't *tell* you anything, for God's sake!"

"How would they know that?" asked Slade.

"Oh, Jesus! I've already got the extra printed. I'd be hawking it by now, except the fire distracted me. What should I do?"

"It's your decision," Slade replied. "But I'd advise you not to make them think you're running scared. Coyotes love the smell of fear."

"Jesus! I have to go now."

Ridley turned and fairly sprinted for his office. Slade frowned after him, remembering his poker hand and wishing he could go back to the game.

Too late. Another game was starting now. The stakes were life and death.

15

"I think he looked quite handsome," Melody O'Hara said.

"Who would that be?" asked Harmony Maguire, as if she didn't know her sister's mind, her wants and needs.

"No one," said Melody, embarrassed now.

"You're saying *no one* in Gehenna was quite handsome? Well, I must say, I agree with you. They've always seemed an ugly lot, to me."

"Why must you taunt me, Sister?"

"Taunt you? I declare, the very —"

"You *know* well enough to whom I was referring. It's pure cruelty on your part to make me spell it out."

"In that case, please forgive me." Harmony could not resist a smile.

"See, there! It *pleases* you to torture me."

"*Torture?* Dear Sister, I believe you are the princess of exaggeration."

Melody ignored her, saying, "But he *was*

handsome. Don't you agree? The marshal?"

"I admit he has a certain quality about him," Harmony allowed. "If it was my choice, though, I'd pick a man who doesn't live by pistols and his wits alone."

"That isn't fair! He lives by *law.*"

"Out here, Sister, the two are indivisible. My lands, you make him sound like an attorney or a judge."

"I never said that! And he works for one, in any case."

"Does *dirty work* for one, you mean."

"Say what you will. *I* think arresting villains is an honorable trade."

"Perhaps. It also has a short life span. Why, he's in gunfights every time he turns around."

"It doesn't have to be that way," said Melody.

"You think the villains he's pursuing will surrender and confess the error of their ways?"

The buckboard lurched beneath them, thrown off balance by a stone or gopher's burrow. Harmony clung tightly to the reins to keep the horse from shying.

"What I *mean* to say," Melody answered, "is that men and jobs can change. He doesn't absolutely *have* to be a lawman, does he?"

"Why ask me, Sister? *He* chose the trade, not I. You barely know the man, and here you are, daydreaming that he'll cast off his career for you and settle down . . . to what?"

"I haven't thought that far ahead, if you must know."

"It's loneliness you feel, not love," said Harmony. "Perhaps some gratitude mixed in with it, because he saved our lives and virtue."

"Oh, who asked you, anyway?"

"You did, when you began soliloquizing on his beauty."

Melody blushed the color of a ripe strawberry, but it faded swiftly as a group of horsemen suddenly appeared, breaking from cover in a copse of trees off to their left and moving in to block the road.

Harmony yanked the reins and reached between her feet to grab a pistol. At her side, Melody had a rifle clutched against her chest.

"Now, ladies," said a dark-haired rider with a waxed mustache and day-old stubble on his cheeks, "it's rude to point your weapons at a lawman. It's a crime, in fact."

For the first time, Harmony saw the badges they wore pinned to vests and shirts.

"Lawmen?" said Melody. "Then, you must know —"

Harmony interrupted her. "What sort of lawmen are you? I see from your badges, you're not federal."

"You've got sharp eyes, ma'am. And you're right. We're sheriff's deputies."

"There hasn't been a sheriff in Gehenna for a year or more," said Harmony. She kept her thumb pressed to her pistol's hammer, ready to cock it and fire in a heartbeat.

"You're right again, ma'am. We were handpicked by the marshal who's in town, right now. I do believe y'all are acquainted with him."

"Jack Slade?" Melody said.

"The very one, sweet thing."

Blushing again, she said, "Why, I'm surprised he didn't mention —"

"Hush, Sister! What business do you have with us?" asked Harmony.

"There have been threats against your safety, ma'am, and Marshal Slade — your Jack — sent us to make sure you were unmolested on your way back home."

Harmony eased her six-gun's hammer back, saying, "I find that curious. Particularly since I saw *you* lounging with some other thugs outside the Rosebud when we passed this morning. None of you were wearing badges then."

"Well, ain't you the attentive bitch?"

Harmony raised her pistol, suddenly confronted by six weapons pointed at the buckboard where she and her sister sat. One was a sawed-off shotgun that would spray them both with buckshot, even if the other shooters missed with their revolvers.

"Ma'am," the spokesman for the riders said, "my orders are to bring you in alive, *if possible.* You wanna make it possible, or not?"

Gehenna's Western Union office was a boxed-off corner of the hardware store, with wiring stapled to the wall and running through a hole cut in the ceiling to the pole outside. When Slade walked in, the clerk was waiting on a customer who wanted nails but wasn't sure what kind. Slade told him not to hurry, using the spare time to compose his message to Judge Dennison.

His first attempt was too long-winded, so he tore it up and started over, printing clearly on the message form. His final draft read:

TROUBLE IN GEHENNA STOP CONFIRM HARASSMENT OF HOMESTEADERS STOP TWELVE DEAD SO FAR INCLUDING PREACHER STOP BELIEVE BOTH PARTIES NAMED BY YOU IN-

VOLVED STOP SEEKING FURTHER
EVIDENCE FOR TRIAL STOP ONE MAY
COOPERATE STOP MAY NEED REIN-
FORCEMENTS FOR ARRESTS STOP
NEXT MESSAGE WILL ADVISE STOP
SLADE GEHENNA ENDIT

Reading over it, Slade thought his cable
ought to stir up some response on both ends
of the line. *Twelve dead so far* would tell
Judge Dennison that he was in the middle
of a wicked situation with the gloves off, no
holds barred, and would save later explanation of the body count, if Slade lived to
submit a field report.

Slade took for granted that the hardware
clerk–cum–Western Union agent would
reveal the contents of his message to Cartwright, Bjornson, or both. His shop was on
the north side of the street, which ought to
make him Cartwright's man, but as the only
telegraph agent in town, he'd likely struck a
deal with both camps to supply whatever
information they required.

Why not?

In fact, Slade counted on it.

Cartwright and Bjornson would assume,
correctly, that they were the "parties
named" by Dennison, when he had briefed
Slade in Lawton. Slade's reference to "fur-

ther evidence," when he had none at all, should make them think that he had *some,* and was about to gather more. In theory, that should spur his enemies to action, while Slade's plea to hold off reinforcements for a bit should put the local warlords under pressure. If they took his message at face value, one or both should try to move against him soon.

His snare was hidden in the phrase, "One may cooperate." With any luck, both Cartwright and Bjornson would believe the other had provided Slade with evidence against him. That, in turn, could launch both ego-driven men into a rage and spark a shooting war between the hostile sides.

Slade's job, in that event, would be to minimize civilian casualties and mop up any stragglers, locking up those who survived until Judge Dennison could hear the charges filed against them.

Charges, right.

Before Slade filed a case, he'd have to find a willing witness or observe a crime in progress *and* arrest the perpetrators without killing them. From what he had experienced around Gehenna so far, he suspected that would be a major stumbling block.

The clerk finished his business and approached Slade with apologies, which Slade declined. "You're just in time," he told the clerk and pushed his message form across the counter. "This goes to Judge Isaac Dennison in Lawton, at the federal courthouse."

The clerk kept his face blank while scanning the message, then nodded and answered, "Yes, sir." He took another moment, getting settled at the telegraph key, then started tapping out the message in code.

There was a chance, Slade realized, that the helpful clerk might send the *wrong* message on purpose, distorting or changing entirely Slade's words. On balance, though, he thought it was a small risk, next to what he faced when Cartwright and Bjornson got their copies of the cable. To facilitate matters, Slade left his copy with the clerk after he paid his bill and left the shop.

Standing outside, Slade scanned the two saloons, each with its knot of gunmen on the sidewalk, facing off across the street.

"Over to you," he said and started back toward his hotel.

Buck Bjornson downed his second shot of whiskey in five minutes, waiting for his throat to open up again before he said, "You're absolutely sure it wasn't us?"

"I swear, Boss," Damon Shakespeare said. "I had in mind to ask some questions of the preacher, after Slade stopped by to see him, but I hadn't got around to it."

"None of the men got overeager? Maybe jumped the gun?"

"No, sir. You got my word."

Bjornson stopped his pacing, settled in the rolling chair behind his desk. "All right, then. That means Cartwright's lost his goddamned mind."

"Or Eulis. That'd be my bet."

"He's mean, I grant. But Jesus Christ! To kill the *preacher?* That's a country mile beyond pure meanness."

"I could drop him for you." Shakespeare sounded eager at the prospect.

"Why not let the marshal do it for us?" Bjornson countered.

"How's that, Boss?"

"Suppose some little birdie told him Baker was responsible. That means *Cartwright's* responsible. If Slade believes it, then he's honor bound to deal with them — which takes the heat off *us.*"

"*If* he believes it," Shakespeare emphasized.

"Correct. We have to set it up just right. Our little birdie must be *credible,* not someone he'd suspect of setting up a trap. Who owes us one hellacious favor, Day?"

"That could be half the town, Boss."

"No. I want a *special* little birdie. Honest. Upright. Female wouldn't hurt us any."

"He's already got the Abbott woman, and them sisters."

"Ah. The sisters, I believe, we can dismiss from further thought. As to the sweet Sabrina, I have reason to believe her charms are wasted on our Marshal Slade."

"You think he's queer?"

"Don't be ridiculous! I'm *thinking,* here."

"Sorry."

"You've had our people watching him, as I instructed?"

"Yes, sir."

"Tell me everyone he's spoken to in town," Bjornson ordered.

"Well, there's you and Cartwright. Miss Sabrina. Me and Baker. One of Baker's boys. Don't know his name."

"Pass that."

"The preacher."

"Who can't help us now," Bjornson said.

"That Ridley, at the *Beacon.*"

"No. Too risky."

"Your clerk, at the hotel."

"Aha! A possibility."

"Some waitress at the Longhorn, too. That's all we've seen."

"One of the latter two, I think," Bjornson

said. "I'm leaning toward the waitress, frankly, since she probably talks to Slade."

"Why'd she wanna turn Cartwright in to Slade?"

"Why does anyone do anything? Self-interest or civic duty, take your pick or roll them up together in one package."

"Um . . . okay."

"Don't be afraid to tell me when I've lost you, Day."

"You lost me, sir."

"Try this. The waitress might tip Slade because she likes him, maybe wants him in the sack. Or she might spill the beans because she thinks Cartwright has done a dreadful thing, killing the preacher man. If all else fails, we might see fit to pay her what she makes in six months at the Longhorn, for five minutes' conversation with the marshal. Take your pick."

"I'd go the money route," said Shakespeare.

"I'm inclined that way, myself," Bjornson said, "but feel her out in any case."

"I don't know if she'd go for that."

"Not feel her *up,* for Christ's sake! Find out how she feels about the preacher getting roasted and the rest of it. Use someone who won't scare her shitless in the process and defeat the whole damned purpose."

"Maybe Trixie, from downstairs?"

Bjornson thought about it. "That's a notion. She cleans up all right. Be sure she understands the job, though. I don't want her telling stories out of school."

"I'll make it plain to her."

"We're finished for the moment, then. I want to know immediately when our boys are finished with the sisters."

"Right, Boss."

"Do me proud, Day. Do *yourself* proud."

"Yes, sir."

When his gunman had departed, Bjornson sat and glowered at the office door. He muttered to himself, "Dumb bastard. Do it fucking *right* this time."

"They oughta be here," Early Somers said. "I'm purty sure they oughta *be* here."

Billy Bauer checked his pocket watch, put it away, and said, "We wait."

"How long?" asked Jubal Cole.

"Until I tell you differ'nt," Bauer replied.

"It's goddamned *boring*," Jubal's brother whined.

"You're getting paid for it," Bauer reminded him and all of them.

"Still boring," Jared Cole retorted.

"And your blathering about it doesn't make it any better," said Hank Murphy.

"Listen, now —"

"Shut up, the lot of you!" snapped Bauer. "The next one I hear bitching, Shakespeare cuts his pay in half."

"Says who?" the Coles echoed in unison.

"Says *me,* the sumbitch that he put in charge of you. Now, let me hear you gripe again."

To that, no answer but a sullen glare.

The silence let him think. Somers was right about the sisters being overdue, but Bauer had no explanation for their tardiness. They might've thrown a wheel, or stopped somewhere along the way to pick wildflowers. Who could say what women might get up to on their own, unsupervised?

He recognized the fierce frustration brewing in his men, felt some of it himself. They'd ridden out from town excited by the prospect of some looting, raping, killing — and they'd wound up sitting on their asses far past time for their intended victims to arrive. It put a strain on young, impulsive bucks like Jubal and his brother. Hell, it put a strain on old dogs, too.

But they would wait.

The only two alternatives were fraught with peril. Shakespeare's orders were explicit: Grab the sisters at their spread and find out what had happened to the other boys who visited them earlier. There'd been no mention of pursuing them around the countryside, and Bauer damned sure wasn't going back to Shakespeare empty-handed, telling him they couldn't do the job because his men were goddamned *bored.*

That was a sure way to get neutered, maybe killed, and Bauer wasn't having it.

He couldn't ride off looking for the sisters by himself, leaving the other men behind, in case he missed them on the trail and they came home to find his boys, with no hand to restrain them. Bauer knew exactly what would happen then, and by the time he circled back, smart money said the sisters would be in no shape to tell him anything.

Same story if he sent men out to backtrack, looking for the women, while he stayed put at the farmhouse. None of them were trustworthy right now. Their blood was up, and Bauer wouldn't stake his life on any one of them.

Not even close.

Waiting was all that he had left, and after sunset, they would have to do it in the dark. They couldn't show a light, to warn the sisters of their presence. Couldn't even make a pot of coffee, since the chimney smoke would instantly betray them.

Where in hell *were* they?

Bauer began to list the things that could go wrong for women riding on their own, through open, hostile country. They were armed, as he had plainly seen in town. Their guns could handle any snakes or other animals they met along the way, including pumas. Bullets wouldn't help them if their horse went lame or something happened to the buckboard, but the only way for him to check that was in person, and he had already ruled it out.

The wild card was an ambush on the road. Not Indians, who hadn't shown their painted faces in the neighborhood for two or three years, anyhow — but someone else. Maybe some border trash.

Or Cartwright's men.

What were the odds of *that?* Bauer had given up on guesswork lately, with the way things seemed to be unraveling around Gehenna. If it got much worse, Bauer decided on the spot, he'd give some thought to running for it, getting out while the getting was good.

Go now, a small voice whispered in his head.

He knew just how to do it. Tell the others he was going back to check the road alone and leave them gloating that they'd have the sisters to themselves, if they showed up while he was gone. Head westward toward Gehenna, until he was out of sight from the farmhouse, then pick another compass point and ride like hell until he was beyond the reach of Bjornson, Shakespeare, and the rest.

Not yet.

"How's that?" Hank Murphy asked.

"How's *what?*" Bauer demanded.

"You said somethin', there."

Jesus!

"Forget it," he replied. "Just talkin' to myself."

Slade took his time, dawdling along Main Street and letting both sides get their fill of watching him. He'd made no secret of his visit to the Western Union office, and it wouldn't take much time at all for others to come sniffing after him, wanting a look at what he'd written.

Perfect.

Slade was one block short of the Bonanza when his stomach told him it was time for lunch. He doubled back and crossed the street, entered the Longhorn Restaurant, and took the same place where he'd eaten breakfast, safe from anybody coming up behind him.

"Marshal," said the waitress as she smiled

her way across to him. "Not tired of us by now?"

"Good food, good scenery," he said, returning smile for smile. "What's not to like?"

"Well, we appreciate the business, that's for sure." She handed him a menu as she asked, "Coffee to start?"

"Sounds good."

The Longhorn's lunchtime offerings that day included steak and trimmings, pan-fried chicken, and beef stew. He'd eaten heavily at breakfast, but between the poker game and the excitement of the fire, Slade felt as if he'd gone all day without a morsel.

When the waitress brought his coffee, Slade declared, "I'll try the stew. And is there any of that Texas toast?"

"Marshal, there's *always* Texas toast."

"All right, then."

"Saving room for pie?"

"I might, at that."

"I like a man who knows his mind," she said and left him with a swirl of skirt.

Slade sipped his coffee, watched foot traffic on the street, and pictured shooters drifting toward the hardware store, bribing the clerk if necessary, maybe pushing him around a bit. Judge Dennison would likely have his wire by now, and soon its contents would be common knowledge to Slade's enemies.

Stirring the pot, to help it boil.

The stew and Texas toast arrived five minutes later, and Slade devoured it at leisure. There was no point rushing back to his hotel. He didn't plan to hole up in his room, but wouldn't mind a nap before he faced the afternoon and evening ahead.

How would his enemies react? Slade reckoned it was even money, whether they came hunting him or turned against each other with a vengeance. One thing that he *didn't* count on was a quiet night at the Bonanza, dozing in his rented bed.

The waitress came back half an hour later, when his plate was clean, his mug empty. She wasn't smiling this time as she asked, "Was everything all right?"

"Perfect," Slade said.

"Well, then." She set his bill down on the table, picking up his plate and coffee cup. "You have a *safe* day, Marshal. Please?"

Slade watched her go, then focused on his bill and saw the small note folded underneath it. Casually, he slipped the note into a vest pocket, left two new silver dollars on the table, and moved on to deal with the cashier.

Outside, Slade walked a half block from

the Longhorn, then stopped in an alley's mouth to read the note. It was a hasty penciled scrawl that told him *Kartrite's peepul did the preechur.*

"Well, now."

From the shift in attitude, Slade knew someone had reached out to the waitress in between the service of his meal and the collection of his empty plate. They'd trailed him to the Longhorn, then arranged to have the note passed as he left.

Slade had no way of determining whether the note's message was true or false, but he could use it, either way. Maybe he ought to call on Cartwright, let him read the note without explaining where it came from, and find out what Cartwright had to say.

But first, that nap.

Slade stopped and listened in the hall, outside his room, but nothing stirred beyond the door. He stepped inside and locked the door behind him, had his hat off when he saw another folded piece of paper lying on the floor between his feet.

16

Slade stooped to get the paper, feeling from its weight alone that it was larger than the note already tucked into his pocket. He unfolded it reluctantly, with caution, as if it contained an angry scorpion.

The message was longer than that he'd received from the waitress, more carefully written by someone who knew how to spell.

We have the sisters. If you want them free again with no harm, come alone and unarmed at midnight. Ride six miles north from town. X marks the spot.

It was unsigned, of course. Most of the space below the note was filled with a rough hand-drawn map of territory Slade had missed on his ride to Gehenna. Hills were indicated, with what seemed to be a river, but could just as easily have been a winding road. Landmarks were labeled as a rock pile, chimney (with no house to hold it upright), and a "devil tree." A tidy *X* was drawn beside what seemed to be a house, its roof a plain inverted *V*.

Slade sat down on the bed to think.

First thing, the bait was obvious. Whoever wrote the message must've known he'd smell a trap, but they were counting on him to submit for mercy's sake. Slade cursed the moment when he'd seen the sisters in Gehenna, when he'd crossed the street to speak with them in front of watchful eyes.

His fault . . . unless the threat itself was false.

He couldn't *know* if Melody and Harmony really had been abducted. Not unless he rode out to their place immediately, or went on to keep his midnight rendezvous with their alleged kidnappers.

Midnight.

That was classic, but Slade knew already that he wasn't playing by some faceless adversary's rules. If he kept the appointment, he'd go well ahead of time to scout the territory and create his own plan of attack.

Alone. Unarmed.

The first part wasn't difficult, since there was no one in Gehenna he could trust, either to keep a secret or to watch his back.

As for reporting to the enemy unarmed, Slade wouldn't think of it. More to the point, he couldn't make himself believe his enemies would think of it. They'd order him to leave his guns behind, hope for the best — and gun him down on sight, no matter what he carried with him.

So, the trick was not to let them see him when and where he was expected. Slade assumed that he would be outnumbered at the killing site and staked his hopes on the advantage of surprise.

How well that worked wouldn't be known to him until he'd seen the layout of the killing ground. If there was cover, then he had a chance. If not . . . well, maybe there was still a little something he could do to shift the odds.

Slade's mind circled back to the threat itself. Had the sisters been snatched? And if so, were they already dead?

Slade checked his pocket watch. He had eleven hours and thirteen minutes left before his scheduled rendezvous with death. That didn't give him time enough to visit Melody and Harmony at home, assuming they were at the homestead, safe and sound.

Of course, they might be lying dead inside their house, or in the yard. It was the easy way to handle them, while banking on

Slade's guilt or curiosity to make him keep the midnight date.

The cold part of his mind told Slade the sisters didn't really matter. If they were alive or dead, kidnapped or safely tending to their chores at home, his enemies expected him to act as if their lives were hanging in the balance.

Fine. Why not?

Slade had been hoping to provoke a move from one side or the other. Now he had it, and he couldn't let it go to waste. Whatever waited for him six miles north of town, he'd meet the challenge more or less head-on.

But on *his* terms.

Slade did the calculations in his mind. Six miles was a two-hour drive. Sundown, based on the past two days, would come at half past six o'clock. Leaving at dusk, he could ride west from town until no one could see him, then turn back to the northeast and get his bearings, use the map's landmarks to find his way.

With any luck, Slade would reach the destination sometime between nine and half past, with ample time to spare before his deadline. He could check out the lay of the land, find his angle of attack, and maybe strike when they were least expecting it.

It would be *they,* he realized, because the

plot — or bluff — was too elaborate to be a one-man game. If Cartwright or Bjornson had a shooter who could take Slade in a stand-up fight, they would arrange an incident, then plant him in an unmarked grave somewhere and have a story ready for Judge Dennison when he sent reinforcements to Gehenna. Maybe tell the next marshals that Slade had ridden out of town to question homesteaders and never made it back.

The plan they'd picked was cleaner, though. Slade guessed that everyone in town would lie for one boss or the other, out of fear or obligation, but most liars can be cracked. If Slade rode out of town, there would be witnesses who didn't have to lie.

Slade thought about it for another moment, made his choice, then lay down for a nap. Within a minute, he was fast asleep.

"What will they do with us?" asked Melody O'Hara, barely whispering.

"I don't know," Harmony replied with equal caution.

They were seated on a narrow, sagging bed in the smallest chamber of a smallish three-room house. Their wrists were tightly bound, with hands behind their backs, and more rope hobbled them in case they tried to run.

"They must want *something*," Melody persisted.

When the guns were pointed at her, hours earlier, she had expected death — even allowed herself a heartbeat of excitement, mingled with her fear, at the prospect of seeing her lost Mickey once again.

When the riders didn't fire at once, and Harmony lowered the hammer on her pistol, Melody began expecting rape. It was an unprotected woman's constant fear among rough men. And what man wasn't rough, when he had rutting on his mind?

Jack Slade.

They'd been disarmed, with smiles and whistles of appreciation as the riders counted up their weapons. Brooding silence fell, after one rider named the missing owner of a Colt revolver with four notches on its grip. Melody saw the riders treat them with more care, once that discovery was made, and the hostility of their abductors markedly increased.

One of the riders had dismounted then and climbed onto the buckboard's seat, taking the reins from Harmony and clucking at their horse to follow its companions northward. As they set off on the new course, riders flanked the buckboard and another trailed behind it, watching out for any shady move.

She had lost track of time, couldn't have said how far they traveled north, but guessed it must've been two hours, anyhow. The house where they had stopped was small and plain. Melody had never seen it before, but that didn't surprise her. There were countless things she hadn't seen.

And now, she guessed, she never would.

The gunmen *had* to kill her now, and Harmony. They'd shown their faces, and no matter what transpired from that point onward, if they let the sisters go alive, they must have known that charges would be filed against them. Death would mute the sisters for eternity, while Cartwright or Bjornson gloried in defeating justice once again.

And Jack would never know.

That thought had barely taken shape when Melody knew why they had been kidnapped, kept alive, instead of being shot outright.

"We're bait," she hissed at Harmony.

"Explain, Sister."

"They want someone to come for us, so they can kill him. Then, we're next."

"But who . . . ? Oh, Lord! The marshal?"

"Jack will come for us. I know it!"

"Only if they tell him how to find us," Harmony replied. "And they'll be waiting for him, if he comes."

"It doesn't matter." Melody felt almost giddy with relief. "He's *far* too clever for them."

"Let us hope so, for our sake *and* his."

A rapping on his door roused Slade at five minutes past two o'clock. He bolted upright on the hotel bed and cocked his pistol, calling out, "Who is it?"

"Me," a soft, familiar voice replied. "Sabrina."

Slade crossed to the door on stocking feet, unlocked it, holding his Peacemaker ready as he opened it a crack.

"Are you alone this time?" he asked.

"See for yourself."

He leaned out far enough to check the empty corridor, then said, "What do you want?"

"To come inside, for one thing."

Slade stepped back to let her pass, then closed the door and locked it with his free hand. He thumbed down the hammer on his Colt but didn't lay the gun aside.

"You don't need that with me," Sabrina said. "I promise you."

"What brings you here?"

"I wanted you to know that I'm not staying at the Rosebud. I'll be slipping out as soon as I can manage it."

"Why's that?"

"I overheard some talk about the Reverend Trowbridge. Cartwright's shooters killed him. I'm not sure if Baron told them to or not. Maybe it just got out of hand, but there it is. I've had enough."

Slade took the small note from his vest pocket and showed it to her. "Not your writing, I suppose?"

She frowned and shook her head. "I know my letters. How'd this reach you?"

"Someone left it at the desk downstairs," Slade answered. She would only know that he was lying if she'd passed the note herself. "And then," he added, turning up his hole card, "I found *this* under my door."

Sabrina read the second note, shaking her head. "You've had a busy day," she said.

"Know anything about the second one?"

"It's news to me," Sabrina answered. "But I think I know the place."

"Oh, yes?"

"That chimney, now. It has to be the Johnson place. They had a so-called accidental fire, about six months ago. Their house burned to the ground and sparks flew over to the barn, some say. They had a solid

307

chimney, though. It's all that's left, aside from ashes."

"And the house across the river, by the *X?*" Slade pressed her.

"First, it's not much of a river. More a stream, I'd say, unless we get a really heavy rain. There were some more homesteaders out that way. I don't recall the name, but they pulled out after some stock went missing and their little boy was snakebit — in his bed."

"No accidental fire?"

"You never heard that saying, that variety's the spice of life?"

"I missed it," Slade replied. "Who would you say ran off those families?"

"What difference does it make? One side's no better than the other, in Gehenna."

"If this goes to court, I'd like to have you testify."

"Not me," she told him. "Positively not. I'm leaving Cartwright, but I'll need to find work somewhere else. That kind of thing hangs on and follows you. Word gets around. Snitches don't live long in my world."

Slade knew Sabrina must have seen and suffered things that he'd have trouble putting into words, maybe a few beyond the reach of his imagination. And he had a feeling that she wouldn't cave.

"All right," he said at last. "But if you're leaving, make it soon. After tonight, I don't know how much time you'll have."

"Hold on." She pushed the note and map at Slade. "You're going through with this? It stinks of treachery."

"My nose works fine," he said. "I have no choice."

"You *always* have a choice. Don't go."

"And let the sisters suffer in my place?" Slade shook his head. "That isn't me."

"They're likely dead already," she replied. "Or, by now, wishing that they were."

"In any case, somebody pays."

"And you collect?"

"Unless they kill me first."

"Well, I'd say that's the plan."

"Planning and doing are two different things."

"It's your life, Marshal. But I hate to see you throwing it away."

"What if I said the same to you?"

"I made my choices, way back when. It's too damned late to change my mind and wish it all away."

"Same here."

"Well, then, I guess we're two damned fools. Good luck," she said and rose on tiptoes, lightly kissing Slade's left cheek.

"The same to you," he said.

"You'll need it more than I do," she replied. "I'm just running away. You're walking barefoot, right into a nest of rattlesnakes."

Buck Bjornson read the lawman's message once again, this time aloud, for Damon Shakespeare. "Trouble in Gehenna, stop. Confirm harassment of homesteaders, stop . . . Believe *both parties named by you involved,* stop. Seeking *further evidence* for trial . . . *One may cooperate.*"

He turned on Shakespeare, livid. "What in hell is this supposed to mean?"

Shakespeare blinked at him. "Well, he's writing to the judge."

"I *know* that, damn it! Do you take me for an idjit?"

"No, sir!"

" 'The parties named by you.' Who would that be, do you suppose?"

"Well, um . . . I reckon . . . you and Cartwright?"

"Bet your ass, that's who it means. *Parties* means more than one, for damned sure. Who else could it be?"

A helpless shrug from Shakespeare.

" 'Seeking *further evidence* for trial.' That has to mean he's got *some* evidence already, right?"

"Or thinks he does," Shakespeare replied.

"Thinks, nothing. This one's smart enough to know Judge Dennison will tear him a new asshole if he screws around. Old Isaac's famous for it. So, he must have *something*."

"I dunno, Boss."

"I dunno, Boss," Bjornson mocked his shooter. "Jesus! What about this shit: 'One may cooperate.' One *who,* for Christ's sake."

"Somebody he's talked to," Shakespeare offered.

"Not just anybody, though. See how he's set it up, not wasting any words he'd have to pay for? First, he says, *both parties named by you,* and then, *one may cooperate.* He's pointing right at me or Cartwright."

"Then, it must be Cartwright, yeah?"

"Of *course,* it must be Cartwright! Jumping Jesus, who else *could* it be?"

"Good thing you had the idea for that note, then, Boss."

"If he believed it," Bjornson answered, pacing. "If he hasn't got a deal in place with Cartwright to forget about the parson and come after me, like I'm the only one to blame for everything that's happened."

"That don't sound right, Boss."

"Can you tell me what *right* has to do with it?"

"I mean, it seems like Slade's a hardnose. When you tried to buy him off, you didn't even get a nibble."

"That *could* be because he's rock-ribbed honest," Bjornson granted. "Or it might mean that he struck a better deal before I talked to him."

"From Cartwright." Shakespeare wasn't asking.

"We don't know this Slade from Adam," Bjornson said, half talking to himself. "Could be the sudden sort, who grabs the first deal pitched to him and runs with it. Or maybe . . ."

"What, Boss?"

"Maybe Cartwright *is* cooperating. He could feed this lawman horseshit left and right, make out how he's a plain old honest pimp and gambler, getting by on what he earns the honest way, while I run all around behind him, pulling dirty tricks on settlers and the like."

"But who'd believe it?"

"Maybe Dennison. I won't know that until it's too late and my neck is in a goddamned noose!"

"What should we do, then?" Shakespeare asked him. "Give the word, Boss, and I'll take 'em all out. Slade, Cartwright, the whole damn mess of 'em."

"Let's not be hasty, Day." Bjornson stopped his pacing, sat down on a corner of his massive desk. "Slade's cable doesn't say which one of us he's counting on to make his case against the other. If the marshal has an accident, I can reach out to Dennison myself, come on all sorrowful about his loss, and help him put our buddy Baron on the scaffold."

"That's good, Boss. Should I go deal with him now?"

"There's no rush, Day. Tonight is soon enough."

"Okay. I'll get some boys together."

"You do that. And Day?"

"Yes, sir?"

"This is your second chance. It's do-or-die. If Slade's still breathing when the sun comes up tomorrow, I expect to find you at the undertaker's, in a box."

After Sabrina left his room, Slade changed his mind about waiting for dusk to leave Gehenna. Any way he timed it, shooters from both sides were bound to have an eye on him. It was a given, and he knew two other things with certainty.

If Harmony and Melody were prisoners, they should be under guard already at the place marked on his map.

And any spies from town who tried to warn the ambush party of his premature departure had the same two-hour ride ahead of them. Six miles due north, beyond the rock pile, chimney, and the devil tree — whatever *that* was.

Even if someone saw him leave Gehenna and rushed off at once to warn the kidnappers, he'd still have a head start. Suppose the shooters manning the abandoned farmhouse knew that he was coming early. Did it matter?

Slade supposed, on balance, that the warning might wind up working against them. Say a rider burst in on them, all excited, saying Slade was on his way . . . but nothing happened. In a while, the bushwhackers would start to wonder, getting extra tense and crotchety among themselves, wishing he'd rush them and be done with it.

A waiting game could work both ways.

They would've had arrangements plotted out before they grabbed the sisters, Slade supposed. Judging how many men they needed, telling each one where to wait and what to do when Slade arrived. They might expect him to come early, try to fool them, and be ready for it. But that strategy had built-in problems of its own.

Waiting was hard work for a nervous bunch of gunmen, when they didn't know for sure exactly when or how their prey would show itself. Knowing that Slade was on his way ahead of time, they'd tighten up, then feel the tension gnaw away at them as hours passed, with no sign of their target. When he was a couple hours late, some would begin to think that he'd decided not to come at all. They'd seethe with anger and frustration, maybe bleeding off into relief.

Whichever side had snatched the sisters, they must know that Slade had killed nearly a dozen shooters from Gehenna, as it was. Each pistolero would be second-guessing his ability to deal with Slade, wondering if they had enough men for the job.

And they might make the sisters suffer for it.

Slade refused to chase that thought, coldly suppressed the images that came to mind when he imagined Melody and Harmony alone with six or seven shooters, maybe more.

If they were still alive, he'd do his best to keep them that way. If they weren't, or if they'd suffered any degradation from their captors, he would make the bastards pay. Kill them, if they resisted him, or hold them for the judge's hanging rope.

Dead meat, whichever way you sliced it.

But Slade couldn't help the sisters, or himself, if he was dead.

Caution was paramount from that point forward. Every move he made required consideration of its likely consequences for himself, the sisters, and his enemies. He had to turn the trap around, somehow, and let it snap on *them.*

But he would have to see it, first.

The map told Slade where he was going, more or less, but it did not reveal the forces that would be arrayed against him when he got there. Numbers mattered, as did placement, attitude, the talent and experience of his selected adversaries. Two determined shooters with a slew of kills behind them were more dangerous than fifty yokels who could barely load their guns.

And he knew the big men of Gehenna would be fielding their best guns this time. At least, the best ones they had left.

17

"They'd be here now, if they were comin'," Early Somers grumbled.

Sitting in the dark, afraid to light a lamp and thereby give away the fact that they were camped out in the farmhouse, Billy Bauer silently agreed. He would've bet his last dollar that something wicked had befallen the two sisters on their slow ride back from town.

His last dollar, but not his life.

"How long we gonna wait?" asked Jared Cole.

"Till I say differ'nt," Bauer answered.

"This is stupid," brother Jubal said.

"Awright, then," Bauer told him. "You just ride on back to town and tell Day what a fool you think he is."

"I reckon not," Jubal replied.

"I didn't think so. Anybody else having a bright idea?"

Hank Murphy tried a reasonable tone.

"Billy, you know as well as I do, you can *walk* from here to town inside four hours, give or take a bit. We been here *five,* at least. Them sisters got a buckboard, and they ain't here yet. They's either lost or dead."

By Murphy's standards, that was quite a speech, and Bauer couldn't disagree with him. "We got our orders," he replied, no longer trying to defend them. "I ain't goin' back and tellin' Day that we give up. Whoever wants to do that, I won't stop you — and I won't bring no damned flowers to your funeral, either."

"How about this, then." Murphy leaned a little closer to him in the dark. "Say two of us rides back along the road to look for 'em. If we run into 'em along the way, we scoop 'em up and bring 'em right back here. But if we *don't* see anything, then one comes back and tells you, while the other rides back into town and talks to Damon. How'd that be?"

It made good sense to Bauer, but he didn't want to cave too easily. "Who'd go?" he asked.

"I'm thinkin' me and Early," Murphy said.

Again, Bauer could think of no good argument against it. He was just about to say so when the sound of rapid hoofbeats sounded from the yard outside. As one, the shooters

318

rose and drew their pistols, pressing toward the cabin's door and windows.

Peering through a crack between the shutters on one window, Jubal Cole whispered, "That ain't no buckboard. It's a rider."

Bauer shouldered Cole aside and scanned the narrow slice of yard that he could see. It was, in fact, a man on horseback, reining in before the cabin, sitting with his face in shadow from the wide brim of his hat, while moonlight bathed the yard.

"Billy?" the rider called. "You boys inside there?"

"Who the hell is *that?*" asked Jared Cole.

"I know that voice," his brother said. "Gimme another look."

"No need," Bauer replied. "It's Eddie Frasier."

Moving to the door, he threw it open, stepping out into the moonlit yard. The others ranged behind him, staring up at Frasier on his pinto.

"Well, you found us, Eddie," Bauer told him. "Right where we're supposed to be."

"Not anymore," Frasier replied. "Day sent me out to fetch you back."

"How come?" asked Murphy.

"Sisters won't be comin' home," said Frasier. "Some'un grabbed 'em off the road, most likely Cartwright's men. The word's all over town."

"I *knew* somethin' was wrong," said Early Somers.

"Are we goin' out to look for 'em?" asked Bauer.

"Hell, no! Day says, let the marshal spring 'em, if he can. Should Baker's people drop 'im, all the better."

"And suppose they don't?"

"I reckon there'll be hell to pay," said Frasier. "May be, anyhow. Wait till you get a whiff of town. It smells like war."

Slade didn't wait for dusk. He walked down to the livery at five o'clock, taking his Winchester and saddlebags along with him. The hotel clerk asked nothing as he left, and Slade offered no information on his own.

The hostler granted Slade a wary welcome, doubtless thinking of the way Gehenna's people had a tendency to die when he was near. He helped Slade saddle up the roan and took another couple of dollars off Slade's hands.

"I'll be back late," Slade said, not adding *if I make it back at all.*

"Time's all the same to me," the hostler said. "I got no place to go."

Slade rode out Main Street as he'd

planned, westbound, until Gehenna was a mile behind him and its many prying eyes no longer had him covered. Next, he turned northeastward, urged the roan into a steady trot, and started ticking off the mileage in his head.

The detour added nearly three miles to his ride, but Slade was in no hurry. He had seven hours to complete a trip that should take three, at the outside. The extra trail time offered him a chance to think, refine his plans, although Slade knew he couldn't put the final frosting on until he'd seen the battleground.

Slade had no reason to believe the kidnappers would free their hostages, whether or not he willingly surrendered to their custody. With that in mind, he brushed off any thought of playing by the rules they'd dictated, resolved that he would have to kill a few of them, at least, to rescue Harmony and Melody.

Judge Dennison would understand, although he much preferred live prisoners before the bar of justice, where he could decree their fate.

Still, disappointment was a part of life.

At six fifteen, with sundown closing fast, Slade found the rock pile from his map. It was a new addition to the landscape, mud still clinging to a few stones where they'd been uprooted, heaped on top of one another like a stack of cannonballs.

From there, Slade rode along the bare suggestion of a road until he reached the former Johnson farm, its blackened chimney standing like a totem pole as night fell on the badlands. Half an hour later, as he reached the stream depicted on his map, a bright three-quarter moon rose in the east to light his way.

Slade stopped and thought about the stream awhile. It wasn't deep or swift, but drowning wasn't his concern. Across the way, no more than fifty yards distant, a mini-wood composed of ten or fifteen trees provided perfect cover for an ambush party, if the kidnappers desired to drop him on the road instead of waiting for their rendezvous at the abandoned homestead.

Slade had time to spare, so he rode west along the winding stream and found another place to cross, a half mile from the brooding stand of trees. From there, a straight line back to intersect the almost-road would put the trees behind him. Anyone who waited there, and wanted to pursue him, would be forced to cover open ground.

The devil tree surprised Slade, stark and eerie in the moonlight, but he would have known it anywhere. It *did* look something like a demon etched in wood, bare arms or tentacles hoisted above its knobby head. The damned thing even had a face of sorts, knotholes arranged into a pair of crooked, deep-set eyes above a yawning maw that prepared to roar with rage or pain.

Slade was relieved to see the last of it. He had enough devils to deal with, as it was.

"You ladies nice and comfy, here?" the gunman asked, leering.

"We don't need your attention, thank you all the same," said Harmony Maguire.

He winked and gave a sharp tug at his gunbelt. "You might have it all the same, before too long. Enough for both of you."

A taller man loomed up behind him, overshadowing the lecher. "Time for you to go on watch, Frank," he announced.

"Aw, Eulis, why can't I —"

"Get moving. Now."

The shorter gunman glared, but didn't argue. After he had gone, the leader of the kidnappers moved closer, crouching down before the bed where Harmony and Melody sat hobbled. When he spoke again, his voice was lowered almost to a whisper.

"I suppose you know who I am?" he inquired.

Harmony thought of lying, but she reckoned it would do no good. "You're Cartwright's man," she said. "That Baker fellow."

"Call me Eulis, if you want to," he replied, smiling.

"No, thanks."

"So much for bein' friendly, then. For what it's worth, I don't hold much with harming women."

"Don't hold much," she echoed him. "I guess that means you only do it now and then?"

"Only when necessary," Baker said. "And with regret."

"Why are you after Jack?" asked Melody.

"Your hero's meddling in things that don't concern him, ma'am," Baker replied. "He's got a lesson coming, and you're helping me with the instruction."

"You may have a surprise in store for you," said Harmony.

"That so?"

"The trash you sent to kill us, four days back, weren't men enough to take him. There were six of them, as I recall."

"Not mine, ma'am. And you have my word on that."

"For what it's worth," said Harmony.

"Not much to you, I'll bet. But fear not,

ladies. This will soon be over."

"When you kill us?" That from Melody, a tremor in her voice.

"Why would I do that, ma'am?"

"Because we've seen your faces. We can testify against you."

"You'd do that, would you?" Baker asked.

"I'll see you hang for killing Jack," said Melody, defiant now.

The gunman shook his head, rising with eyes downcast. Harmony thought, for just a moment, that she read a hint of sadness in him, there and gone.

"Well, if you put it that way," he began — and suddenly the front door opened with a squeal of unoiled hinges. Rushing toward them came the short man Baker had dispatched moments earlier to serve as lookout.

"They're gone!" he blurted out to Baker.

"What? *Who's* gone?"

"Who d'ya think, goddamn it? Doc and Arnie. Neither one of 'em is out there!"

"Frank, I swear to God, if you've been drinkin' —"

"Smell my breath, for Christ's sake! Then, go have a look outside, yourself!"

"Calm down," Baker replied, already moving toward the main room of the cabin, where the others waited, guns in hand.

"What's happening?" asked Melody.

"I don't know, Sister. But if we mean to survive this, you must help me with these knots."

Killing wasn't difficult, in Slade's experience, but killing *silently* required some skill — and luck.

He'd ridden once around the cabin from a distance, cloaked in darkness, studying the various approaches to the place. Along the way, Slade marked the two lookouts on duty: one who smoked a cigarette and didn't hide it well enough, the other who made happy sounds as he relieved himself behind a tree.

They were the only two outside. Slade satisfied himself of that on his reconnaissance. He also saw their tethered horses and a buckboard he'd last seen on Main Street in Gehenna. Counting nags, he made it four guns in the house, with Harmony and Melody.

Then it was time to shave the odds.

Slade tied his own horse to a tree, took his Winchester from the saddle boot, and made his cautious way back to the smoker. Halfway there, Slade dropped into a gully cut by flash floods in the not-so-distant past, a scar across the landscape running in the same direction he desired to go.

Slade's target sat behind a slab of granite thrust up through the soil in one of Earth's upheavals, weathered now and cloaked in lichen. The boulder offered decent cover from the south, and it was Slade's good fortune that his adversary lacked the common sense to guard his flanks. The spotter was expecting Slade to ride in from Gehenna, and he never stopped to think that his intended prey might stoop to misdirection.

Good.

Slade left his rifle in the gully, drew his bowie knife, and crept with slow, painstaking movements from the wash. When he was on the rim, he rose into a crouch, no more than half a dozen paces from his enemy. Slade's shadow, cast by moonlight, stretched away beyond him, toward the farmhouse on his left.

His rush was fast and furious, slamming the lookout heavily against the rock slab that had sheltered him, driving the breath out of his lungs. Before the gunman could recover, Slade had jammed the bowie's heavy blade beneath his jawline, twisting sharply as he drew it back and out.

Silenced forever, fumbling at his open throat before the final darkness overtook him, Slade's would-be assassin dropped into a fetal curl and shivered out the final seconds of his life. In parting, Slade relieved the dead man of his six-gun, tucked it down inside his belt, then dragged the corpse back to the gully and reclaimed his Winchester.

One down, and five to go — but only one of those outside where Slade could reach him, without tipping off the rest.

If he was quick enough.

There had to be a changing of the guard sometime, Slade reckoned, but with no idea of when the lookouts had been posted, he could not guess when their shift might end. That meant he must work faster, or risk meeting reinforcements from the house before the first round of his work was done.

Slade's gully ran behind the house, veering away from it a yard or so for every six or seven of his loping strides. When he was level with the north, or rear, side of the farmhouse, Slade was thirty yards away from his next target, standing lookout in the shadow of a weeping willow tree.

Slade couldn't see the spotter well, but took a chance and trusted that his full attention would be focused toward Gehenna and the pale thread of a road meandering away southward. If Slade was wrong, he'd know it when the sniper's first shot slammed into his chest.

He scrambled from the gully like a lizard, then fell prone and lay immobile for a moment, waiting for the lookout to respond if he'd been seen. When nothing happened, Slade rose slowly and began his crouching trek across the forty yards of open ground that separated him from the next man he meant to slay.

The grass soil helped smother Slade's footsteps, no grating sand or rattling stones to spoil his harsh surprise. From twenty feet, he smelled the urine that his enemy had spilled onto the ground when Slade had ridden past him, unobserved.

It was the shooter's last mistake.

Slade threw one arm around the gunman's head, blocking his air supply, crushing thin lips against his teeth, then cut the lookout's throat before he had a chance to struggle. When the life ran out of him, Slade turned the corpse and let it sag across his shoulder, lurching toward the gully with his burden.

It was all of three long minutes later, when another man emerged, hissed toward the willow tree, then moved into the shadows there. After a moment's futile searching, Slade saw him emerge and run full tilt around the cabin, toward the boulder where his other friend should be.

Slade waited, smiling as he heard the

shooter come back breathless, raising the alarm.

"All right, now, listen up!" said Eulis Baker to his men. "Unless Arnie and Doc went off together for a moonlight ride, Slade's out there waitin' for us."

"Jesus! What are we supposed to do?" asked Virgil Meade.

"What Mr. Cartwright paid us to," Baker replied. "We came to kill him. That's the plan, and nothin's changed."

"Except that he's *out there,* and we're penned up *in here,*" Duke Henson said.

"And he's done kilt two of us," Frank Pullman added, spinning his revolver's cylinder for no good reason Baker could determine.

"Quit that!" he commanded. "It's still four of us to one, and we've got what he came for. Don't forget it. He can either come in, nice and quiet, or we go to work on them and let him listen to it."

"Who's to say he gives a damn about them women?" Virgil asked.

"He's here, okay? That has to tell you something," Baker said.

"Tells me he means to kill us like he done those boys at the Bonanza," Pullman said.

Baker grabbed Pullman's shirt and

snatched him close, so they were nose to nose. "You feel like running, Frank? Go on, then. Waltz out there and tell him you give up. If that works out for you, we just might try it."

"Lemme go, damn you!"

"As soon as you quit squealin' like a little bitch."

"We gonna kill each other, now?" asked Henson.

"Not unless one of you tries to cut and run," Baker replied.

"We're *with* you, Eulis, goddamn it!" Virgil said. "Where are we gonna run, with *him* out there?"

"My point, exactly," Baker snapped. "Now, watch and lemme show you how it's done."

A nest of squirming snakes had settled in his gut, but Eulis Baker still found nerve enough to cross the cabin's main room, ease the door open, and stand upon the threshold.

"Slade!" he called into the night. "Looks like you dropped a couple of my boys. Thought I'd return the favor with your lady friends, unless you leave your weapons where they are and come on in!"

Silence.

Baker stepped forward, one long stride,

and raised his voice. "I'm warning you, law dog! You've got one minute, then I set the boys loose with their skinning knives!"

A flash of orange light in the darkness caught his eye, but there was no time to determine what it was. The rifle bullet struck Baker dead center in his forehead, lifted him completely off his feet, and pitched him backward through the cabin's open door.

Slade rushed the house before the echo of his rifle shot rebounded from the nearest hills and trees. He pumped the lever action on his Winchester and had the open doorway covered, narrowing the gap, while Eulis Baker's corpse still twitched and wriggled on the bloodstained wooden floor.

Shadows pitched and yawed inside the cabin, cast by lamplight. Slade heard frightened voices cursing, asking panicked questions. There were three men still alive in there, unless they'd come with extra mounts.

As for the women . . .

Someone tried to shut the cabin door, but Eulis Baker's legs were in the way. One of the shooters took a chance, reaching around to drag Baker aside, and Slade triggered a shot that peeled long splinters from the floorboards near the outstretched arm.

"Goddamn it!" someone yelped.

When Slade was almost to the porch, a gunman leaned around the doorjamb, rapid-firing three shots from a double-action gun. The bullets zipped past Slade, well to his left, and he returned fire with the Winchester, knocking a chunk out of the jamb but missing flesh.

A heartbeat later, he was on the porch and flattening himself against the wall of heavy logs, between a shuttered window and the door. His early circuit of the property had shown him two windows in front, one each to east and west, with no means of escape in back. He had two-thirds of all the exits covered, and if anyone escaped through the remaining windows, they would have to come around in front, exposed, to take him down.

"Slade, listen!" someone called out to him from inside. "Let's make a deal!"

Convinced that bullets couldn't pierce the logs he leaned against, Slade answered, "Speak your piece."

"You want the ladies, right? How 'bout we send 'em out, and you just ride away. This was Baker's show, to start with, and you done kilt him."

"Throw out your guns first," Slade replied.

"And I mean *all* of them."

"So you can walk in here and kill us? Man, that's crazy talk," the faceless voice came back at him.

"No crazier than me ignoring that your deal would let you shoot me in the back."

"You got our word we won't do that. I swear!"

Slade let them hear his laughter. "Trusting you sounds like a bad idea, to me," he said, when it had passed.

"You'd rather we start cutting on the women?" asked a second voice. "It's your call, lawman."

"You need to think about that, long and hard," Slade answered. "None of you's done anything that warrants hanging yet, as far as I can testify in court. You harm the women, I can promise you a noose in Lawton, if I don't just burn you out and shoot you on the run. That's *your* call, and I'm finished talking."

Muttered conversation reached his ears, but Slade deciphered none of it. He was about to try the same hat trick he'd used the first time that he fought for Melody and Harmony, before he'd even known their names, when the first voice he'd heard called out, "All right, we give!"

"Give *what?*"

"We're throwin' out our guns, goddamn it! Hold your fire, now!"

"Get to it," Slade replied.

A pistol sailed out through the open doorway, landing in the yard. Two more came after it, one landing with its hammer stuck into the dirt, so that the gun was balanced on its grip and sights.

"That's all we got! We're coming out now!"

"Come ahead," Slade offered.

He was ready when they lurched out through the doorway, and the first one clear reached for his hideout piece. Slade shot him in the chest and swung around to nail the next one, tugging at a sawed-off shotgun he'd shoved down inside his trousers for some unknown reason. Slade's round struck him in the cheek, before the dying shooter's index finger found the shotgun's double triggers and his legs were blasted into stew meat.

"Jesus, wait!" the last man screamed. "I swear to Christ, I got no gun!"

The shooter's hands were empty, raised above his head, when Slade stepped up and clipped him with the rifle's stock, a solid blow beneath his chin to put him down. When he was satisfied another wasn't needed, Slade called out, "Ladies, are you all right in there?"

"We're fine, thank you," said Harmony, from somewhere in the back. "But we could use some help with these damned knots."

18

Buck Bjornson felt the whiskey he'd been drinking intermittently over the past five hours. It was churning in his gut and in his head, making him wobble just a bit when he stood up to pace his office. He fought through the dizzy spell and hoped that Damon Shakespeare hadn't noticed.

"Day," he said at last, "it troubles me that I don't understand what's going on around this goddamned town tonight. That shouldn't happen. I'm supposed to be *in charge!* And you're supposed to get the information that I need to *stay* in charge!"

"I know, Boss."

"Shit, you know! You come and tell me Cartwright's people grabbed the women *you're* supposed to deal with so that we get this lawman off our backs. You can't say *why* he took them, just that *we* can't reach them. That's no use to me at all."

This time, the gunman didn't speak, just

stood and nodded with his eyes downcast.

Bjornson swerved in the direction of the bottle on his desk, was reaching for it when he changed his mind and clenched his hand into a fist.

No more.

"You're looking worried, Day," he said.

"I reckon so."

"Well, here's the good news, boy. I figured out what's happening, no thanks to you."

"You did?"

"It's obvious," Bjornson said. "So god-damned obvious I couldn't see it." Bjornson giggled. "Don't you think that's funny?"

"Do I, Boss?"

That made Bjornson laugh harder. When he was able to control it, dabbing at his eyes, he said, "Hell, yes, you do. Why not?"

Shakespeare put on his most ingratiating smile, hands fidgeting around the curved grips of his pistols.

"Well," Bjornson prodded, "don't you want to *know* what's happening?"

"Sure, Boss."

"All right, then. You recall the lawman's telegram, I guess."

"Uh-huh."

"He told Judge Dennison that one of us was helping him. Remember?"

"Meaning you or Cartwright. Sure."

"And since we *know* it isn't me, it must be Cartwright."

"Yeah."

"Well, this is it! He means to screw us with the sisters."

"I don't —"

"Jesus, Damon, it's plain as the nose on your face. He stashes them somewhere, then has 'em tell the marshal that I sent your boys to run 'em off their land, or worse. The marshal takes 'em back to Lawton with him, where they tell the judge — and guess who's screwed?"

"You, Boss?"

"*Us,* Damon. Don't forget your part in this. You think Judge Dennison will stop with me, once he starts cleaning house, you need to have your head examined."

"Yessir." Finally, the gunman seemed to understand. Or was he faking it?

"No matter, Day. Here's what we have to —"

Sudden hammering on the office door distracted Bjornson. "What!" he shouted back at the intruder.

One of his bouncers entered, looking skittish. "Boss, you told us keep an eye peeled for the law dog? Well, he's ridin' right down Main Street, and he's got somebody with him."

Bjornson turned and rushed past Shakespeare, opening the door that served his private balcony. He stepped outside, glanced down into the street, and saw Jack Slade astride his roan, leading a pinto by its reins. The pinto's rider looked unsteady in the saddle, with hands bound behind his back.

Hands tied, and something strange about that face, beyond its vague familiarity.

"Do we know him?" Bjornson asked. "The other one?"

"He's one of Eulis Baker's boys," Shakespeare replied. "Name's Virgil Meade."

"Looks like he caught a beating." Leaning on the rail to get a closer look, Bjornson asked, "Is that a *badge* he's wearing?"

"Sure looks like it, Boss."

"So, what's *that* all about?"

"I don't —"

"Have any goddamned clue? I didn't think so."

As they stood and watched, Slade led his prisoner down Main Street to the constable's abandoned office. There, Slade first dismounted, tied both horses to the rail outside, then helped his prisoner down from his saddle.

It surprised Bjornson when Slade unlocked the office door and opened it. Slade shoved his prisoner inside and shut the door behind them. Moments later, lantern light spilled through the window, but Bjornson couldn't follow what was happening inside.

"I need to think," he told Shakespeare. "Get out, and take that bottle back down to the bar."

Slade's last stop in Gehenna, prior to leaving from the livery, had been at the abandoned jail. He'd found the back door standing open, with some damage to its lock, and let himself inside. No guns remained in the wall-mounted rack that once held several, but he'd found a set of keys in one of the desk drawers. Two fit the iron-barred doors on back-room cells. A third fit both doors, front and back.

He'd claimed the keys, because it had occurred to him that some of those involved in crime around Gehenna might wind up surrendering. Despite the bloody nature of his latest mission, Slade brought more defendants in alive than dead. Judge Dennison preferred to mete out lethal justice from the bench, as ordained by the statute books, and while he hadn't second-guessed the times when Slade was forced to use his guns, word of another killing always seemed to make him . . . sad.

Now Slade possessed a prisoner and was

prepared to charge him with kidnapping and attempted murder. Either charge would send him to the lockup at McAlester for ten to fifteen years, based on Slade's and the sisters' testimony.

Slade had sent the women home, with still more captured guns and orders to be doubly careful for the next few days. He'd left them primed to testify against Slade's sole surviving prisoner, including details of their captors' conversations that linked Baron Cartwright to the kidnapping.

Slade was prepared to jail the big man, next.

But not just yet.

When Virgil Meade was locked securely in his cell, Slade stood outside and studied him through rusty bars. "How old are you?" he asked at last.

" 'Bout twenny-five, I reckon."

"You'll be pushing forty when they let you go," Slade told him. "If you last that long."

"Guess I'll just have to try," Meade said.

"Or we could make a deal."

"What kinda deal?" The shooter was suspicious now.

"We both know picking up the sisters wasn't your idea," said Slade. "Tell me who put you up to it, and maybe I can get Judge Dennison to shave some of your time."

"How much?"

"That's up to him. But *any* time you spend inside McAlester is *hard* time. I can guarantee it."

Meade paused to think about it, chewing on his swollen lower lip until it pained him. Finally, he said, "You're right, Marshal. It damn sure wasn't me behind it."

"Who, then?"

"Eulis picked us out to ride with him."

"That's Eulis *Baker*?"

"One you kilt back at the cabin, right."

"That doesn't help you," Slade replied. "I can't file charges on a dead man."

"Well, you know who Eulis works for, don'tcha? Should I say *worked* for?"

Slade knew, all right. But simply knowing wouldn't count as evidence in court.

"Did Baker tell you lot who ordered *him* to grab the sisters?"

"Man, he didn't *have* to say. We all work for the Man."

"And you'll say that in court?"

"Depends," Meade answered. "How'm I supposed to know you can protect me from the likes of *him?*"

"If you're alive tomorrow," Slade replied, "that should be proof enough."

"Tomorrow, maybe. What about *tonight?*"

"I still have work to do," Slade said. "You

should be safe in here."

It sounded lame, even to him, and Meade was not deceived. "*Should be* don't cut it, lawman! I'm as good as dead, you leave me here alone."

"Let's see what happens, shall we?"

"Can you lemme have a gun, at least?"

Slade smiled and shook his head. "I don't think so," he said. "But maybe I can help distract your so-called friends."

"I've got good news and bad news," Baron Cartwright told the scruffy young man standing near his desk. "You want the bad news first?"

"Suits me, Boss."

"Eulis Baker's dead, with four of his best men. The *good* news is, you've got his job — if you can handle it."

The shooter grinned. "No worries, Mr. C."

His name was Coney Walker. Cartwright didn't know what kind of name that was, nor did he care. Walker was said to be the fastest gun among his dwindling troop of shooters, and he wasn't flat-out stupid, like so many of the rest.

"You know how Baker got it?" Cartwright asked.

"I heard the law dog dropped him an' the others."

"All but one."

"That Virgil," Walker said. "He's dumb as dirt, you ask me."

"Dumb enough to tell the marshal what he wants to hear?"

"You're thinkin' he might give you up, for movin' on the sisters," Walker said.

Or something else, thought Cartwright, while he said, "It crossed my mind."

"Best thing would be to shut him up, before he spills."

"Not get him out of town?" asked Cartwright.

"Well, we *could* do that," Walker replied, "but what's to stop the law dog runnin' after him and catchin' him again? Then, when the little bastard squeals, he'll blame you for the sisters *and* a jailbreak."

"That's good thinking, Coney."

"Mama Walker didn't raise no idjits, Boss."

"I see that. Can you do it? Silence him, I mean?"

"Don't see why not. You want the marshal taken care of, while I'm at it?"

"You get the chance, why not? But first things first."

"I hear you."

"And we'll have to deal with Bjornson's people soon."

"The more, the better," Walker answered, smiling.

"So, you're not . . . concerned . . . about Shakespeare?"

"Afraid of him, you mean to say? He don't scare me."

"I'm glad to hear it. While you're taking care of Meade, I'll think of something that will help us get a handle on Bjornson."

"How 'bout I just shoot his ass, next time he steps out on his widow's walk across the way?"

"It's food for thought," said Cartwright. "Meanwhile, when you see Meade, tell him he's a disappointment to us all."

"It's good as done," said Coney Walker, and the office door closed quietly behind him as he left.

The clerk at the Bonanza looked as if he'd seen a ghost when Slade came back to drop his saddlebags and wash up in his room. Slade guessed that in Gehenna, more news spread by word of mouth than in the pages of the *Beacon*. Both sides had supposed he would be dead by now, and his return had thrown Slade's enemies off balance.

But he knew that they weren't finished

with him yet.

Nor he with them.

Before he stirred things up between Gehenna's warlords, Slade had to prepare an ambush. Riding into town with Virgil Meade behind him, Slade had guessed that the arrest would worry Baron Cartwright. Meade was primed to squeal, and he could send Cartwright to prison — maybe to the gallows — if he lived to meet Judge Dennison.

It didn't take a genius to decide that Cartwright would do anything within his power to help Meade escape from custody, or kill him in his cell. Slade would've put his money on the latter course of action, since it was the only certain way to shut Meade up for good.

Which brought Slade to perch atop the feed store, situated next door to the jail. He'd found a ladder propped against the store's back wall, used it to reach the square, flat roof, then pulled it up behind him to avoid alerting any would-be lynchers to his presence in the neighborhood.

His silent vigil lasted thirty-seven minutes, by Slade's pocket watch. The watchers would've seen him leave the jail, walk back to his hotel, and disappear inside. Once he had doused his lamp, they'd give him time to fall asleep, then make their move, not knowing Slade had ducked out through the back and crossed Main Street where it was darkest, farthest from the two saloons, to make his way back eastward and to stand watch.

Now here they came.

Slade didn't try to count them, couldn't risk showing himself before they slipped in through the jail's broken back door. Once they were all inside, he had to scramble with the ladder, nearly dropping it and fairly leaping down the rungs to plant his feet on solid ground.

If he was too slow, and they executed Virgil Meade, Slade would've lost his only living witness. On the other hand, he still might capture one of them alive and hold a noose over his prisoner until the shooter talked.

Slade trailed the interlopers, following their voices, intercut with protests from the holding cell.

"I swear, I didn't tell the law dog nothin'," Meade was saying. "Please, just get me outta here."

"We got our orders," said another voice, intractable.

"Damn it, I'm on your side!"

"Coney says you're a loose end, Virgil."

"Coney *Walker*? What'n hell's *he* got to

do with this?"

"He calls the shots for Mr. Cartwright now," one of the shadow shapes replied.

Slade filed the latest name for future reference, then raised his Winchester and barked, "Lay down your guns!"

Three shooters turned to him as one, and none of them made any move to drop his weapon. Rather, they were swiveling their six-shooters toward Slade, crouching to make less tempting targets of themselves.

Slade didn't wait for them to fire. He shot the nearest of them somewhere in the torso, heard him grunt in pained surprise, then swung his rifle toward the second shooter as the first one fell.

A pistol shot slammed past him, while Slade pumped his rifle's lever action and returned fire, taking down the second gunman at a range of six or seven yards. The wounded man lurched backward, reeling through the door that separated Meade's cell from the former marshal's office at the front.

Slade let him go, dropping and rolling underneath the final gunner's spray of bullets. Rapid-firing with a single-action handgun butchered accuracy, but the slugs were passing close enough to make Slade thankful that he'd changed position. Firing from the floor, he drilled the shooter through one thigh, then caught him with a bullet to the upper body as his target fell.

"Are you hit?" Slade asked Virgil Meade.

"I don't think so."

"You'd know it if you were."

Slade rose, stepped past the nearest of the fallen, for a look into the office. There, the second man he'd shot was sprawled beside the desk, unmoving. Slade bent over him, checked for a neck pulse, and found none. He backtracked, checked the other two as well, although he knew it was a waste of time.

"You know these three?" Slade asked.

Meade nodded.

"Cartwright's men?"

"They was supposed to be my friends," said Meade.

"Something to think about, when we get back to Lawton. Maybe your old boss doesn't think that highly of you, after all."

Buck Bjornson watched a small crowd gather at the jail, people with coats thrown over nightclothes, bare feet stuffed into their boots and shoes. He saw the undertaker come and go, dressed as he always was, and wondered if the buzzard ever took off his black suit. At last, after the best part of an hour, Jack Slade stepped outside and sent the gawkers home to bed.

Five minutes later, Damon Shakespeare rapped on Bjornson's door, then entered on his order.

"Well?" Bjornson demanded. "What's that all about?"

"Seems three of Cartwright's boys went after Meade. Slade caught 'em at it, and he put 'em down."

"Trying to bust him out, were they?" Bjornson asked.

"Could be. Or else, make sure he doesn't tattle on his boss."

"He's still alive?"

"So far," Shakespeare replied.

"Maybe that's something we can work with. Get a friend to visit him, let's say, and offer our support."

"Money?"

"It couldn't hurt," Bjornson said. "He'll need a lawyer, at the very least. Who knows what else?"

"And in return for that . . . ?"

"He tells the truth about Cartwright. That's all we need."

"Good thinkin', Boss."

"I have my moments," Bjornson said. "First thing tomorrow, I want you —"

The window shattered then, imploding,

and Bjornson dived headlong behind his desk. He heard the echo of a rifle shot, before a second bullet, then a third, whined through his office, scarring furniture and walls.

"You hit, Boss?" Shakespeare asked him when the firing stopped.

"I'm fine," Bjornson snapped. "Put out that lamp, for God's sake!"

Shakespeare scuttled toward the sideboard, where a slug had missed the standing lamp by inches. Darkness enveloped Bjornson and his office as his gunman doused the wick.

"We're okay now," said Shakespeare.

"Prove it!"

Rising from the floor, Shakespeare advanced with pistol drawn to stand before the shattered window, peering out into the night. Below the balcony, excited voices rose, responding to the new alarm.

Bjornson crouched behind his desk, still seeking cover. "Where in hell did it come from?"

Shakespeare came back, finding the bullet scars, turning with arms outstretched between them and the windows, like a tight-rope walker.

"High, across the street," he said at last. "I'd say the Rosebud. Maybe on the roof."

"Or from the goddamned balcony?"

"Could be. It's hard to say."

"Trust me on this one," Bjornson said. "It's Cartwright, damn his eyes."

"He's not a shooter."

"So, one of his stooges, then. What difference does it make?" Bjornson rose, raging. "Get all your men together, Damon. If the bastard wants a war, we'll give it to him!"

Slade scrambled down the last rungs of the borrowed ladder, jogging back through darkness to deposit it behind the feed store. Racket from the street told him that he had roused the town again.

The hard part of a shot through window glass was trying to make sure the bullets weren't deflected, drilling Bjornson or his gunman when Slade meant to leave them breathing and unharmed. His first round had been close enough to put them on the floor, the others added for effect, while taking care to miss a lamp that would've sent the Rosebud up in flames.

Slade knew Judge Dennison wouldn't approve of his technique, this time, but it would be his little secret, shared with no one. As to what might happen next, his best guess was that Buck Bjornson would blame Cartwright for the attack and seek revenge.

Moving along the darkened strip behind Gehenna's Main Street shops, Slade replaced his spent Winchester shells with loose rounds from his pocket. Whatever came next, he was ready to meet it head-on . . . or to stand back and watch, if it suited him better.

Slade reckoned that Virgil Meade was safe for now, whatever happened next. Cartwright had lost three men trying to silence Meade, and if Bjornson struck back in retaliation for the sniping, Cartwright would be fully occupied with self-defense.

As for Gehenna's innocent civilians, Slade assumed that they would stay indoors and keep their heads down when the trouble started. If any joined the coming fight, for reasons of their own, he'd be compelled to treat them as combatants for whichever side they chose.

Slade hoped it wouldn't come to that, but anything was possible. His mind flashed to Sabrina Abbott for a moment, and he wondered if she'd manage to escape from Cartwright's headquarters in time to save herself.

Slade wished her luck, then put her out of mind.

Gehenna — Helltown — was about to self-destruct. Slade couldn't say exactly how or when, but he could feel it coming. If the fault was his, at least in part, so be it.

He would face whatever came and do his best.

With any luck, he might survive to see another sunrise.

19

"So, let me get this straight," said Baron Cartwright, speaking through teeth clenched in anger. "You lost three men at the jail, accomplished nothing there, and now you can't say who was shooting at Bjornson's place from *my own roof?*"

In spite of everything, the look on Coney Walker's face still smacked of arrogance. "The jail thing wasn't my fault," he replied. "They got inside okay, but somebody snuck in behind 'em. Took 'em by surprise."

"*Someone?* Do you have any thoughts on who that might've been?"

A lazy shrug. "I reckon it's the lawman."

"And you didn't think he might be hanging out around the jail, where he'd deposited a prisoner *within the hour?*"

"Nope. Boys watched him go on back to the Bonanza, down the street. Had no reason to think he'd double back, now, did I?"

Not unless your brain was functioning, thought Cartwright. "What about the shooter on the roof?"

"I wasn't up there when it happened, Mr. C."

Cartwright was in his face a heartbeat later, leaning close enough to spray Walker with spittle as he raged, "I've had enough of your smart mouth, goddamn it! Understand me, boy? You call me 'Mr. C.' once more, I'll beat your sad ass to a bloody pulp and leave you in the street!"

Recoiling from his wrath, Walker collided with the nearest wall, looking as if he longed to melt through it and slip away. "I'm sorry, Boss," he fairly whispered.

"Are you?"

"Yessir! Truly am, for sure."

"All right, then." Cartwright smoothed his satin vest with both hands, swallowing an urge to smile. "Now, what about the roof?"

"We found some rifle shells up there, but nothin' else. Whoever done the shootin' got away before the boys clumb up there. That's the truth."

"Why would I doubt you, Coney? Have you ever lied to me?"

"N . . . n . . . no, sir!"

"Well, there you go. Now, using that sharp mind of yours, who do you *think* might want to fire on the Valhalla from my roof? Assuming that he wasn't one of ours?"

"No, sir, it weren't. I axed 'em all, first thing."

"Same question, then," Cartwright replied.

"Why . . . uh . . . I reckon somebody who wanted them across the street to *think* you done the shootin'."

"Yes," said Cartwright as he poured himself a solitary whiskey. "I believe you're on to something, there."

"Somebody stirrin' up a fight, to hurt you both."

"That's my thought, too." He sipped and mused, "Who could it be?"

"I'd say the law dog, but . . ."

"But what, Coney?"

"Well, he can't do that, can he? I mean, bein' criminal and all, when he's suppose to walk the straight'n narrow?"

"Even saints stray off that path from time to time," Cartwright reminded him.

"I guess so, Boss. But Slade sounds purty goldarned straight, from what I heard."

"I know one way to settle it. Let's ask him!"

"Boss?"

"Why not? You take a few hands with you. Run along and find him for me. Tell him we have something urgent to discuss, back here."

"S'pose he don't wanna come?" asked Walker.

"Then convince him. I trust you can —"

Sudden gunfire echoed from the street as bullets peppered Cartwright's balcony and windows. Shattered glass deluged his Oriental rug, a shower of glittering blades. Across the room, a painting he'd brought all the way from Kansas City took a hit and clattered to the floor.

Cartwright and Walker, hunched together in the shadow of his heavy desk, rode out the first barrage, then heard a harsh voice calling from across the street.

"You shoot at me, sumbitch? Guess what? I shoot right back at *you!*"

"Bjornson?" Walker asked.

"I think so. *Shhhh!*"

The outside voice continued, not addressing Cartwright any longer. What it said was, "Go ahead and light 'er up!"

Cursing his understanding of that order, Baron Cartwright bolted to his feet. He saw a whiskey bottle with a burning wick of cloth attached to it come sailing from the darkness, arcing toward his balcony. It burst on impact, spewing kerosene that stung his nostrils in the instant prior to catching fire.

Slade watched the first moves of the battle from the recessed doorway of the barbershop, one block due west. Business had slacked off at the Rosebud since the latest round of shootings half an hour earlier. Slade wasn't worried much about civilians in the cross fire, but he knew anything could happen as the fighting spread.

Holding his Winchester, his pockets tight with extra cartridges, Slade moved along the sidewalk on Bjornson's half of Main Street, toward the battle zone. He'd barely started when a Bjornson gunman in the street hurled a bottle with a burning rag attached toward the Rosebud's second floor. Slade blinked as it exploded, setting Cartwright's balcony ablaze.

Another pair of gunmen ran from the Valhalla to their comrade standing in the middle of the street. They lugged a wooden crate between them, bottles jingling in it as they ran. Slade had already halved his distance to the rival sporting houses when they set the crate down and began extracting bottles, striking matches on their boot heels.

"That's enough!" Slade shouted at them,

shouldering his rifle as he stepped into the street and let them see him. "Put the bottles down and step away!"

Too late.

One of the shooters had his wick lit, bright flames licking up around his hand. At Slade's command, he tried to shake it out but couldn't do it. Cursing, he spun on his heel and pitched the homemade fire bomb straight at Slade.

It fell a dozen paces short, losing its wick on impact, spilling kerosene or coal oil in the dirt. The fumes caught quickly, small flames dancing on the surface of the street, but no explosion followed.

"Raise your hands!" Slade ordered. "Now!"

Instead, two of Bjornson's gunmen went for pistols, crouching slightly as they drew. Slade shot the one who'd thrown the bottle at him, scoring a body hit that made his target kick back like a cancan dancer as he fell.

The second gunner froze, hand halfway to his six-shooter, then straightened up and raised both hands above his head. Behind him, number three already had his hands raised, pleading with his eyes by firelight for a chance to live.

"Take off your gunbelts," Slade commanded. "Drop them where you stand, and get the hell away from here. If I see either one of you again, I'll cut you down on sight."

They didn't argue, fumbling with belt buckles for an instant, then discarding weaponry and fleeing past Bjornson's club, seeking a safer place to hide. Slade questioned his own impulse to be merciful, fully aware that one or both of them could find new weapons quickly, double back, and blast him from the shadows, but he had more pressing things to fret about as shots from the Valhalla started raising spurts of dust around his feet.

"You *missed* his ass, goddamn it!" Damon Shakespeare raged, shoving at men on either side of him. "What's wrong with you?"

They muttered lame excuses, none of any interest to him at the moment. Battle had been joined with Cartwright's men — long overdue, in Shakespeare's estimation — and the marshal had seen fit to interrupt.

For that, he had to die.

"Want something done right," Shakespeare said, "do it yourself." He rounded on his men, snarling, "They got a whole saloon across the street. Can any one of you hit *that?* Well, *can* you?"

"Yessir."

"Sure, Day."

"Then, for Christ's sake, *do* it!"

They were firing at the Rosebud when he left them, snatching up a scattergun before he started down the stairs.

Bjornson called out to him from the landing, asking, "Where in hell are *you* going?"

"I'm gonna take care of the law dog," Shakespeare answered and ignored whatever else Bjornson shouted after him as he was rushing down the stairs and out of the saloon.

He cleared the swinging doors, hearing the gunfire hammering above him, bullets peppering the Rosebud, opposite. A few of Cartwright's men were firing back now, making Shakespeare duck and dodge until he reached the nearest alley's pitch-black mouth and lost himself inside it.

Panting, Shakespeare paused to sort his thoughts and tried to scan the street without giving Cartwright's snipers anything to shoot at. On the Rosebud's balcony, two men with blankets were about to finish beating out the flames from Shakespeare's first firebomb.

He hadn't lobbed the deadly cocktail personally, but it had been his idea, a little trick that he'd been thinking of for some time now, useful for torching homesteads if the sodbusters were stubborn about leaving when their betters told them to. The Rosebud would be burning bright by now, he thought, if Jack Slade hadn't butted in and ruined everything.

Another reason why the law dog had to die.

Along the street, some of the same shopkeepers who had rallied to the jailhouse shooting scene were out again, some having donned their normal street clothes in the meantime. They were catching on, he guessed, that this would be a cataclysmic evening for Gehenna — one that changed the world for certain people, ending it for others.

Like Jack Slade.

Shakespeare went hunting, clinging to the shadows on the south side of Main Street. When worried merchants recognized him, calling out to ask him what was happening, he either cursed them or ignored them altogether, watching for the man he'd pledged to kill.

Somewhere, close by, he knew Slade would be waiting, maybe peering out at him right now from a convenient vantage point. The scuffling sound of boots on wood behind him made him spin and nearly fire his shotgun at the balding, forty-something owner of the dry-goods store.

"Don't kill me, please!" the merchant begged.

"Get off the goddamn street," Shakespeare replied, dismissing him.

His mind was churning as he stalked the boards.

Where are you, Slade, you slick son of a bitch?

Slade saw Bjornson's top gun moving west, along the sidewalk on the Swede's side of Main Street. Shakespeare was carrying a sawed-off shotgun in addition to the twin six-shooters dangling from his hips.

Three guns, and possibly a hideout tucked away somewhere, but Shakespeare only had two hands. Whether he carried one or twenty weapons, all that really mattered was his skill.

Slade hadn't seen him draw, but he supposed there was a reason why Bjornson had promoted Shakespeare to command his other gunmen. Whether he was just that good or had bamboozled Bjornson in a pinch, Slade wouldn't know until he faced the man.

Why bother?

He could snipe his target from the shadows that concealed him on the north side of the street, at no risk to himself. One shot, and he'd eliminate a threat that might prove deadly, if unchecked.

Why not?

Because it didn't *feel* right.

Slade had no compunction about ambushing his enemies in situations like his rescue of the sisters earlier that very night, when he was critically outnumbered. If his life was riding on the line, fair play went out the window in a flash.

But here, right now, he didn't feel that threat.

Two blocks away, shooters employed by Cartwright and Bjornson were engaged in full-scale warfare. Gunshots hammered back and forth between Valhalla and the Rosebud. Since he'd shot the firebomb thrower, two more fighters had been cut down in the street, their bodies sprawled like sacks of dirty laundry fallen off a wagon.

Slade wondered where the boss men were, and if Sabrina Abbott had fulfilled her promise to escape before the killing started. He would have to answer both those questions, Slade decided.

Once he'd dealt with Damon Shakespeare.

Shouldering his Winchester, Slade stepped

out of the shadows into moonlight. Shakespeare hadn't seen him yet, so Slade called out to him across the street.

"That's far enough," he said. "Put down the scattergun, then drop your gunbelt, nice and slow."

"Unlikely," Shakespeare answered, smiling as he pivoted and fired both barrels of his shotgun from the hip.

Slade hit the sidewalk, feeling buckshot sting his left thigh as he dropped. The problem with a sawed-off weapon was its range. Shakespeare had grazed him with a single pellet out of twenty-odd that peppered windows, walls, and doors for several yards on either side of Slade.

Slade fired his rifle from the prone position, seeing Shakespeare lurch a little as the bullet found him, but he didn't fall. Dropping the empty shotgun, Shakespeare drew both of his pistols, whooping out a rebel yell as he rushed toward his enemy across Main Street.

Slade gave him points for guts and put a bullet through them at a range of forty feet or so. The impact staggered Shakespeare, dropping him to one knee, but he hung on there, cursing and leveling his six-guns for another try.

Slade rolled out to his right, while .45

slugs hammered slivers from the sidewalk close beside him. Coming out of it, he rapid-fired two shots and scored with one of them, at least. Shakespeare went rigid, gasping like a fish hauled out of water, then fell over backward in a crumpled heap.

Slade lay a moment longer on the boards, waiting to see if Shakespeare had some life left in him, but the gunman didn't rise again. At last, with sounds of combat raging from the west end of the street, Slade rose, reloading on the move, and went to join the fight.

Sabrina Abbott hadn't gotten out in time. She'd lingered, wondering if she should speak to Cartwright, maybe leave a note, or slip away without a word to spare herself his wrath. Her bag was packed already, hidden underneath her bed, and she was reaching for it, finally decided on the silent getaway, when shooting started in the street outside and someone shouted, "Fire!"

It went to hell from there, with gunmen running up and down the hall outside her room, Cartwright moving among them, bawling orders, asking questions that were half profanity and half insult to those he grilled. No one could please him, and she'd known instinctively that it was not the time for him to catch her leaving, carpetbag in hand.

So, she had stalled, heard someone say the fire was out, while gunfire escalated, blazing back and forth between the Rosebud and the Valhalla. This was it, she realized, the fight that had been brewing since the moment Cartwright and Bjornson met and staked competing claims over Gehenna.

Only one of them would walk away this time.

Or maybe both would die.

She wondered where Jack Slade was, then dismissed the marshal from her mind. Drawing a small revolver from her pillow case, Sabrina checked its load, confirming that she had a round in all six chambers.

Finally, holding the shiny pistol in her right hand, heavy bag clutched in her left, she slipped out of her room into the rush of shooters running back and forth along the corridor. Where were they going, when the fight was obviously out in front?

Sabrina spoke to no one, kept her pistol hidden in the deep folds of her skirt as she moved down the hallway, her right shoulder brushing wallpaper. Most of the shooters lusted after her, and some of them had paid to bed her, but they all ignored her now, caught up in a survival drama that transcended sex.

She reached the stairs and jostled down among descending soldiers, cursing with the best of them when she was pushed against the wall or nearly tripped by clumsy feet. Downstairs, the customers had fled, while the bartender and piano player stood behind the bar, both holding shotguns leveled toward the bat-wing doors.

Good thing I'm going out the back, Sabrina thought, and turned right at the bottom of the staircase, gaining speed along the hallway that would take her to the kitchen, liquor storeroom, and back door.

She met no challenge passing through the kitchen, and the storeroom was deserted. Pushing through the back door into darkness, she relaxed a little when the door clicked shut behind her, muffling the sound of gunshots from inside. The building's bulk buffered the battle noises rising from Main Street.

Sabrina turned left, took a step — and found a pistol pointed at her face.

"Well, now," said Coney Walker. "Where'n hell are *you* off to, sweet thing?"

Slade slowed his pace as he approached the Rosebud, kneeling under cover of a water trough outside the jail. He thought of ducking in to check his prisoner, but reckoned Virgil Meade could wait. He had the safest room in town right now, unless the buildings on the north side of Main Street caught fire, and if that happened, Slade could always double back to set him free.

If Slade was still alive.

And if he wasn't, what the hell? Let the kidnapping would-be murderer fend for himself.

Counting the men and muzzle flashes visible on each side of the street, he guessed that Cartwright's and Bjornson's teams were more or less well matched. Slade couldn't vouch for quality on either team, but *someone* on the firing line was good enough to drop two shooters after Slade had cleared the scene ten minutes earlier.

Slade couldn't see the dead men's faces, and he likely wouldn't know them anyway, which barred him from guessing which army had suffered the losses. As it was, Bjornson's men had either given up on firebombing the Rosebud, or they'd gone off looking for another angle of attack, while snipers kept their adversaries busy on the street.

Slade wondered how to tackle it, when both saloons were fortified and bristling with guns. If he was suicidal, he could step into the street and call on everyone to cease fire, but the end result would likely be a fusillade from both sides that would leave him looking like a colander.

No good, he thought.

Which meant that he would have to deal with one side at a time, the hard way, multiplying risks with every step he took. But *which* side should he tackle first?

The Rosebud loomed before him, thirty feet away and on the same side of the street. If he chose the Valhalla first, it meant retreating to a safer distance and then crossing Main Street, which could tip gunmen on both sides to his whereabouts.

The Rosebud, then.

Slade knew he couldn't enter through the front door, crossing Cartwright's guns, while Bjornson's peppered him from the south side of Main Street. That decided, he retreated to a nearby alleyway and ducked into its shadows, shielded from pale moonlight by two-story walls on either side.

Slade cursed the sand and gravel rasping underneath his boots, wishing that he could travel silently, then realized that gunfire from the street would cover any passing noise he made. His next hurdle would be the Rosebud's back door if Cartwright had posted men to guard it. Otherwise . . .

Reaching the alley's end, Slade knew his next step could mean death, but he was stymied if he didn't budge. Taking a breath and holding it, he made his move.

20

Baron Cartwright seethed with anger, lying on the glass-littered floor of his office while bullets plunked into the walls, the ceiling, and the furniture. The place was literally shot to hell, but the worst part was knowing that he couldn't reach the man responsible.

No, make that *men.*

He had been feuding with Buck Bjornson for the better part of two years, but they'd mostly kept it out of town, between themselves, and relatively subtle. This explosion, Cartwright reckoned, was primarily the fault of one Jack Slade, who had upset the balance and accelerated matters to an unexpected flashpoint.

Cartwright would've loved to kill both men, starting with Slade, but he had been reduced to crawling on his belly like a lizard in his own damned office, bloodied by the glass cuts on his hands and elsewhere.

Cartwright's contribution to the battle so

far had been half a dozen shots fired through the window, from a rat's-eye view, uncertain whether he had even hit Bjornson's saloon, much less a living enemy. It galled him, being pinned down in that manner, when he should be leading men across the street to storm Valhalla and extract its owner for a necktie party.

Just thinking of it, picturing Bjornson dancing at the short end of a rope, made Cartwright almost giddy. He could do it, if he wanted to. Well, maybe not the *leading* part, but he could offer juicy bonuses to those who followed orders and impressed him with their martial skills.

Get on with it!

Three pistols lay before him, one already emptied through the window. As the voice inside his head goaded Cartwright to action, he picked up the other two, then wriggled backward to the cover of his desk. When he was relatively safe behind it, Cartwright struggled to a crouch, then duck-walked from his office, past the tall door with its bright new bullet scars.

When he was safe outside the line of hostile fire, Cartwright stood up, feeling a momentary rush of dizziness as he regained full altitude. It passed with stuttered heartbeats, and he moved along the second-story landing, calling for his new top gun.

"Coney! Where are you? Coney Walker!"

When no answer came, he buttonholed a gunman passing by, clutched at his arm, and snapped, "Where's Coney?"

"Dunno, Boss."

"Stay here, by me," Cartwright instructed. "I've got work for you to do."

"Okay."

Four times he asked the question, each time drawing negative replies, keeping the shooters with him as he moved on, searching. On the ground floor, one of Cartwright's wounded flagged him down.

"I seen him, Boss," the gray-faced gunman said, while keeping pressure on a thigh wound. "He was headin' out the back."

"What for?" Cartwright demanded.

"Looked to me like he was runnin,'" said the shooter, "but I can't be sure."

"Son of a bitch!"

"Yessir."

"How badly are you hurt?"

"Can't walk so good right now."

"Well, hobble over by a window, then," Cartwright instructed. "You can cover us from there."

"Cover?"

Dismissing his confused employee, Cartwright started shouting at the others, most of whom were either firing through the Rosebud's doors and windows toward Valhalla, or reloading weapons under cover while the other side returned fire.

"People! Listen to me now!" he cried. At first, the gunfire smothered his entreaty, then he started moving through the barroom, man to man, snatching at vests and sleeves, demanding their immediate attention.

When he had it, and the fire was all incoming, Cartwright told the huddled troop, "We can't go on like this. We need to fight our way across and take Valhalla, root those bastards out, and give them what they asked for, starting with their goddamned boss. Who's with me?"

Silence.

"Right! A thousand dollars each for every man who fights, and double that for Bjornson's head. Two thousand for the lawman. Anyone who doesn't fight, you're fired! Now, once again, *who's with me?*"

Cartwright thought he heard more snarl than cheer in the collective answer, but he took it for agreement. "Good!" he told them. "Form up ranks around the door, there, and be ready on my signal. Those who can't walk, man the windows. Give us cover fire. On three, now! *One . . . two . . .*"

■ ■ ■ ■

Slade didn't recognize the man who had Sabrina Abbott pressed against the Rosebud's wall, near the back door, but moonlight showed a revolver in the stranger's hand. He drew its muzzle slowly, teasingly, across Sabrina's cheek.

"Is this a private party?" Slade inquired.

The shooter flinched away from him, half turning, cocked his piece, and hauled Sabrina off the wall to stand before him as his shield.

"Private? Hell, no," he said. "You're just in time, law dog."

Slade held his rifle steady at his shoulder, watching every move the gunman made over its sights. "I'm glad to hear it," he replied.

"Truth is," the shooter drawled, "I hoped we'd get together."

"Do we need the lady for it?"

"Lady? I don't see no lady. Just another whore."

"You're short on manners, boy," Slade said.

"Reckon you'd like to teach me some?"

"Be happy to, if there was time," Slade answered. "As it stands, the best that I can do is kill you."

"That's big talk," the shooter said, eyes blinking rapidly.

"You'll want to test it, I suppose."

"Just do it, Jack!" Sabrina blurted out. "Don't worry about —"

"Shut it!" snapped the gunman, giving her a sharp rap to the temple with his six-gun.

Slade felt anger churning in his gut and swallowed it, maintaining focus on his enemy, watching the shooter's weapon and his nervous eyes.

"You're pretty tough with unarmed women," Slade observed. "Is that about your limit?"

"Guess not, since I'm Cartwright's number one," the gunman sneered.

"I smoked his number one tonight," Slade said, "and three more with him. That makes you his second choice, at best — maybe his fifth, depending how you look at it."

"Think you can take me, law dog?"

"Well," Slade said and shot him through the right eye socket, ruffling Sabrina's blond hair with his bullet, "let's find out."

The dead man folded like an empty suit of clothes, but the clenched fingers of his left hand held Sabrina's hair and dragged her down on top of him. The slug that drilled his brain short-circuited the message to his trigger finger, leaving Slade to pry the pistol from the corpse's grip before he freed Sabrina.

"God!" she whimpered, standing in the circle of Slade's arms. "You cut it close."

He pushed her back to arm's length, studying her ashen face. "Reckon I'd say the same for you."

"I didn't have a chance to get out earlier," she said, recovering and stooping for her carpetbag. Sabrina nodded toward the nearby door, saying, "You won't be going in there, will you?"

"That's the plan," Slade answered. "Will you be all right?"

"Hell, yes. Just watch your back, okay?"

Already moving toward the door, Slade said, "I always do."

"They're coming, Boss. It's crazy, but —"

A lucky shot struck the excited gunman in his left arm, dropping him to one knee on the barroom floor. He blinked upward at Buck Bjornson's face in stunned surprise.

Bjornson crouched behind his wounded shooter, more for cover than from any great concern. He made a show of peering at the young man's bloody arm, then nodded, frowning. "You're all right," he said. "Get back into the firing line and hold them off."

"My *arm!*" the gunman whined.

"Are you left-handed?" Bjornson asked him.

"N-n-no."

"Well, shit, you're good as new. Get up there now."

To emphasize the order, Bjornson rose, dragging the whiner to his feet, and shoved him toward the windows facing Main Street, where the noise and stench of gunfire steadily increased.

They're coming!

It *was* crazy, Cartwright and his men leaving the Rosebud to attack Valhalla, but Bjornson couldn't doubt his eyes and ears. Outside, the enemy was gaining ground. They wouldn't have an easy time of it, but he had twice as many dead and wounded now as when the shooting had started some ten minutes earlier.

Ten minutes was a lifetime. In the next ten, Bjornson knew he might be dead, unless he used that time to good advantage for himself.

Leaving his men to hold the ground floor if they could, Bjornson made his way upstairs, half crawling on the staircase to present a smaller target for his enemies outside. The barroom had been shot to hell, but it could still be worse — and would be if Cartwright's raiders forced their way inside.

It was too late to think about that now. His top gun's plan to burn the Rosebud down had failed, and now Shakespeare himself was missing — gone to hunt the marshal down, one of Bjornson's men had told him. If he wasn't back by this time, Bjornson guessed he never would be.

Screw him!

In his office, Bjornson removed one of the paintings from its hook and set it on the desk, revealing a wall safe. He spun the combination dial, first right, then left, and right again, until it clicked and Bjornson pulled the bulky door open.

Neat stacks of banded greenbacks filled most of the safe, sharing a portion of their space with deeds to plots of land in town and various surrounding farms. Hauling an empty satchel from the knee well of his desk, Bjornson filled it with the contents of his safe until the bag was difficult to close. Unwilling to abandon anything, he stuffed the last two packs of currency into his pockets.

Ready.

Now, the trick was getting out alive, but Bjornson had prepared for that.

Rushing downstairs, ducking the slugs

that whispered past him, smacking into walls and whittling down the banister, Bjornson reached the ground floor, turned his back on the defenders of his worldly kingdom at their posts along the Main Street firing line, and made a beeline to the kitchen pantry.

There, a certain "closet" was secured with a dusty padlock, and Bjornson had the only key to fit it. No one presently in his employment knew what lay beyond that padlocked door.

Bjornson paused outside the door to light a lamp, then used his key, entered, and locked the door behind him. Lamplight showed ten wooden steps, descending into darkness.

Chinamen on loan from an obliging railroad man had dug the tunnel for him, then were sent back to their dreary life of labor on the rails in Texas, California, or wherever they were in demand. No living person in Gehenna knew the secret of Bjornson's tunnel, running underneath the shops on Main Street's southern side. He would emerge behind the livery, from a neglected tool shed, which the hostler had strict orders to ignore.

"So long, suckers," he told the people of Gehenna and began his steep descent into the pit.

Slade half expected to be ambushed as he entered through the back door of the Rosebud, but he found no guards awaiting him, no frightened whores milling about to squeal alarms at his appearance. Gunfire echoed from the barroom, as before, but now some of it had a distant, muffled quality about it.

When he was halfway down the service corridor, a creaky floorboard brought his head and Winchester around to face a young Hispanic woman, staring at him wide-eyed. Moving cautiously, she raised a finger to her lips, the universal sign for silence, then retreated, closed the door, and vanished from his sight.

Slade thought of checking out the kitchen, making sure no one concealed there could come rushing at him from behind, but then decided that he didn't need to fear Cartwright's domestic staff. If one of them approached him with a weapon, Slade would deal with it. Until then . . .

Emerging into the Rosebud's combination barroom and casino, Slade saw half a dozen gunmen crouched before the shattered Main Street windows, firing steadily at the Valhalla. It seemed to Slade that all of them were wounded, dangling useless limbs or sporting bloodstains on their clothes.

Edging to his left, Slade ducked behind the bar for cover, braced himself, and raised his voice. "Enough! Throw down your guns and raise your hands!"

Slade wondered for a heartbeat if they'd heard him, then the heads began to turn in his direction, recognition dawning on their anxious faces.

"Nice and easy," Slade amended, wondering if that was even possible.

"Easy, my ass!" one of the shooters growled, turning to aim his pistol at the bar.

Slade fired instinctively, before his brain could flash a cogent message to his arm and hand. His shot wasn't a perfect kill — off center, high, and to the left — but it was adequate to put his target down.

And then, all hell broke loose.

The five remaining gunmen vented fear and anger through their weapons, adding new scars to the Rosebud's pockmarked bar, smashing the few undamaged bottles ranged behind it on ascending shelves. Hunkered below their line of fire, Slade wondered whether breathing fumes of alcohol could make him drunk.

That way, at least, he thought it wouldn't hurt so much when Cartwright's shooters rushed the bar and gunned him down.

Secrets.

Gehenna harbored many, and indeed, as Baron Cartwright now discovered, it was literally *built* on secrets. It was knowledge that achieved what no man had accomplished since Cartwright was twelve years old.

It frightened him.

He'd known about Bjornson's tunnel for a year or more, had bribed the livery hostler for a peek inside the run-down shed behind his stable, and took care picking the lock by candlelight, leaving its face unmarked.

Alone, Cartwright had plumbed the tunnel's depths that night, traced it to the Valhalla, then retreated and secured the shed as if its secret were inviolate. He'd kept the information to himself, against the day when he might need it for survival's sake.

Like now.

But still, Bjornson had surprised him.

Sometime in the twelve or thirteen months since Cartwright had explored the hidden passage, its creator had returned and added new refinements. Cartwright's first trip through the tunnel had revealed no crates of dynamite, with fuses linked to detonate them in a deadly chain of rapid-fire explosions underneath the southern tier of Main Street shops.

Cartwright stood gaping at the stacks of high explosive charges in the light cast by his bull's-eye lantern, until scuffling footsteps in the distance made him close the lantern's shutter, letting darkness fall around him like a shroud.

He had dispatched his men to storm Valhalla, saw them off en masse, then used the diversion to sprint along Main Street, lantern in hand, until he reached the livery and ran around behind it. Cartwright had used brute force, this time, to spring the shed's padlock, planning to outflank Bjornson and give him the last great surprise of his life.

Too late.

Almost.

Who could it be, except Bjornson, toiling toward him through the tunnel? In another moment, Cartwright saw the light cast by another lantern, held aloft by his most ardent adversary.

Cartwright waited until Bjornson was within ten feet of him, then shone his lantern in Bjornson's face. The tunnel walls were marked by giant shadows of their pistols, leveled toward each other at a range from which it would be difficult to miss.

"Cartwright?"

"None other, Bucky Boy."

"How did you know?"

"I'm smarter than you give me credit for."

"I see that. Well? What do you want?"

"The same thing that I've always wanted," Cartwright answered. "Everything."

"All right," Bjornson said agreeably. "You've got it. As you see, I'm leaving town. My shooters may give yours some trouble, but that's life."

Cartwright ignored Bjornson's patter, asking him, "What's in the bag?"

"Necessities. For traveling."

"I'll have a look."

"Think so?"

"You're in a tight spot, Buck. Nowhere to run."

"*We're* in a tight spot, Baron. Look around."

"I have," Cartwright replied. "How do you think the people will react when they find out you're storing TNT under their very beds?"

"*What* people?" Bjornson mocked him. "All I see up there are sheep. Some of them answer to you, the others flock to me. I don't care what they think, or *if* they do."

"The bag," Cartwright repeated. "Leave it, and you're free to go."

Instead of answering, Bjornson squeezed his six-gun's trigger. The report was thunderous inside the tunnel, hammering at Cartwright's eardrums, while the bullet plucked his lantern from his grasp.

He dropped into a crouch and fanned two shots at Bjornson. One of them struck home and staggered Cartwright's human target. Gasping at the sudden pain, Bjornson dropped his lantern and it burst on impact with the nearest crate of dynamite. At once, flames caught hold of the dry and dusty wood.

Cartwright was up and running by the time the nearest fuse began to sputter, racing back along the way he'd come and praying he'd be fast enough to outrun death itself.

Slade was about to rise and meet his adversaries with a final blaze of gunfire, when the earth moved underneath his feet. It seemed to tremble first, then *shifted* with sufficient force to drop him on his backside in a spreading pool of whiskey and tequila.

The titanic, thunderous explosion came a heartbeat later, rolling down the southern side of Main Street in a cloud of smoke, debris, and dust. Shops vaporized in rapid fire, as if a dragon had awakened underground and was stampeding toward Valhalla at the speed of light.

Slade struggled to his feet in time to peer across the bar and find his would-be killers either sprawled or kneeling on the barroom floor, all gaping through the Rosebud's empty window frames toward the Valhalla, opposite. They saw it detonate, roof rising on a thundercloud of smoke, while shattered walls sprayed shrapnel for a hundred yards in all directions.

Slade was safe below the bar, again, when the infernal blizzard struck the Rosebud. Its facade crumpled, the balcony and roof sagging in front, while a death wind of detritus swept through the saloon. Huddled beneath the worst of it, head shielded with his arms, Slade waited for the storm to pass before he rose, rifle in hand, and looked around.

The men who'd tried to kill him moments earlier were down and out of action. Some of them were likely still alive, but Slade ignored them, carefully maneuvering around the barroom rubble that included dangling ceiling beams. He guessed the Rosebud would collapse at any time, and Slade felt better only when he was outside, standing with trash and corpses in the middle of Main Street.

The south side of that boulevard was

devastated, stores and offices replaced by a trench large enough to swallow a freight train. Somehow, he saw, the livery and other buildings at the far end of the street had managed to escape with only minor damage to their walls and shingled roofs, though panic noises issued from the stable.

Watching out for snipers on the way, Slade walked down to the livery and went inside. The hostler had lamps lit, and he was comforting the animals as best he could. Slade freed his roan and led it from the stable to the street, where dust was settling at last.

Sabrina found him standing there, surveying what remained of yesterday's Gehenna. She set down her carpetbag and stood beside him, watching dazed survivors wander up and down Main Street.

"There'll be no coming back from this," she said.

"Don't be so sure. Have you seen anything of Cartwright or Bjornson?"

"Only that," she answered, nodding toward the dusty, smoking trench.

"Their work?" asked Slade.

"Bjornson had a tunnel dug between Valhalla and the livery," she said. "Baron discovered it some time ago, snooping around, and kept it to himself."

"Except for telling you?"

"Just pillow talk, while he was trying to impress me."

"Tunnels normally collapse," Slade said. "They don't explode."

"Can't help you there, Marshal," she said. "It's something for you to investigate."

"What makes you think they're both down there?" he asked.

"When he was mad at Buck for something, Baron used to say he'd like to sneak in through that tunnel and surprise him, maybe cut his throat while he was sleeping."

"Pillow talk." Slade shook his head.

"Whatever gets you through the night."

"I'll have to verify that they were in there, if I can."

"Good luck," she said. "I'm on tomorrow's weekly stage, if it shows up on time."

"Where to?"

"I'm thinking Dallas, maybe Houston. Somewhere I can get lost for a while, forget all this. And you?"

"I've got a prisoner in jail, maybe a few still breathing in the Rosebud. I suppose I'll have to take them back to Lawton."

Or, he thought, *sit tight and press Judge Dennison for reinforcements.*

The hardware store–cum–Western Union

office was located on the north side of the street, and thus was spared all but superficial damage from the blast. Unless its wires were down, he could reach Lawton in the morning and request assistance.

"Are you staying at the Rosebud overnight, then?" he inquired.

"I might as well," Sabrina said. "It still looks safe enough, in back. There's no one left to bother me."

"Maybe I'll see you in the morning, then," said Slade.

She smiled and said, "I wouldn't be surprised," then turned away from him and walked back toward the leaning hulk of the saloon.

Townspeople were already picking through the wreckage there, seeking survivors or whatever they could carry for themselves. Slade saw no reason to deter them, guessing they could be more help to any wounded men from Cartwright's side than he could.

Those with injuries would be available tomorrow, if he wanted to arrest them. Virgil Meade, still locked up in the jail, was going nowhere overnight.

Slade felt a sudden need for sleep. He took his horse back to the livery, then walked toward the Bonanza, wondering what would happen to Gehenna and its people in the days ahead. A host of critical decisions lay in store for those who still remained — whether to stay or go, rebuild or try their luck elsewhere.

Whatever happened to them, they would have another chance.

He thought next of the sisters, sleeping safely in their cabin, and decided it was only right for him to stop and fill them in on what had happened since their rescue. Maybe it would mean a fresh start for the two of them, as well.

Slade smiled, to think of seeing them, then thought of Faith, Judge Dennison, and home.

Wherever that was.

We hope you have enjoyed this Large Print book. Other Thorndike, Wheeler, and Chivers Press Large Print books are available at your library or directly from the publishers.

For information about current and upcoming titles, please call or write, without obligation, to:

Publisher
Thorndike Press
295 Kennedy Memorial Drive
Waterville, ME 04901
Tel. (800) 223-1244

or visit our Web site at:

http://gale.cengage.com/thorndike

OR

Chivers Large Print
published by BBC Audiobooks Ltd
St James House, The Square
Lower Bristol Road
Bath BA2 3SB
England
Tel. +44(0) 800 136919
email: bbcaudiobooks@bbc.co.uk
www.bbcaudiobooks.co.uk

All our Large Print titles are designed for easy reading, and all our books are made to last.